DEATH AL DENTE

Also by Peter King

The Gourmet Detective
Spiced to Death
Dying on the Vine

Peter King

DEATH AL DENTE

St. Martin's Press ✻ New York

Library of Congress Cataloging-in-Publication Data

King, Peter (Christopher Peter)
    Death al dente: a gourmet detective mystery / by Peter King.
    p.   cm.
    ISBN 0-312-19891-4
    I. Title.
PS3561.I4822D39   1999   98-44611
813'.54—dc21   CIP

First Edition: April 1999

10   9   8   7   6   5   4   3   2   1

ACKNOWLEDGMENTS

My sincere and enduring thanks are due to Jeff Gerecke of JCA Literary Agency, New York and Charles Spicer, Senior Editor, St. Martin's Press, New York, whose expertise, advice, and encouragement have been of inestimable value throughout the Gourmet Detective series.

I would also like to express my appreciation to the following for their help with this book: Bill Froug, Emmy-winning writer and producer whose intimate and expert knowledge of what it is really like to be on a film location was invaluable in writing the final chapters of this book, and Roberto Mei, owner of Fontana di Trevi in New York City and Cafe Baci in Sarasota, Florida, for his contributions, corrections, and suggestions on all matters pertaining to Italy and Italian cooking.

CHAPTER ONE

He looked just like he did on the screen—both the big one and the smaller one. Wavy hair, light reddish gold in color, solid, reliable features, light blue eyes that crinkled at the corners when he smiled. He had the same mild manner and the deliberately unconcealed Cockney accent that was a reverse of the usual movie star image.

I knew he had played for years in British second features before his international appeal had been discovered. His name and face were now known all over the world and I knew that he ran his own production company. He still appeared in a remarkable number of films though—most of them in Hollywood. He played laid-back secret agents, historical heroes, dedicated scientists, improbable lovers, and most recently, affluent business executives.

"Was it some of those roles that gave you the idea of opening a restaurant?" I asked him.

"Not really," he said with that lazy East London drawl that was his trademark. "I bought a half share in that first restaurant because I liked the idea of being able to eat and drink in my own place and share it with others."

"It wouldn't have been nearly as popular without your name behind it."

He smiled. A producer had said of him, "He's the only person I know in Hollywood who hasn't been spoiled by success—with the exception of Lassie," and I could see why. Desmond Lansdown was aware of his fame but did not flaunt it. Where his name was likely to be a drawing card, he was ready to use it. He was under no illusions concerning the value of having *Desmond Lansdown* attached to anything whether it was a film, a business, or a restaurant.

"Quite true," he agreed affably. "It has done very well."

It had indeed done very well. We were sitting in Benson's Brasserie, probably London's most famous restaurant and perhaps even the most famous restaurant in the Anglophile world. Most of this fame was due to heavy patronage by film and television stars—a direct result of Lansdown's participation. The original brasserie had been the entry of a struggling chef entrepreneur called Paul Benson into the restaurant business. It had been popular because of its food, but when Lansdown bought a half share and spent a a good part of the next few months here— while he was "resting" between roles—the brasserie had rocketed to the top. More remarkable, it had stayed there.

Restaurants in major cities today are complex beasts and have to fill many roles to stay profitable. They are simultaneously feeding troughs for the nondomestic, showrooms for culinary wizardry, posing parlors for the would-be and almost-are famous, and a meeting place for those who have already achieved fame. Benson's had achieved the first two goals but it had been the arrival of Lansdown that had provided the latter two and put it on the global eating map.

One of Desmond Lansdown's personal assistants had phoned me. He sounded like a young man and had an Oxford accent that you could cut with a dull fork, chosen no doubt by Lansdown in a whimsical moment. I would have bet that his background too was as uppercrust as it could be—a further deliberate contrast to Lansdown's own upbringing as the son of a Billingsgate fish porter and a charwoman.

The young man had confirmed my identity. "You call yourself the Gourmet Detective, I believe."

I confined my agreement to a plain, "That's right." He might have sniffed but it was barely audible. "I am sure you recognize the name of Mr. Desmond Lansdown?"

"The actor? Of course. I'm one of his fans."

"He would like to talk to you. Over lunch at his restaurant. A confidential matter for which you were recommended by Sir Charles Willesford. Would tomorrow be convenient?"

A free lunch at Benson's Brasserie! And an assignment too!

"Let me look at my appointment book," I said and rustled the pages of Sri Owen's *Indonesian Regional Food and Cookery*, which happened to be open on my desk. "I have a couple of things," I said in one of those musing voices, "but I can move those . . . yes, I'll be there. About noon?"

So here I was, in what some claimed to be a close second to the Ritz as the most beautiful dining room in London. The paintings on the walls were framed in a baroque style that gave the place the look of a Parisian restaurant of a few decades ago. It bustled with a casual grace that probably hid careful organization and efficient planning. The lighting was good, as if to emphasize that there was nothing to hide, and the acoustics were excellent—points overlooked in too many restaurants. We were upstairs, the more secluded floor.

"You've done a wonderful job here." I said and meant it.

"Paul Benson gets most of the credit," he said with a modesty that in a movie star was as rare as caviare in a fish-and-chip shop. "Of course, he had the sense to bring me in as his partner"—he flashed that winning smile for which he was famous—"but at the same time, he remodeled and updated here."

A waiter came with two gin and tonics, which Lansdown had ordered when we sat down.

"Here's to your continued prosperity," I said, raising my glass. He nodded in acknowledgment, took two large swallows, savoring each, and said, "That's where you come in."

No small talk? Well, I'm a man of few words myself— except when more are called for.

"Sir Charles Willesford recommended you highly."

"Ah, I did a job for him in France recently. He seemed quite pleased with the result." I saw no reason to add that I had come extremely close to having my career ended—permanently—on that assignment.

"We buy a lot of our wine through his company."

I nodded and sipped gin and tonic.

"He told me that you specialize in culinary investigations."

"That's right," I agreed. "I find rare foods, unusual spices and herbs, advise on the use of little-known food specialties, locate markets for exotic ingredients—that kind of thing."

"Sir Charles told me a little about the job you did for him." There was more than just a twinkle in those world-renowned light blue eyes. "Bit of a private eye too, aren't you?"

"Not deliberately," I told him, a little alarmed. "If you're looking for a two-fisted, gun-toting gumshoe who can do a racing turn at eighty miles an hour, I'm not your man. It's turmeric—not turmoil with me. I'm into marjoram—not mayhem. I was scared out of my apron a couple of times there in France . . ."

He grinned engagingly. "If they decide to make a film of your life, I'll volunteer. Not to play you, no, getting a bit too long in the tooth for that. I'm doing some directing now though . . . still, that's not why you're here."

I waited for him to tell me why I was here but instead he said, "But first, let's order. The chef tells me the lobster balls are very good today—didn't know they had them, did you? I'm going to have what I had the other day—it was great. A warm salad of duck livers with sherry vinegar and then filet of lamb with Madeira sauce and rosemary butter. You can choose anything you want from the menu, of course."

"I'll go along with your choice. Sounds good."

A photographic flash sizzled and Lansdown frowned. He caught my look and then grinned. "I don't mind an occasional photo, but it has to be of me," he said. I was trying to connect the line of the flash to a table when Lansdown said, "Third table over."

The subject caught sight of us, waved, and called out a cheery, "Hi, Desmond!"

"Julia Roberts," Lansdown said to me just as I recognized her. "She's off to Rome tomorrow—they want her to play the Vatican's first woman cardinal. Typecasting, I told her, but warned her not to try for Pope."

The waiter came, took his order, and waited. "I had an excellent Amarone with it the other day," Lansdown said. "A lot of them are a bit too 'big' for lamb, but this one—it's from the Fabiano vineyard—was just right. That okay with you?"

I agreed and he nodded to the waiter. "And a couple more of these." He motioned to the gin and tonic. "They make mine with Bombay gin—yours will be the same," Lansdown had come a long way from his barrow boy origins.

"That's fine."

"Right," he said. "Let's get to business. Here's why I wanted to talk to you. We've done very well here, that's true. Now I've got another idea—I'm not bragging, this one really is mine—and Paul agrees with it. See, the way I figure it, French cuisine is a bit over the hill, so to speak. It's still wonderful and there are some magnificent restaurants in France, here and elsewhere. But in recent years, the Italians have been more imaginative, more progressive, more innovative." He paused and eyed me for a moment. "Any comment on that?"

"I agree. I've made similar observations myself."

"Good. Then when I tell you that Paul and I are going to open another restaurant, it won't be any great surprise when I tell you that it's going to be Italian."

"I can't think of a better choice," I told him. "You can hardly lose."

"Most new restaurants opening these days are trying to be different and offer the diner something he doesn't get every day and certainly doesn't get at home. As a result, we've got Thai, Vietnamese, Afghan, Korean, Moroccan, and God knows what else. Now, the way I see it, they're all a bit gimmicky. Oh, the food's good in many of them and some are even authentic. But I don't think too many are going to last, and I want to be in this for the long run."

The waiter brought two more gin and tonics and the salads.

"That kind of commitment is vital in a restaurant's success," I said. "It shows in the way the place is run."

We both drank, and as Lansdown put his glass on the table, he turned it slowly, clinking the ice. "Just one more thing . . ." There was a silky tone to his voice that told me something critical was coming.

"This isn't going to be just another Italian restaurant," he said slowly and took another swallow. "It's going to be the best Italian restaurant in London. It's got to be the best, or we don't do it." His voice hardened just the way it had when he'd played that SS colonel who was trying to kill Churchill.

"A tall order," I said, just managing not to add "Herr Oberst." "London has a number of outstanding Italian restaurants right now. There's La Famiglia, Orso's, Zafferano, Del Buongustaio . . ."

Lansdown emptied his glass, gazed regretfully at it for a second, then sternly resisted the thought that had tempted him. "Excellent, all of them," he agreed.

"And there are several more not far behind."

"True, but let me ask you this: which one is really superior to all the others? Which is *the* Italian restaurant in London? I mean, which one stands head and shoulders above all the rest?"

"There isn't one," I answered after the briefest reflection. "Not one that really stands out."

"Exactly!" He thumped the table, just missing his gin and tonic. "That's the one we're going to open!"

He pointed to the salad. "Try this. Then tell me it's great."

I tried it. It was. I told him. He was partway through his already. "I'm a fast eater. Always have been. Probably stems from my early days in the East End when if you didn't eat fast, someone would snatch it off your plate."

The waiter brought the wine, opened it and Lansdown tasted, nodding with approval. We held up the glasses, their glowing ruby-colored contents inviting us.

"Here's to the best Italian restaurant in London."

"I'll drink to that," said Lansdown and we did. "What do you think of it?" he asked.

I took another, more analytical sip and considered. "Rich and well rounded," I said. "It has a great texture and the tannin comes in strong a little later, and I like that long, lingering finish. Too many red wines today cut off short."

"Couldn't have put it better myself," he said and this time his accent came through without any camouflage at all. "They tell me they use a special process for making Amarone of this quality," he added.

There was something in his tone that made me suspect he knew quite well what it was. If so, this was his way of making sure that I was sufficiently well informed to undertake this mission and earn the steep fee I intended to charge him. It was an appropriate moment to convince him he was making the right choice.

"Yes, they call it 'appassimento.' It's used only for Amarone. The grapes are left to dry on racks in a well-ventilated room for up to three months after harvesting. This concentrates the sugar and adds flavor. That plus a long fermentation raises the alcohol content higher than most. A good one like this has fifteen to eighteen percent alcohol—nearly half as much again as a typical red wine."

He nodded, apparently satisfied with my answer, drank some more, and nodded again.

"Now you're going to ask me where you come in."

"I am."

"I want you to bring me a chef."

I put down my fork and stared at him.

"Me?"

"Yes, you."

"You've noticed I'm not Italian, haven't you?"

"Sure. I played an Italian myself once in a film. Didn't

convince anybody. So I can spot other non-Italians with no trouble." He grinned and disposed of the rest of the salad in two mouthfuls. "No, you don't have to be Italian. You do have to go to Italy though."

He drank some more wine and I decided not to point out that it was a shame to risk affecting the taste of such a fine wine by eating salad at the same time. He reached inside his jacket pocket and took out a folded sheet of paper. "See, here's what we did, Paul and I. We wrote down all the chefs we could think of who would qualify as candidates for running the best Italian restaurant in London. We looked everywhere—even one in San Francisco and one in Copenhagen. Then we started to eliminate one here, one there, one for this reason, one for that reason. We kept on until we had three left. Happens they're all in Italy, even all in the same general area."

I was returning to the excellent salad as he asked, "You can see where I'm heading now, can't you?"

"I think so. You want me to check all these three out and rate them for you."

He grinned his devil-may-care grin—the one that he had used so often and to such good effect in that movie where he was a con man in Monte Carlo.

"I want you to eat at the restaurants where these three cook. I want you to find out everything you can about how they operate, how efficient they are, how ingenious they are, what kind of people they are. I want you to learn anything about them that you think is necessary for making a final decision— that decision being which one is the best chef for the best Italian restaurant in London. Hey, why just London? England, sure, maybe Europe!"

———

It sounded like a tough assignment, but obviously somebody had to do it. I took the list and studied the three names. I recognized all of them, though I had never visited their restaurants. They were good choices, every one. All had extremely impressive reputations and all were chefs with a brilliant future ahead of them. But where would that future be?

"Do you have any reason to believe they're all willing to come to London?"

"We've done some very preliminary checking. I spent the best part of a year in Italy not too long ago making that film on the life of Don Juan, and I made a lot of friends there at the Cinecitta Studios in Rome. I had them do some minor espionage for me. I think all of these will come for the challenge, the opportunity—and, of course, the money."

I recalled the film, a stinker of the first order and a resounding box-office crash. I thought it better to step clear of that subject—especially the casting of Lansdown as Don Juan.

"Sounds like an interesting assignment," I said cautiously. "There might be a problem, though. I can assess their food and cooking from a few visits, but they'll be suspicious if I'm found prowling around their kitchens and asking questions."

He drank some Amarone with relish as the busboy took the salad plates away.

"Spent quite a bit of time working that one out." He smiled with satisfaction and went on. "I've put a fair amount of money into a new eating guide. It's time Michelin and the others had some further competition anyway. You'll be our inspector in Italy, researching for the guide. Once they find out who you are, they'll all be willing to cooperate. But bear in mind, they will think you're working for a guide book. There mustn't be a clue as to why you're really there."

He sat back and watched the waiter bring the main course. "I don't always eat this much at lunch," he said, "but I'm going to one of those buffet reception affairs tonight and I never get enough to eat at them. All those little bits of this and that on slivers of toast. Oh, they're tasty enough, but how can you fill up on anchovies, capers, and caviare?"

He chuckled. "It's a hard life, my lad. Problems, decisions everywhere. Did you know they want me to play Churchill? He's one of my heroes, how can I do that? Even if they have got—no, I can't tell you—to play Stalin."

A waiter was firmly shooing away a girl who looked like a reporter as we attacked the lamb. It was succulently tender and the Madeira sauce and the rosemary butter complemented one another surprisingly well.

"At the bottom of that sheet is a number where you can reach me."

"Country code thirty-four—that's Spain, isn't it?"

"Yes. I'm shooting some episodes for a television series, *Richard the Lionheart* it's called."

He eyed me in a challenging sort of way and that gave me just enough forewarning not to say "Surely you're not playing him!"

He smiled. "Yes, I'm playing Richard. The writers have made him an older man. Richard was only thirty-two years old when he left on his first crusade, did you know that? We're shooting all the battle scenes in Spain. I'll be a physical wreck when I come back. I went up to Lincoln last week to see that bloody great sword he used. It's still there, in the Guild Hall, you know. I could hardly lift it—it's over six feet long and weighs a ton. Feels like it anyway."

He had a reputation for collecting unusual and little-known facts and I could picture him going up to Lincoln just to swing Richard's sword.

"They've made me four aluminium and plastic replicas," he went on, chuckling. "The way I wield that weapon, I'm sure to break one or two."

He had an engaging way of chatting. There was no boasting and none of the domination of a conversation that many movie and TV stars had. The things he talked about were interesting to him and he liked to share that interest with others.

"Nigel is taking care of travel and hotel arrangements for you. Have you met him? He's here somewhere . . ."

"No, I haven't. Is he the fellow who phoned me?"

"Yes, that's Nigel."

"Fine," I said. "Well, I'm ready to swing a sword or two in my own way. A dinner knife, anyway."

"Good man." The way he said that had been used by impersonators who liked to depict him in a command post on the battlefield, nonchalantly sending unwilling volunteers off on impossible tasks.

That was not a real parallel with me though, I reflected. This job would be easy, a real pleasure—with no risks involved at all . . .

CHAPTER TWO

The airport at Bologna is not large but the Alitalia Boeing 737 landed smoothly without even using up all the east-west runway. Traffic into Bologna has increased at a faster rate than airport expansion, with the result that the terminal always seems crowded. Then I remembered that the entire country always seems to have many times more people than it has in reality. I was watching for my suitcase when I spotted a board among the many being held aloft in the baggage claim area.

"Perseus Travel," it said. Lansdown had told me that he was laying on a service to get me to my hotel. Perseus Travel turned out to be a lanky young man with long black hair that he had to keep pushing out of his eyes. His dark eyes showed no interest in me as he took my one suitcase and told me he had a limo out front.

It was parked in the absolutely-no-waiting-or-stopping zone and the way in which he passed a couple of banknotes to the police officer on guard there was clearly the outcome of much practice and in-depth experience.

It had been about two years since I had been in Italy, and as always when I came here, I was glad I was not driving. Every Italian seems to have aspirations of being a Grand Prix contestant. They drive faster and there seem to be more cars, louder horns, more gestures, and more close calls than anywhere else in the world.

Ignoring the traffic and concentrating on enjoying the countryside was easy to decide, not so easy to do, but I persevered. Away from the airport surroundings, all the familiar impressions returned: the fields of manicured olives, the dusty sideroads leading into small vineyards, and the unfinished houses. Only Mexico can compete in the percentage of houses begun and never finished, They seem to be everywhere, many of them bearing the unmistakable signs of many owners. Brick has been used here, stone there, concrete block elsewhere; then the next buyer, convinced he has a bargain, has a better idea and uses another construction material.

The intermittent row of cypress trees stamps *Italy* indelibly on any scene it adorns. Then from a bony ridge of hills, I could see a squat, ugly, but once-formidable castle, gray with age, still proud and now lonely. In a knife-thin valley, concrete mixers were standing in line, ready to pour the foundations of yet another housing tract, probably new homes for the thousands of East Europeans now finding Italy the next promised land after Germany.

The limo slowed marginally as a sneering condescension to entering the suburbs of Bologna. A church behind iron railings had red and white banners outside proclaiming a clerical congress, and next to it was a row of crumbling almshouses. Just beyond was Il Banco del Spirito Santo, the ubiquitous chain seen throughout Italy. *The Bank of the Holy Ghost* is a name that astounds tourists who see it for the first time, but closer acquaintance with the country brings the realization that only the Italians could blend the spiritual and the financial so blithely.

The traffic thickened as we penetrated the town. My driver shouted curses at a bus that refused to get out of his way, then swerved violently in front of an ambulance with flashing lights.

It was no doubt on its way to a hospital carrying an unfortunate pedestrian who had unwisely ventured out of his house. My driver yelled curses which did not reflect well on the personal life of the Holy Family and stamped on the accelerator so that he was not too many seconds late in a race with a traffic signal.

It was with relief that I arrived at the Ambasciatore Imperiale Hotel. The severe stone façade made it appear a little grim on the exterior, but inside, the spacious gray-and-white marble–flagged lobby was divided with mirrors and curved walls. Large modern oil paintings and wrought-iron stairways flanked a wall of stainless steel–fronted elevators while the room was larger than usual, colorful in soft beige and light orange. Every convenience was provided, including a phone and TV in the bathroom, while the minibar was well stocked.

I had unpacked, taken a shower, and dressed when there was a knock at the door. I opened it to find one of those gorgeous girls who have given Italian glamour such a good name.

She flashed me a dazzling smile. "Hello, I'm Francesca from the escort service," she said in English that carried only the faintest trace of a charming accent. She pushed the door further open and came in before I could protest, although that thought had not crossed my mind. She closed it with a provocative flick of a well-rounded hip.

"Desmond sent me," she said.

I had not expected Lansdown to supply any auxiliary services of this nature but she broke into a giggle and went on, "He told me to say that. Actually, he explains in this fax. May I sit down?"

She handed me a sheet of paper and sat in the armchair by the window. She crossed a pair of elegant legs and leaned back to watch me read. Lansdown's fax explained that he had retained her agency to furnish me with an interpreter and guide for as long as she was needed during my stay in Italy. He had added a note to me stating that he had used her services while he had been making the Don Juan movie. He said she was extremely efficient, has a thorough knowledge of the area, knew a number of people in influential places, and he was sure she would give maximum satisfaction in every regard.

A writing table was handy, and I sat in the chair beside it and looked at her. She wore a light sandy brown–colored business suit with wide lapels and a skirt just to the knees. It was a spectacular fit and I found her a credit to the Bolognese commercial community.

"He speaks very highly of you," I told her.

She had big, dark eyes, almond-shaped, and a generous mouth. Her nose was unmistakably Roman but only proud not dominating. Luxuriant black hair had probably once cascaded down her back but was now cropped a half inch short of severe. Her figure was curvaceous, with a slim waist that accentuated her bosom and hips. She had long showgirl legs, which she uncrossed then crossed the other way.

"We had some fun times together," she said in a musical voice that is found in so many Italian women and confirms the nation's eminence in opera. "I was working in the Cinecitta Studios in Rome when Desmond came to make *Don Juan*. I was assigned as his personal assistant. Sometimes I work as a script girl—I want to be a director but nobody has given me the chance yet."

"You were born in Rome?"

"No, here in Bologna. I grew up in this region, in Verona, Parma . . . I work for the escort agency in between films—times are hard in the movie business here in Italy just now. American films are what everybody in Europe wants to see."

"Well, I'm glad to have you," I told her. "My Italian is passable, but it's much better to have someone who is a native speaker."

"It sounds like a pleasant task for you," she said demurely, and I wondered how much she knew.

"Your presence will make it even more pleasurable," I told her. Italians should not be allowed to think they are the only ones who can be gallant. Before she could respond, I asked swiftly, "What exactly did Lansdown tell you?"

"He has put a lot of money into a new food guidebook. For the Italian section, you are going to review restaurants in this region—where the best Italian food comes from," she added loyally.

"Good. I am sure you will be very helpful." So Lansdown had not told her the real reason I was here. Did it really make any difference? was my fleeting thought. Perhaps not.

"Desmond also sent me this list." She handed me another fax. Eight or nine restaurants were listed. The three belonging to the candidate chefs were among them but not together. Lansdown had evidently added the others as a blind. I noted that the first name on the list was underlined. It was the Capodimonte, owned and operated by Giacomo Ferrero, one of the three chefs on Lansdown's list.

Francesca was a sharp-eyed girl. She saw my perusal of the list return to that name at the top. "At this time of year, it is not difficult to get a table at these restaurants, but Desmond does not want any of your time to be wasted so he suggested that I make a reservation at Capodimonte. I made this for tonight. For two, of course," she added with a delicious smile.

"Good planning. Yes, I want to visit as many restaurants

as possible. Let me see, will you make reservations at some others for the following nights?"

"Of course." She took a tiny electronic organizer from her bag. "Which ones?"

The computer had arrived in Northern Italy. She even looked as if she knew how to use it. Sexist! I reprimanded myself, naturally she does. I scanned the list.

"In the order Desmond has put them?" she asked innocently.

The other two chefs were down the list but there was no need to be too cloak-and-dagger about this. I wanted to check out all three promptly so as to allow time for repeat visits if required.

"This one, the Palazzo Astoria in Padua," I said casually. "Isn't that the restaurant run by Ottavio Battista?"

Her eyes glowed. "Yes! You know him?"

"He has a reputation," I said, "even in England. They say he is the enfant terrible of Italian cuisine . . . er, do you speak French?"

"Of course. I know what it means. They also say that he is absolutely divine!"

"As a chef?"

"Yes—as a chef and also as a man."

"Well, it's his restaurant I'm interested in," I said, which was a partial truth at least. "Let's go there next."

She nodded and her fingers flew over the minuscule keyboard. She looked up before I had time to admire her dexterity. I looked back at the list. "There's another restaurant with a wonderful reputation . . . I keep seeing the name . . . it should be next—ah, here it is, San Pietro."

"In Verona, yes, it is one of the best at the moment." Her fingers twinkled again. "And after that?"

I picked a couple at random, names I did not know.

She rattled them off on the keyboard and reached into her bag again. Her hand came out with a cellular phone and she was squeezing out numbers. She said a few brief sentences and nodded to me. "We're okay for the Palazzo Astoria tomorrow night." I did not have time to congratulate her on her efficiency before she had repeated the performance. "Alas, the San Pietro is fully booked the next night, some special function but I can make it for the following night. The others can be arranged later."

Lansdown certainly knew how to pick a good personal assistant. "Let's see, it's nearly five o'clock now," I said. "What time is dinner tonight?"

"I made the reservation for eight-thirty. It's a little early but I thought I should allow plenty of time for you to assess the place."

Eight-thirty is not early by American or British standards, but this reminded me that the Italian stomach operates on a later schedule. Francesca stood up. "I will go now. Pick you up about eight-forty-five. Capodimonte is not far from here."

"I thought you said our reservation is for—"

"Eight-thirty, yes. But no Italian ever arrives on time."

She swung her bag on to her shoulder and strode to the door. She fluttered fingers.

"Ciao."

CHAPTER THREE

B ologna the Fat, it is called in Italy," she said.

Francesca looked charming in a close-fitting dress in black shantung with a tiny shoulder cape that achieved the maximum of exposure despite a pretense at modest coverage. Ebony and gold earrings and simple black high heel shoes completed a stunning effect.

I had heard that description of Bologna before but had forgotten it. The town lies in a buffer zone between the olive oil country and the butter culture where animal fat reigns supreme. Bologna's location in the heart of Emilia Romagna means that it accepts both styles of cooking, striving simultaneously to maintain the old traditions and explore new horizons.

Not too new though . . . Lean Cuisine? Forget it. Diet? That's for invalids. The Italians are not stick-in-the-muds in food, however, and are well aware of the trend towards more healthy eating that is still sweeping much of the Western world. That is to say, they are apprised of the trend but their reaction to it is cautious. Extra virgin olive oil has replaced lard and the harshest description they apply to a food is to call it *pesante*, heavy. Beyond that, their venturing is tentative—a contrast to the French who leapt eagerly on to the Cuisine Minceur bandwagon only to have a wheel or two fall off. Now they are trying to find a way back to some middle ground.

"In the inimitable way of Italians, you manage to keep

abreast of modern trends in cuisine without emulating them," I told Francesca. "You hold on to tradition without being a slave to it."

"It is also called Bologna the Red," she said. "It threw away political tradition in the fifties and sixties and became the center of Italian communism."

"A change that the rest of the world found baffling," I pointed out.

"That was understandable," she agreed. "No one expected a predominantly Catholic country to embrace Communism. But that was only the viewpoint of foreigners who did not have a deeper knowledge of the Italian temperament. We Italians are too realistic to expect a revolution to eliminate poverty, hunger, and inequality. We did not want a revolution, but we love the role of strutting rebels. We love the bands, the parades, the noise, the posturing, the food, the spectacle, the fireworks."

I smiled at her exposition. "You like the trappings of revolution but not the ideology. You know, Francesca, you have a sound comprehension of the Italian people—for an Italian. Most nationalities do not see themselves as clearly as that. Patriotism usually gets in the way."

She shrugged delightfully. "I have lived in America and in England. That helps."

"To come back to Bologna the Fat. Do Italians still consider this region as dominant in cuisine?"

"Oh, yes," she said firmly. With a smile, she added, "Unless they are Sicilian or Piedmontese or Tuscan or Lombardian . . ."

"The old rivalries still exist?"

"Of course. They do not die. But overall and from an objective point of view—"

"If such a thing exists with food—"

"Yes, then Emilia Romagna still reigns."

She had been only twenty minutes late picking me up so it was nearly nine-thirty when we arrived at Capodimonte. An hour late was nothing. She swept in as if she were the Queen of Sheba and was doing the restaurant a favor by appearing at all.

The sommelier appeared and invited us to have an aperitif.

"I'll have a *Rabarba*," I said.

Francesca clapped her hands in delight. "You know Rabarba?"

"An Italian friend introduced me to it years ago. I'm still not sure if I like it but I always order one."

"I'll have one too," she said.

The Italians have a bewilderingly large selection of aperitifs. Many are made from unlikely vegetables and fruits. Rabarba is made from rhubarb and has a unique taste, sort of sweet and bitter fruity at the same time.

The aperitifs and the menus arrived. I studied the latter carefully, for I was at work already. There are several things you can learn about a restaurant from its menu. For instance, you should be suspicious if the menu offers crab bisque but no crab dishes. It probably comes from a can. Skepticism concerning quality is justified when the menu is as thick as a magazine, for it means that many of the products are frozen.

Francesca engaged in a detailed conversation with the maître d' about several of the menu items and then ordered different ones altogether. First she had tiny squares of smoked eel on a bed of cooked Treviso radicchio while I had the *bocconcini*, a Bolognese specialty—vol au vents filled with chicken giblets and truffles. The tiny puff pastries literally melted in the mouth. We both went for pasta dishes for the second course. The region around Bologna is the pasta center of Italy, the maître d' reminded us, so it was an inevitable choice. Francesca preferred the *crosetti*, rounds of egg pasta, while I had the *frittalloni*, which I had never encountered before. Small pasta cups were filled with spinach, cheese, and sultanas, the sweet seedless raisins, then deep fried. Francesca said she liked them sprinkled with sugar so she could eat them as a sweet course.

The sommelier, a jolly fat man, was a profound source of advice on local wines, and perhaps recognizing that we were not complete neophytes, said that while the Emilia Romagna region was paramount in food, that was not the case in wine too. Still, it was third in Italy as measured by volume, so naturally they had some very good wines. Most of these came from the foothills of the Apennines, he said. Many were light and bubbly, as they were drunk young, but several fine still wines were in the cellars.

Some Trebbianos were among his recommendations as well as the Albana di Romagna, Italy's first white wine to gain the coveted DOCG designation. A couple of Pinot Biancos and some Chardonnays from the Terre Rosso also received consideration but I eventually decided on a wine from the Colle Piacentini zone. Francesca wisely chose to leave the choice to me so that she could not be held responsible, she said with a grin.

The pastas were excellent, as we might expect from the pasta center of Italy. "Don't they have a funny idea about pasta in the USA!" said Francesca. "They serve it with the meat or the fish or the chicken of the main course."

"In place of potatoes or rice. Yes, they do. Much better to have it first, like this."

By the time we were mulling over possible main course dishes, several tables had been filled. Next to us, six people were enthusiastically discussing the menu. Some of them had been here before and were offering recommendations. They were presumably locals of some stature as two waiters were promptly assigned to their table.

Francesca had suggested we delay ordering the main course until after we had had the earlier ones. "You think the first and second courses may be filling," I suggested.

"You told me it is two years since you were in Italy. Maybe you have forgotten that we eat heartily here."

I thanked her for her concern. "What are you having?" I asked her.

She chose fish while I ordered the lamb sweetbreads with prosciutto. My choice was intended to challenge the chef to the limit, for this is a dish that is usually prepared with plenty of small white onions. These tend to obscure the delicate sweet-bread taste so I had carefully asked how Giacomo cooked it, and the maître d' assured me that it was onionless.

The wine came and was expertly opened and served. The conversation from the next table was growing in volume as food was being consumed. When our dishes arrived, Francesca and I eagerly surveyed them. Her sole Florentine simmered gently, a sprinkling of nutmeg on the sole giving it a pleasant aroma. With it, as side dishes, she had a slice of oven-baked polenta and some tiny green beans. My sweetbreads justified the chef's reputation. We each tasted the other's food. I wanted to confirm that the Capodimonte served a high quality sole and they did. This area has no coastline, so fish like this, caught in the Adriatic, has to be transported and handled with speed and efficiency.

I looked at the surrounding tables to see what they were all eating and, as far as possible, confirm that the diners looked satisfied. The service tells a lot about how a restaurant is run.

Waiters have to look around their area and be sure that a diner is not getting impatient for attention after several minutes of arm waving.

We were just finishing eating when there was a bustle on the other side of the room and a big, bearded man in white came in, transforming the whole restaurant by his very size and personality.

It was *il patrone*, Giacomo Ferrero. He looked like a well-fed Pavarotti.

He stopped at the next table, where the diners were evidently good friends of his. One of them was a burly man with a smooth well-fed face and a voice of authority. Chef Giacomo called him Silvio. He also greeted his wife, Elena, effusively. She was a woman of stunning appearance, dark and voluptuous with a well-developed bosom and hips. Giacomo knew the other couple but to a lesser degree evidently.

Francesca was on the side of our table nearest to them, leaning over so as not to miss a word of their conversation. I raised my eyebrows to portray a question and looked over there to denote that I was asking who they were but she frowned and gave a tiny headshake that I supposed meant she could not tell me now or she might miss something important.

We were able to finish our meal just as Giacomo left the next table and came over to ours. He kissed Francesca's hand, saying it was nice to see her again and remarking on the German diplomat she had been with the last time she was here. She slid past that by introducing me.

Giacomo shook my hand enthusiastically. He seemed the kind of person who did everything enthusiastically.

"Welcome, signor! Welcome to Capodimonte!" He

leaned forward to ask solicitously, "Tell me, how was your meal? Please be absolutely honest."

I assured him that it was one of the finest meals I had eaten in a long time.

"Wonderful!" he boomed. "Let me introduce you to my good friends here." He waved in the direction of the next table.

Half an hour later, the eight of us were as close as if we had just spent a week together on a cruise ship. Silvio Pellegrini was a supplier of many of the products used by Giacomo. He owned a pasta factory and buffalo farms where the milk was obtained for the manufacture of mozzarella cheese. His wife, Elena, was dark eyed and black-haired and said little. The male half of the other couple was Tomasso Rinaldo, Pellegrini's lawyer, a striking-looking man with silvery hair and beard. He looked capable of swinging any jury, and his careful grooming and beautifully cut suit and silk cravat suggested a lucrative business. His wife, Clara, was pleasant and smiling and took an instant liking to Francesca.

They were chatting away as I said to Pellegrini, "It's fascinating that you have buffalo farms. I know that some mozzarella is made from buffalo milk but most people associate the animal with the open plains of middle America. It's difficult to associate it with Italy."

"We make the finest mozzarella in Italy," Pellegrini said proudly. "We export more and more all the time."

"Isn't it hard to milk buffalo?" I asked. "They are such big animals—it must make it dangerous."

He laughed. "You must come and see them. Our cheese factory too. It is one of the finest in Europe."

"I'd love to," I said and meant it.

"What would you love to see?" Francesca wanted to

know, determinedly keeping track of several conversations at the same time and within a couple of minutes, we had arranged to go out the next day and visit the Pellegrini farms and factory.

"I have a thought," said Pellegrini. "What are you doing the day after tomorrow? The reason I ask is that is my birthday and Bernardo Mantegna, one of our most famous chefs, is giving a big party for me in his restaurant. I would like for you to come."

Francesca and I exchanged glances. I saw no reason not to be truthful. "As a matter of fact, we tried to get a reservation there that night and could not."

"Excellent." Pellegrini beamed. "Please come as my guests."

"Haven't you had dessert yet?" asked Giacomo in concern. "We have some magnificent concoctions of mascarpone. I will send some over."

He shook hands with the two men, kissed all three women, and turned to me.

"I believe you will leave here tonight, signor, convinced that I am the man for Mr. Lansdown's restaurant."

CHAPTER FOUR

I was madder than a wet hen. I was boiling over like a forgotten stew.

We were going back to my hotel, this time with a different driver. She was a middle-aged lady with hair in a bun and the look of a schoolteacher. She drove at reasonable speeds, obeyed traffic signals, and was nonagressive.

"How could he have found out?" I raged. "Somebody must have told him! Who was it?"

"I don't know," Francesca said as if she could not have cared less.

I had found it difficult to concentrate on the magnificent sweetened mascarpone that Giacomo served us for dessert. This is the soft cheese used in the preparation of tiramisu, one of Italy's more recent export successes. Giacomo used a more simple approach. He mashed crushed walnuts into the mascarpone, folded in some whipped cream, and chilled. I told him he was omitting telling me something, for I detected an unmistakable flavor, and he admitted having stirred in some brandy. "I am always trying to be a little different." He beamed.

My stomach triumphed over my head, though, and I was able to enjoy the dessert and congratulate him on his cuisine. I had said nothing about his bombshell, saving all my anger for Francesca. It did not bother her a bit. She shrugged a curvaceous shoulder at my question about the leak.

"You Anglo-Saxons worry too much about secrets. You are in Italy now. Here, everyone knows everything that goes on."

"Did *you* know?"

She gave me a tantalizing look, leaned back in her corner of the big, comfortable limo, and crossed her legs. She must have Roman blood in her, I thought. She looked about as unconcerned as the Empress Calpurnia on hearing that a dozen legions had been lost in the African desert.

"Lansdown will be furious," I told her, determined not to let her off the hook. "If it wasn't at his end, then it must have been your people."

"I showed you the fax," she said languidly. "There was nothing in it." She straightened to a pose of hauteur as she added, "If anyone is angry, it should be me. You didn't tell me the truth. You are only supposed to be writing a guidebook."

"But did you know?" I persisted.

"What is there to know?" She was all wide-eyed innocence. "That Desmond has restaurants in London, New York, and Miami. So he is hiring a chef. What of it? What is—as you put it in English—the big deal?"

A streetcar cut us off, bell clanging furiously. We swayed, but the powerful suspension of the limo righted us immediately, and our driver resumed her smooth control. At least we didn't have the alpine circuit chauffeur of yesterday taking us on a mad night ride through the streets of Bologna.

It was time to exercise what the crew of the U.S.S. Enterprise call "damage control." Perhaps it was not that serious. After all, they always survive. I was still puzzled over how Giacomo knew though—and what about the other two chefs? Did they know too?

"Desmond will be calling in a few days—he'll call you first, of course," Francesca said, adding the last part as a conciliatory afterthought. "I'll tell him that I know about the chef business."

"He will ask how you know," I told her.

She stared out at the brightly lighted shop windows as we went through what was evidently the fashion district. She giggled. Sophisticated women cannot giggle and maintain their sophistication but Francesca was the exception. "I'll tell him you talk in your sleep," she said and giggled again.

We reached the hotel before I could compose an answer to that.

"Do you want me to come with you to Pellegrini's farms tomorrow?" she asked.

"No, I think I'll go alone. Why don't you take a day off? Pick me up tomorrow evening for dinner at the Palazzo Astoria."

I got out of the limo. She leaned across the seat. "Are you mad at me?" she asked, her eyes large and childlike.

"No," I said. "I was but not now. Well, not mad at you anyway—I was so annoyed that someone knows. I still can't figure out who and how."

"It's like I told you, this is Italy. We all know our neighbors' business. This is probably still a secret—"

"How can it be—"

"A secret not known to more than just a few people." She gave me a pout that might have implied a kiss and pulled the limo door shut as the vehicle rolled away from the curb.

The Ambasciatore Imperiale had a breakfast room big enough to serve the Italian army. It was all marble, glass, and chrome and sufficiently daunting that I walked on through and out on to the Via Novella in search of a *tavola fredda*. These serve snacks, drinks of all kinds, buns, and cakes, plus, of course, coffee. They have a few tables but it is mostly stand-up service. The name means cold table and distinguishes it from *tavola calda*, hot table, where meals are served.

Both are busy all through the day. The food is under large glass panels, the walls are mirrored and covered with bottles, the floors are marble, and the atmosphere lively and fizzing with conversation. Just in time, I remembered one convention that baffles first-time visitors. You have to pay for your food and drink before you can buy it—and you have to buy it before you can eat it.

Foreigners shake their heads in astonishment at what seems like a cumbersome system. First, you walk around and decide what you want. You pick a person behind the counter, using elbows and shoulders to get there. Forget order and manners. The person rings it up and hands you a sales slip. You take this to the cash desk and pay. The slip is receipted and you now take this back to the sales counter and exchange the slip for your purchases.

There *is* a reason for all this—the larcenous streak in the Italian nature means that it would be financially suicidal for the owner to trust the staff. He knows that they would pocket what they consider a reasonable share of the profits to compensate for their miserable wage. The system as operated puts all the financial responsibility on the sole person at the cash desk, almost always the owner or his wife. If the books do not balance at the end of the accounting period, the finger of accusation is unerring.

The quality of the food is surprisingly high in such places. Pastry is fresh every day and most of the consumption is sweet pastries. Coffee is always fresh and excellent while, particularly at breakfast time, the flow of customers is heavy. A typical way for an Italian to start his day is a glass of brandy, two or three cups of strong black coffee, and a sweet, sticky bun covered with icing and sugar.

I drank a cappuccino and ate an Italian equivalent of a croissant. These are less sweet than most of the other offerings, though not as flaky as the French version. The seat by the window that I had selected gave me an excellent view of the passing parade. People watching is a great pastime in any foreign city but when the city is Italian, it is triply rewarding.

Italians are always active, purposeful, and vital. Every scene portrays the vivacity, the throbbing, pulsating life with its noise, its movement, and its excitement. Anyone observed strolling is certainly a tourist. The streets are jammed with cars, honking loudly and frequently. The sidewalks are crammed with pedestrians, always seeing a friend across the street. Conversations are conducted in loud voices and with expressive gestures. Every opportunity is seized to dash across in the most dangerous places and between impatient cars. Motor scooters dart in and out like wasps, oblivious to signals, narrowly missing pedestrians, and sneering at the angry motorists.

Mothers admonish, scold, praise, cajole, and encourage children watched by admiring relatives. Men lounge, smoke, talk, gesticulate. Voices call from open windows. Snatches of opera drift out from radios. Scales are practiced, smells of cooking flow out on to the sidewalk.

An Italian can stretch a cup of coffee out for an hour but, as entertaining as it was, I strolled back to the hotel and within a couple of minutes, the Perseus limo rolled up to the curb. I was glad to see that Francesca had paid attention to my request and Bella, the driver of the evening before, was at the wheel.

We headed out of town in a northerly direction and picked up the autostrada. On the green hillsides, herds grazed in the shade of leafy chestnut trees. The valley of the Po River is rich in wheat, said to be the best in Italy. We passed through a region where giant trucks loaded with sugar beet hurtled past us at eighty miles an hour. Apple orchards lined the autostrada, then fields of many of the other products of this fertile area whizzed past: pears, strawberries, peaches, asparagus, zucchini, and potatoes.

A huge roadside sign declared that we were approaching the Pellegrini farms, and after some minutes, Bella exited from the autostrada and followed a local road for some distance. Pulling onto a private road, she turned through a massive wooden arch, again with the Pellegrini name in gigantic letters. We drove up a winding incline, past a long fence, and finally stopped before an imposing structure.

In front of it, Silvio Pellegrini sat at a long wooden table talking volubly into a cellular phone. He gave me a wave and resumed his verbal onslaught on the party at the other end who, it seemed, had not delivered on time. He closed the conversation with a blast of orders, shut off the phone, and dropped it into his pocket.

"So, my friend, welcome to the Pellegrini enterprises!"

He was wearing casual clothes today, a gray shirt and blue jeans with ankle boots, but he still looked like the wealthy, powerful landowner and business executive. The smooth, well-groomed face, a little full from good eating, and the sleek black hair seemed more suited to a boardroom than a ranch. His affable manner was obviously one reason for his success—he even seemed genuinely pleased to see me.

He took me into the farmhouse, which had evolved a long way from that humble origin. A large rambling building, it had been enlarged, modernized, and almost rebuilt. Pellegrini had a penthouse in Bologna where he lived most of the time, he told me, but he loved this place, which he had bought when it was a barely livable habitation.

In the added rooms, ceilings were high, with skylights letting in a yellow sun. In the main living room, expensive carpets lay on floors of massive terracotta tile while oil paintings and faded tapestries covered the walls. "I use this room most of the time." Pellegrini said. Just inside the door was a table with an elaborate coffee maker, gleaming chrome and glass. "I drink a lot of coffee." He smiled. Next to it was a drinks cabinet and above it glass shelves filled with bottles of all colors. The outstanding feature by far, though, was the waterwheel.

"Long before I bought the place, this was a mill. We don't have olive trees on this property but there are many groves in the area. They are mostly small and their owners could not afford a press of their own so they would bring their harvest here for the oil to be extracted. It is not used any more but it would have been a shame to destroy such a magnificent feature."

I agreed. It was a massive wooden wheel, so large that the roof and ceiling had to be raised, Pellegrini told me, in order to accommodate it into the structure of the house, which had then been expanded around it. The stream which had powered the wheel was partly dammed, and only a trickle fed a large pool about the size of a home swimming pool. A wooden walkway went over the water, around the pool edge, and into another part of the house.

"The wheel still turns," I noted.

"Yes," said Pellegrini. "It is its natural function. I could not think of stopping it. So I had a small motor installed."

He took me through the rest of the house, then led me out into the back to a Unimog, a small German vehicle very much like a Jeep.

"Now you will see buffalo," he told me with a proud smile.

We bumped over uneven ground. He drove, like all Italian men, too fast, which accentuated the irregularity of the terrain. He had to shout to make himself heard.

"These buffalo are really bison—just like the American buffalo. These were brought here from India several centuries ago."

"It seems strange to think of buffalo here," I shouted back. "They seem so natural on the American plains. In Italy, they just don't seem to belong. Are the two breeds alike?"

"The American buffalo is bigger and heavier than ours. It has shorter, stockier legs, a bigger head, and heavier fur."

We had climbed enough to be able to see a panorama spread before us. It was grassy land with frequent clumps of trees and bushes. A strange feature was the vast, whitish areas. I realized they were moving . . .

"Those are the buffalo herds," said Pellegrini.

"I didn't expect them to be white."

"Like their milk." Pellegrini smiled. "Well, not quite as white, but no, not brown like American buffalo. These have been raised for milking for hundreds of years."

We were close to one large herd now, and I could see the shaggy monsters clearly.

"I had no idea they were so big," I said.

"Males weigh up to a ton, females less than half of that."

Their great heads were lowered to the ground, and the

hump that was so characteristic of them looked enormous. Some of them had short horns, curved and menacing, but they paid no attention to us even as we approached to within a dozen yards.

"They spend a third of their life eating," Pellegrini said. "Anything that important needs their full attention. Besides, they are not curious animals. You know how the Indians in America hunted them? They simply rode their horses into the buffalo herd and shot arrows into them or speared them. They would kill or wound a number that way—as many as they needed. The other buffalo would move away, not even aware of having been attacked, leaving the wounded to fall among those already dead."

"You said as many as they needed—they were conservationists, were they?"

"Without knowing it, yes. It was the white man who decimated the herds from a buffalo population of at least one hundred million so that soon they were on the verge of extinction."

He stopped near some small sheds, close to a dense thicket of trees. I hesitated when I saw Pellegrini climb out of the vehicle. "I suppose it's safe?" I ventured.

"Oh, yes, they're harmless."

There were some tawny calves, but most of the herd were cows. The large bulls stayed on the outer edges. They looked like deformed monsters this close. Red eyes gleamed, although none of them appeared to be aware of us.

Pellegrini led the way towards them. I hung behind. Harmless they may be, I thought, but their colossal size was daunting. Pellegrini stopped to let me catch up to him.

"The Campania used to be where most of the buffalo in Italy were raised. Now, we raise more," he said.

I heard him, but I was nervously watching the animals nearest. "Some of them seemed to have noticed us," I said.

He shrugged indifferently. As he did, a bull bellowed loudly. Muzzles raised and tufty tails waved. Hooves pawed the ground. More and more hoarse roars sounded. I looked at Pellegrini. He was frowning and looking around. "Something seems to be upsetting them. I don't understand—"

His words were cut off by an explosion. It was followed by another, then another. A movement stirred through the mass of great beasts, then a few of them broke away into a run. Others followed, until within seconds, the whole herd was on the move. Several more explosions followed, too strong to be gunshots but deep and heavy, vibrating the ground.

The herd had been heading away but these fresh detonations came from a different source and the herd wheeled . . . and came thundering towards us.

CHAPTER FIVE

A hand grasped my arm and dragged me roughly to the Unimog. There was no time to get in and drive. We had barely taken shelter behind it when the herd hit us like a tidal wave of heaving flesh. Buffalo are evidently not very bright, but they sensed enough not to want to run headlong into a Unimog, so the impact was not as colossal as it might have been. The nearest animals tried to avoid the vehicle, but they were packed so tightly that some of them hit it. It rose into the air, crashed down, and bounced, rocking and creaking. Metal splintered and breaking glass crackled.

The Unimog was pushed towards us and we backed away further, still trying to use it as a shield. Bellowing roars and the pounding of hooves filled our ears, and a cloud of dust swept over us. We retreated again as the vehicle heaved and almost turned over, but it landed on all four wheels. By then the herd had split into two streams and they thundered past us, eyes gleaming wildly and muscles rippling under the dirty white skin. The earth rumbled and vibrated.

It was over as abruptly as it had started. The herd was less than a hundred yards away when the lead animals slowed. Others behind them spread out. The herd was scattered, but a few had already resumed grazing and all had stopped. Some of them were looking around with a Why-did-we-do-that? expression that might have been laughable—only it wasn't.

Pellegrini and I stood there, the dust settling around us. The earth seemed to be still shuddering. He walked around the Unimog, checking the damage. Fenders were bent, the headlights were shattered, and one door was twisted, but it was probably driveable. Pellegrini was shaking his head.

"I can't understand it—those explosions . . ." He walked to the sheds, searching the ground, and I followed him. Suddenly, he stopped and picked up a twisted piece of burnt cardboard. He found another and handed one to me. "Fireworks!" he said furiously. "But who would be setting off firecrackers here?"

He drove back to the house, rattles and screeches causing him to swear in Italian, but the engine seemed intact. He stopped with a jolt, ramming the brake pedal hard in his fury.

"I'm going to get to the bottom of this," he said between his teeth, then he started to recall his duties as host. "I am sorry. We were going to have lunch and then take a tour of the mozzarella factory—"

I noted his use of the past tense. "That's all right. We can do it when you have had the chance to make some inquiries."

He nodded grimly. "I intend to do that. Are you sure?"

"Of course. I'm pretty shaken up too. If I can phone this number and have the limo pick me up . . ."

Ten minutes later, Bella drove up and I shook hands with a stern-faced Pellegrini, who left me in no doubt that his staff was in for a rough day.

Bologna is a compact city and perhaps the easiest of all in Italy to sightsee. Everything worth visiting is in or around the Piazza Maggiore, the heart of the city, so I had Bella drop me there. Some tourists complain that there is no Uffizi or Doges Palace, but it is a spectacle of marbled walkways and churches, fountains and towers.

I recalled seeing the leaning towers some years ago and walked there to find that they were still leaning, just as they had been since the twelfth century. There were dozens of them in those days but only these two remain. They are not as famous as their rival in Pisa, but the taller one is twice as high and appears to lean just as much. I visited the Church of Saint Petronius—still not completed after five hundred years—and the Fountain of Neptune, a never-ending source not only of water but of debate between those who deem it vulgar and those who say it is magnificent.

It was time to eat after that much culture, and near the town hall I found a small trattoria, the Da Mario. The trattoria is a wonderful institution. Mostly family owned and operated, they fill the requirements for a café or a small restaurant. Food is fairly simple, ample in volume, and reasonable in price. Service is friendly and fast, ambience is casual and happy.

I had a *fasioi* called *pasta e fagioli* in some parts of Italy and known in the United States as pasta fazool. It is not a difficult dish to make but the better creators of it take out a portion of the cooked beans and blend them into a paste which is then put back to thicken the sauce. It takes good judgement to get that portion just right and this was. Nevertheless, after I had eaten it, I wished I had selected instead a less common soup—the *jota*, perhaps. This has beans, sauerkraut, and bacon and is usually only encountered in the Trieste region.

While I was waiting for the main course, Mama brought me a saucer with a small taster of *bianchetti coll'uovo* which she was serving to a large party at the next table. This consists of newborn, jellylike sardines with anchovies in a creamy sauce of lemon and egg. I had heard of this but not tasted it and it was most unusual, a specialty of Tuscany, said Mama.

For the main course, I had the *bocconcini di cinghialetto*—pieces of wild boar marinated and cooked in a rich red wine sauce. A small side dish of sauteed potatoes sprinkled with rosemary accompanied it. Surprisingly, for a country with a huge agricultural production, Italy's restaurants do not serve vegetables unless ordered. I enjoyed a half bottle of Tignanello, which combines Sangiovese with Cabernet Sauvignon and is aged in small oak barrels.

Mama had said, "What! No pasta?" and brought out an old Italian saying, something about a day without pasta being a day without sunlight, but then the French said that about wine. I told her that I was eating lightly today as I had to attend a banquet that night. I didn't want to mention the name of the Palazzo Astoria though she would probably not have even raised her eyebrows.

A meal like that needed plenty of walking to ensure complete digestion, and I had not been in the medieval museum for many years so I started there. The weapons of the Middle Ages are fascinating combinations of metallurgical ingenuity and murderous intent while the glass, ivory, and Gothic sculptures are unsurpassed, even in Italy. Posters strung across the street advertised the art show in the town hall so I took that in next. Contemporary artists all want to eschew tradition and be as contrary to the old masters as possible. This show was no exception.

After that, I strolled around the city aimlessly, discovering endless delights of narrow alleys with artisans cutting, filing, painting, grinding, polishing, and finally completing reproductions of furniture of which some percentage no doubt were offered as originals. Smells of cooking hung in the soft air, and laundry fluttered gaily from windows.

I was able to do some thinking as I meandered through the old town. Pellegrini had been genuinely shaken by the incident we had just been through. Firecrackers were common in Italy; it did not need to be a holiday for people to set them off. To do so in a buffalo pasture, though, was another matter. No responsible person would do that . . . unless, of course, they knew the consequences and wanted to—wanted to do what?

Kill or maim Pellegrini? Or me? Or both?

Whichever of those, why?

It was not surprising that Pellegrini should be disturbed by the occurrence. He seemed to be more than just disturbed though—he seemed deeply troubled by it, almost as if he knew more than he was telling me. Did he have some suspicion of who had set off the firecrackers and why? If so, it would indicate that he knew the attempt was directed towards him. That was a comforting thought for it meant that I was not the target.

But I could not be the target of any murder attempt unless it had something to do with my mission here, something that involved the task of selecting one chef from among the three candidates.

That was unlikely . . . wasn't it?

CHAPTER SIX

Francesca's eyes were as big as saucers by the time I had finished telling her of the morning's excitement. "But who would do a thing like that?" she demanded, and I told her that if Pellegrini didn't know the answer, I certainly didn't.

She shook her head reprovingly. "As soon as I let you go on your own, you get into trouble."

"You think that was it? That *I* was the one in trouble?"

She caught my meaning immediately. "You? You mean it might have been an attempt on you and not on Signor Pellegrini?"

"It doesn't seem likely, I know."

"Of course not. All because of hiring a chef! Don't be ridiculous. Oh, chefs are important people, yes, but—"

"But I'm not."

"Well, to you, you are—not as important as a chef though." There was a tiny light dancing at the back of those beautiful eyes that suggested she was teasing me, but I played it safe and changed the direction of the conversation.

"Maybe it was a warning of some kind."

"Maybe." She sounded dubious. "But whoever set off the firecrackers could have no control over the herd. They might have killed you. Buffalo are not very intelligent, you know. Nor are they lenient on foreigners."

We both smiled at that. "Anyway, enough of that. We are here to enjoy ourselves."

"I thought this was business."

"It is for me. If all I have heard about Ottavio is true though, there should be a lot of enjoyment too."

The Palazzo Astoria was almost stark in its design, clearly inspired by the geometric, monochromatic approach of the Viennese. The period when Italy and Austria were closely intertwined politically and each was sending its armies to help crush the other's revolutionaries, coincided with the Biedermeier style of architecture. This had a strong influence in Italy, particularly during a time when alternatives were being sought to balance the country's own heavily classical styles.

Many restaurants followed the Biedermeier pattern, and even when Austria's power declined after World War I, the clean, almost severe lines continued in popularity. In the entryway, walls of racked wine bottles set an opulent tone to offset the strictness. The tables were large, the chairs were comfortable, and the lighting aimed to focus on the food.

We were in Padua, one of the great centers of learning in Italy. Galileo and Petrarch attended the university, and although a number of its treasures were destroyed by bombing in World War II, many still remain. The Palazzo Astoria, just off the Via Squarcione, had several famous and popular restaurants within minutes—"Although a lot of Padovans consider this the best," said Francesca.

As an aperitif, we were both drinking a Bellini. With Venice less than thirty miles away, the influence of this drink naturally prevailed, so closely was it associated with Harry's Bar, where it originated. The richness of the peach juice is cut by the slight acidity of the sparkling *prosecco*.

The waiter came with a silver salver that he set in the middle of the table. *Grancevola alla Veneziana* was the first course, also from Venice, where these spider crabs are caught in abundance. It is not called a salad but to Anglo-Saxons it is, since lettuce leaves line the crab shells, which serve as a bed for the crab meat. The chef had cleverly left a little of the pink coral with the pristine white meat. The sauce contained mayonnaise, cream, ketchup, Worcestershire sauce, and cognac, and the dish was served with diced potatoes and celery stalks.

Francesca and I had agreed on a red wine, even though she said she was determined to have fish. The sommelier, an intense young man, fragile as an Italian bread stick, advised us that as we were having Venetian dishes, we ought to drink either Merlot or Cabernet, the two wines that dominate the region. I thought I detected some caution in his use of "ought to drink," and I said that we had plenty of those among Italy's extensive wine exports. Here, I felt, we should have something more specifically local. He suggested *Venegazzu*, which came originally from a classic blend of Bordeaux grapes, and he brought it now. We tasted and approved wholeheartedly. As we put our glasses down, Francesca gasped, staring across the room, and murmured, "Here he comes."

He came at once to our table. Francesca had told me she had not met him, but Ottavio gave her the full treatment: a small bow, a hand kiss, and that sweeping Italian glance that undresses the mind as well as the body of any female.

"And this is the signor from England. Welcome to the Palazzo Astoria."

I thanked him for his welcome and we all sat, a waiter appearing as if by magic with a chair that Ottavio sat on without even looking to see if it was there.

He looked terrible. His skin was pimply and his face gaunt. The hollow eye sockets were gray, and he had four or five days growth of wispy beard. His hair was long and dangled below his collar, and his lackluster curls were unacquainted with shampoo. If he had not been one of Italy's foremost chefs, he could have modeled for ads depicting the ravages of drug addiction. His wolfish smile was still on Francesca, so I promptly broke that up.

"I am glad you are having an emphasis on Venetian food this week," I said. "I may not be able to go there this time, so instead you're bringing the food to me."

He tore his gaze away from Francesca's charms. She was looking at him with parted, breathless lips and I made a mental note to ask her what she saw in him, although I long ago learned that is a pointless question to ask a woman.

His staff not only knew his habits but were aware of his haughty impatience. One brought him a cup of thick black coffee and another slipped a cigarette between his fingers and produced a lighter. I knew that American and British restrictions on smoking in public places had not yet seeped into Italy. Still, he did not ask if we minded and would probably have gone ahead and smoked anyway.

"Best food in Italy," he said, looking at me as if he expected me to argue. "I cook better Venetian food than anybody in Venice—that's this week. Next week, I'll be cooking food from Abruzzi that is better than any you'll eat there. You know where Abruzzi is?"

He sounded as if he was expecting me to say no but I was not going to get into any kind of argument. "South of here, I think. Isn't it the high mountain country on the Adriatic coast?"

He ignored my answer and went on. "This time of year, I cook food from a different region every week. Know any other chef who can do that?"

"You have a rare talent," I told him, and he stared at me as if trying to find something offensive in my comment. He looked around the restaurant, drank most of his coffee, and took deep drags at his cigarette. Around us, there was the low buzz of conversation, bursts of soft laughter, and the clink of glasses. "This was a coffee shop when I bought it. Coffee and buns, can you believe it? Look at it now—best restaurant in Europe."

"You've done a wonderful job," I said and meant it. "Everyone knows it."

Francesca finally found her voice, though it was a little husky with—with what? Surely not passion?

"It must be very hard work, keeping up such high standards."

"Eighteen hours a day minimum," he said. He seemed to have seen someone across the room.

"Doesn't leave you ~~you~~ much time for recreation, does it?" she said softly.

"Oh, I manage a little—recreation," he replied, sparing her a brief burning look then resuming his gaze across the room. "It *is* them!" he rapped out. "They were in a week or two ago. The stupid waiter got them mixed up with the party at the next table and switched their orders. Would you believe it, they ate right through the meal and didn't even complain! Silly bastards! Not the kind of customers I want in my restaurant. I've got to go and throw them out."

He finished his coffee, put out the cigarette in the saucer, and rose to his feet.

"Anything you want, just let me know," he said, looking at Francesca.

"There is one thing," I said. He turned to me.

"I'd like to look through your kitchen after we've finished the meal."

He looked as though he was about to explode, then his mood switched and he nodded. "All right. Help yourself, Just don't get in the way. It's pandemonium in there—controlled pandemonium," he added quickly. "Controlled by me."

He grinned, the first time he had shown any expression of humor, although it was minimal. "Anyway, I have to keep on the good side of the man who's going to recommend me for the job, don't I?"

Francesca had ordered *crochetti di formaggio* for the first course. It is a dish of Venetian origin, but Ottavio had modified it to accommodate the high production of cheese in this area. The croquettes are made with a thick béchamel sauce mixed with grated cheese and egg then cut into squares, breaded, and fried.

I ordered the "priest stranglers." *Strangolopreti* is a simple dish: gnocchi with spinach. I chose it because it is so simple, to see if a chef with Ottavio's reputation could raise it from the mediocre. He had succeeded admirably. I identified chives, marjoram, and—in addition to onions and garlic—caraway. This was a clever touch and made a real difference to the spinach.

Francesca was carefully silent while we ate. I was fuming but had it under control, and the Venegazzu helped. It was well bottle-aged and could be compared to a fine claret, being silky, just right on the tannin, and balanced, not too robust. When the sommelier asked, I congratulated him on his recommendation.

He bowed in grave acknowledgment, and I hoped he would not break in two.

"Did the *Corriera delle Sera* print the news on the front page?" I asked Francesca despairingly as the sommelier left. "Ottavio knows all about it too."

She dabbed delicately at one cheek where some sauce was adhering. "What else can I say? I keep telling you this is Italy. This is a terrible country for spies. There's so little for them to spy on—everybody knows everything that's happening."

"But how can I do my job? Two of them at least know why I am here. The other one, Bernardo, must know too."

"We'll know tomorrow when we eat there," she said complacently. "Anyway, is it really a problem? Evidently, you came here to recommend a chef for some new restaurant of Desmond's. You have names of three chefs. You're supposed to pick one of them. So go ahead and do it. Pick one."

She took a final mouthful of crochetti, savored it, and took a ladylike sip of wine. She enjoyed the taste so much, she took an unladylike large swallow. She met my glare with a sweet smile.

"You're impossible," I told her.

"I know. You like me though, don't you?"

"You're a very efficient assistant," I told her, but she only pouted and turned it into a smile.

"Just how *do* you decide if a restaurant and a chef are good?" she asked.

Perhaps she was just diverting my anger but I answered.

"The service is a clue to the restaurant itself. Close your menu and someone should be there to take your order. Put down a piece of silverware and a fresh one should immediately take its place. If you leave the table, your napkin should be removed and a clean, folded one should await your return.

"Any waiter must be able to answer any question about the food, its ingredients, and how the dish is prepared. If you eat all the sauce and food remains, you evidently liked the sauce and a good waiter will offer you more. When the bread basket is emptied, it should be refilled."

I would have gone on but the main course arrived. Francesca was having the *branzino,* seabass grilled with a sauce of rosemary, sage, parsley, thyme, chives, and marjoram in olive oil and lemon juice. It looked succulent, the fish cut and opened, and with a long roll of pureed zucchini on top.

As a compromise between what I would really enjoy and what would challenge the chef, I selected the crispy duck breasts with chicken liver sauce and a polenta soufflé. Barrel-shaped turnips and carrots with asparagus tips were arranged in a fan around the thin slices of duck. This is a deceptive dish, not nearly as easy as it looks.

Chopped onion must be combined with chopped salami, chicken livers, capers, anchovies, and breadcrumbs, then stirred until the chicken livers are fully sealed. Flour is added and cooked until just light brown, then white wine goes in and the volume is reduced. Consomme is added, and then egg yolks, lemon juice, lemon rind, and seasonings. This a tedious operation and care is needed. The sliced duck breasts take only ten minutes, but it is easy to overcook or undercook them and the fat has to be really crisp.

Ottavio had done a fine job with this, and his chef had demonstrated a delicate touch while the polenta soufflé was light as an angel's wing. I tasted Francesca's branzino and it was cooked to perfection. We ate leisurely enough that we considered dessert. Italians do not have many desserts. Their tradition has always been to end a meal with fruit—pastries were for festive occasions only. One of the classic desserts, however, is peaches stuffed with a mixture of egg yolks, amaretto, sugar, cocoa powder, and grated lemon rind. Baked for about twenty minutes, it is a superb ending to a meal.

"So, do you want me to come with you tomorrow or do you want to get into trouble by yourself?" Francesca wanted to know.

She just giggled when I told her to watch her tongue. "I want to go to Ferrara," I said. "I've never been there but I've heard a lot about it. I'm also going to drop in on Giacomo and watch his preparations for lunch."

"I hope you'll be careful. Italy is full of dangers besides buffalo."

"Speaking of dangers, let's go see how Ottavio runs his kitchen."

The white-tiled kitchen was cramped and hot. Ottavio, naturally, occupied center stage, standing at a stainless steel–topped table. Behind him was a range of ovens and gas-fired hot plates. On his right, three sous-chefs worked on a long bench above a series of refrigerator cabinets. Another young man with a fifties haircut was feeding plates, dishes, pots, and pans into an automatic washing machine. In an extension off the main kitchen, two pasta chefs were molding dough into a variety of different shapes using a battery of appliances.

Ottavio was meticulously chopping and paring the choicest filets and cutlets out of great slabs of beef, veal, and lamb piled along the front of his table. He worked very fast, pausing occasionally only to brush the sweat from his eyes or push back his long forelocks. When he had finished that task, he went to work on an array of plucked pheasants, slashing and ripping. It looked like haphazard fury at first, but a few moments of observation made it clear that every cut was accurate. A minimum of edible meat was thrown away, while only skin, fat, and an occasional bone went into the garbage barrel.

Ottavio's bony fingers were covered in blood, and some was spattered on his apron. His bare forearms had red burn marks from the ovens. A young apprentice came in with a crate of scallops, and Ottavio went to work opening each shell with a twist of his knife, scraping the contents into a large steel bowl. Another helper came in carrying a tray with several salmon, some sea bass, and turbot, and Ottavio, finishing the scallops, came hurrying over.

He evidently preferred several different implements for this chore. He stood imperiously, waiting for his helpers to put them one at a time into his right hand like some master surgeon in an operating room calling for scalpels and clamps and saws.

Steam was rising from half a dozen pans on the hot plates. Ottavio paused in his task of trimming the fish to dip his fingers in the water and suck them. He waved a commanding hand and a can of salt was promptly pushed into it. He threw the salt in from a height, a technique used by many chefs, and went back to complete his cutting.

He pushed the tray of fish at a sous-chef and went bounding around the kitchen, hair flying, shouting instructions, cursing a young man who dropped a dish, tasting a sauce here and a soup there, yelling invective at everyone within range. "I told you to put the —ing mushrooms on top!" he shouted at a squat, dark-complexioned unfortunate who looked as if he had just heard his death sentence pronounced.

Francesca was taking in this scene of carnage and profanity with her mouth open, although on her that looked good. Her eyes glistened with admiration as she stared at this pyrotechnic display of culinary skill and macho mayhem. Her expression changed, though, when the great chef screamed, "Get out of the —ing way!" and almost knocked her over as he pushed past with a large basket of fruit. I missed the adjective he used here, and also the one that he had used to describe the mushrooms. Presumably they were a profanity that had materialized from the language since my last visit to Italy.

"Thanks for letting us come into your kitchen," I said. "I know it's inconvenient. Hope to see you again soon."

He didn't appear to hear, being too busy castigating an unhappy underling who was slicing vegetables too thin for his liking. I steered Francesca to the door with a hand under her elbow and she did not resist. The bloom seemed to be off the rose now that her wide-eyed veneration had been shattered by being almost bowled over by the master chef and his basket of fruit. She had a stern set to her face and was probably about to hurl some Mediterranean epithet at him, but I got her out the door in time.

We were out in the street when the door opened behind us and a voice shouted, "Don't forget! I'll make it worth your while if you get me that job in London!"

CHAPTER SEVEN

It had been another inquisition all the way back to the hotel. "How could these chefs know?" I asked Francesca again. She shook her head in perplexity.

"How many people in your office knew about this assignment of yours?" I demanded. "One of them must have spilled the beans."

"Beans?" In my recalcitrant mood, I preferred to believe that she was stalling rather than that she was not familiar with the expression.

She explained that she had an independent role in the agency that came from having a small investment in the operation. In this case, Desmond had called and requested her directly. The fax information had given nothing away and only supported the cover story that I was gathering information for an eating guide.

"It's much more likely that it's someone in Desmond's organization," she said in that languid tone that disdained such trivial details.

"How well do you know him?"

She turned in the wide limo seat to face me at this change in direction of the conversation. "What do you mean?"

I picked my words carefully. If I used the wrong ones, I would learn nothing.

"There is a third possibility. Maybe Desmond is up to something."

It was another colloquialism, but she was not baffled by this one. Nor, to my surprise, did she reject it at once. She looked thoughtful. I prompted her.

"I don't what his motive could be," I told her, "nor do I think he's a devious person. But people with money and power are apt to have a lot of irons in the fire." I paused, but her expression did not change so I assumed she knew that one too.

She went back to my first question. "I got to know him very well when he was here. I don't think he does a lot of—what is your word?—shenanigans?" I smiled.

"That's the word and that's how he seemed to me."

"He is very loyal. When he was here, one of his people got into trouble with the police, and it was only Desmond's efforts that kept him out of prison. I can understand what you are thinking though," she said, being surprisingly reasonable. "He is not only a world-famous movie star, he owns restaurants and now he is financing this eating guide. He has his finger in a lot of pots." She smiled. "We say that too—so there may be some angle here that you and I don't know about." She cocked her head on one side in a pretty gesture. "But I don't think so . . ."

I was still thinking about this as I brushed my teeth. The phone rang. A voice, a man's, verified my identity. "This is Brother Angelo. I am a Dominican monk temporarily attached to the cathedral in Modena." He spoke in English, heavily accented but accurate. "I am sorry to bother you this late at night but it is an urgent matter."

I sat down hard on the edge of the bed. "Urgent! What is it?"

"In the confessional, we hear many things. It is not often

that one of them is serious. But now, I have one of these. This is very serious indeed—"

"Yes," I said quickly, "what is it?"

"It is a matter of murder."

His voice sank to a sepulchral level and vibrated with intensity.

"How does this involve me?" I asked, although I had a feeling I was not going to like the answer.

"One attempt on a life has already been made. There is to be another—and this time, it may be successful."

"How do you know this?"

"I told you, the confessional—"

"But I thought you could not divulge anything you learned there."

"Not everyday sins, no," he said indignantly, "but we are talking about murder."

I made a mental note not to accept everything I heard in the movies, even if it came from Hitchcock. I took a breath and asked, "Whose murder?"

There was a pause and in the background, I could hear a low chanting. I assumed it to be Gregorian as I don't know any others. When he answered, Brother Angelo lowered his voice.

"It is difficult to talk. Can you come here to the cathedral tomorrow?"

"In Modena? Yes, I suppose so."

"After morning prayers, ten o'clock. I will meet you by the statue of San Giorgio in the west transept."

I barely had time to agree before he hung up hastily, just as the chant was rising to a glorious crescendo.

Sitting thinking about this provocative conversation, I had pangs of alarm. Brother Angelo must know about the buffalo charge, when Pellegrini and I had a narrow escape. I was still not clear which of us was the target of that attempt and I had noted that Brother Angelo had said "an attempt has already been made on *a* life," not on my life. Pellegrini had no idea who would be trying to kill him and I could not believe that my simple mission of evaluating three chefs singled me out for extinction. So who and why?

After the alarm came doubt. If it was me in somebody's sights, this might be a trick although surely a Dominican monk must be a rarity in a suspect line-up. Was he really what he claimed to be though? I picked up the phone and enlisted the aid of the hotel operator in getting through to the presbytery of the cathedral at Modena.

"Can I speak to Brother Angelo?" I asked.

There was a muttered side conversation and the man answering said, "He has just gone in to evening prayers. He can not be disturbed. Can I give him a message?"

I thanked him, said no, and hung up.

I strolled along Modena's Corso Canale Grande next morning, a thin sunlight trying to build up its energy for a bright and warm day. The city has an extraordinary number of art treasures and is not too well known, so getting around is easy. Its fame lies mainly in the location here of the factories where Ferraris and Maseratis are made and these, sadly, attract most of the tourists.

The lady limo driver had looked a little surprised when I told her that a change in plans meant we were heading for the duomo in Modena instead of the Corso Ercole in Ferrara. Then she nodded and headed for the autostrada. Both cities are less than an hour from Bologna and we were early arriving, so I made my way in the direction of the cathedral, admiring the pink stucco palaces and the beautiful gardens, ablaze with pink hydrangeas, behind magnificent wrought-iron gates.

I walked past a medieval hospital, little changed since the time of the Borgias. Its gray walls bore its five centuries well, testimony to the oft-voiced criticism that Italians are over-whelmed by antiquity. They love it and refuse to change it, which is why they have so many ancient buildings in a state of disrepair. Many of them are amazingly still in service, and this hospital was no exception. Women were hurrying in with covered bowls and trays, for in Italian hospitals it is expected that the patient's family bring in meals.

Modena's duomo is one of the most glorious buildings in Lombardy. Built in the eleventh century, it is impressive in its Romanesque style, and the restoration work that has been necessary over the years has been done with great care and taste so that it appears the same as when it was built. I admired the vaulted ceiling and an outstanding piece of sculpture in which four great stone lions support a long gallery. A rose window threw carmine stains across a floor worn bone white from millions of feet. The place reeked of dust, that unmistakable smell of the past.

I checked the ancient plaques under the statues around the walls, passing batteries of guttering candles, supplications for help or relief plastered above them. Grotesque paintings hung high in dark alcoves. They showed grinning devils jabbing forked spears into pale flesh while, above, winged creatures swooped, herding the damned into the tunnels that led to the underworld. The smell of incense was heavy in the air and the footsteps of a few sightseers clattered on the flagstones. The structure resonated as a bell began to chime ten o'clock.

San Giorgio is a different saint to the Italians. He is not England's mounted knight, who is usually depicted slaying a dragon. This one stood in a niche, blue and white flowers planted around his feet dripping fresh water. A nun, pale face almost hidden in gray and black robes, stood below the saint. She saw me stop and look around. She took a step forward. "You are looking for Brother Angelo?"

I nodded. "He told me to tell you that he would be waiting for you on the bell tower platform," she said softly. I looked up to see an iron staircase winding upwards in a dizzying spiral and thought that he must have something very confidential to impart. My feet clanged on the metal steps. The only lighting came from high on the cathedral walls, and the small bulbs shed only a dim glow.

The handrail was worn smooth and bare. I climbed higher and higher and eventually reached the top—a wide platform which led to a circular stone-slabbed balustrade going all the way around the outside of the tower. Two diametrically opposed archways led out there from the platform. Sunlight came streaming in through these, welcome after the clammy coolness of the cathedral interior.

I heard a voice but could see no one, nor could I distinguish the words. I went out through the nearer of the two archways. The daylight was dazzling and the warmth almost physical, but still there was no one in sight. Perhaps Brother Angelo was on the other side, so I started out to walk around the circular walkway. On the outside was a metal rail and I looked down involuntarily. My stomach lurched—I had forgotten that the tower of Modena's cathedral has a pronounced tilt. The fact is that Italy has many leaning towers but we tend to ignore all the others as the famous one at Pisa has hogged all the publicity.

Vertigo is not something I am usually susceptible to, but looking down almost directly at the ground instead of at the horizon, I came close to a feeling of utter terror. I squeezed back against the inner wall and slid along it as I completed my circumnavigation of the tower. Still no Brother Angelo.

It was as I went back through the archway that I had the stabbing thought that this might be a mistake. After becoming accustomed to the brilliant sunshine, I could see nothing coming back inside. Combined with not finding Brother Angelo as I had expected . . .

There was no further time to speculate. I heard a shuffling sound in the gloom in front of me and a figure materialized as my eyes adjusted. Then I could see brown robes and I asked, "Brother Angelo?"

I realized I was not going to get an answer to my question when I saw the thin-bladed knife protruding from the brown-sleeved robe. I was mesmerized as the deadly-looking weapon moved menacingly towards me. I had the fleeting impression of a pale face largely concealed by a brown cowl pulled well forward, but the knife held the full focus of my attention and no other detail registered.

Backing up hastily was not exactly heroic but it was my first reaction. The knife jerked forward again. I almost lost my footing but I recovered and retreated out on to the balustrade so hastily that my back slammed into the railing and for a sickening second, I thought I was going to topple over. I grabbed the rail to steady myself and a strange thing happened.

The cowled head twitched as if looking past me. The shiny blade of the knife dipped marginally, then the monkish figure turned as if suddenly terrified and ran for the stairs. I could hear sandaled feet rattling on the metal rungs. I turned to see what had frightened my assailant so much, afraid of what I would see.

There was nothing. Blue sky held a little late-morning haze. A few pigeons sailed past and the sun shone. Otherwise, nothing. I went in and stood on the platform, looking down. I could see a figure getting smaller and could hear the patter of hasty footsteps, sounding as if their owner could not get away fast enough.

I felt a profound relief then wondered if I had been too quick to jump to a conclusion. I circled the balustrade again, very carefully but there was no one and no trace of anyone or anything to account for the would-be assassin's abrupt flight. Well, I thought, I really scared him off. I wonder how I did it?

I was in no hurry to get down to ground level and stood for a while regaining my composure and pondering, still baffled. I had a momentary palpitation when I heard footsteps on the staircase from far below, but the voices quickly crystallized into female and childish tones. They were speaking excited French and were surprised to see me up there alone. A grandmother and three grandchildren, they took a lot of photographs of the city below. Before they started on a downward journey, a small German group had made the climb and we all went down together.

Outside, I looked around carefully but there was no sign of any brown-robed figures. I saw a sign over an adjacent door that said "Cathedral Offices," and I went in. An elderly man in clerical habit looked at me questioningly. "Do you have a Brother Angelo here?" I asked.

"Why, yes, we do," he said, turning to point. "He's here right now." He indicated a venerable-looking man, very tall and gaunt, who was surely pushing the age of ninety.

"Thank you," I said. "I must be mistaken."

CHAPTER EIGHT

It was fortunate that Francesca was Italian. She loved opera, she had told me, and what is more dramatic? Being accustomed to opera, she did not burst out laughing when I told her of an attempted murder in a cathedral—she had probably watched that scene on the stage a dozen times. She did show the right amount of concern too, making sure I was unmarked by that wicked-looking knife.

"Now that I think about it more objectively," I said, "I don't think his intention was to stab me. I think the knife was supposed to frighten me into backing into the rail and falling over it. That way, it would look like an accident."

"Then stampeding the buffalo must have been an attempt on you and not on Signor Pellegrini."

"But why? You don't usually try to kill off writers of eating guides, do you? Not until after you see what they have written anyway."

"Very strange," she murmured, still looking very solicitous about my health. She looked almost regal in an ivory linen sheath with high-heeled sandals and chunky gold designer earrings. Her hair shone and her eyes were alluringly bright.

We were on our way to the Ristorante San Pietro where the owner-chef was Bernardo Mantegna, "the philosopher of food" as the Italian media liked to call him. His fame was already spreading to other countries, and I had seen him in a guest appearance on BBC television in a program on Italian food. If he was the man for Desmond Lansdown's new restaurant, now was the time to sign him up before he grew to be even more famous.

He greeted us at the door, a lean, spare man with sad but wise eyes. He was almost bald but had a trim short beard and resembled one of the hermits depicted living in caves in early Italian paintings. He was probably at least ten years younger than his appearance suggested. His wife, Vanessa, was small and dark, gentle in speech and movement. She handled the "front," the reservations, the publicity, and the finances.

Bernardo's influence on the decor was obvious: sparse and simple, it just avoided the grim and serious. The light gray walls had a subtly silver tinge that kept it from being austere, and a fresh bouquet of wild flowers at the reception desk gave a personal touch. Handsome glass vases adorned shelves, and antique glass horses, dolphins, and birds in exotic colors, probably from Murano, near Venice, stood discreetly in wall niches. Largely hidden light sources made them glint and shimmer, giving the whole place a soft warm glow.

A banner over the entrance to the kitchen wished Silvio Pellegrini a happy birthday, and a large photograph of him in a happy mood adjoined it. The party was already under way, and we greeted Pellegrini and his wife, Elena. Pellegrini's lawyer, whom we had also met at Giacomo's restaurant the first night, was there with his wife—Tomasso and Clara Rinaldo. The lawyer, distinctive with his silvery hair and beard, said he hoped I was enjoying my stay in Italy. I did not think it was appropriate to tell him that there had already been two attempts on my life.

I wanted to tell Pellegrini, though, and at least set his mind at rest that I was the target and not him. The festive atmosphere and the proximity of other people made it difficult, and I decided to wait until later. In the meantime, I was kept busy meeting friends of the Pellegrinis and tasting Bernardo's antipasti. Trays were being carried around the room by Bernardo's staff, and the first tray to catch my eye was piled with violet-colored delicacies. "Ravioli potentina," the waiter explained. "They are filled with ricotta and pecorino cheese and chopped prosciutto is added."

"But the color—" I protested, and the waiter smiled.

"Bernardo adds violets to the dough after it is kneaded and rolled. The famous Parma violets."

I should have remembered that Bernardo was passionate about the use of edible flowers, surpassing even the famous Frenchman Marc Veyrat who was a shepherd until he came down from the mountains and opened the famous Auberge de l'Eridan in Annecy, experimenting with the inclusion of wild plants and flowers in the dishes of his native Savoy. Another tray came by containing grilled shrimp with yarrow, the plant with known antibiotic and anti-inflammatory qualities and now being used to treat arthritis. "Many plants currently being used in cooking have medical values also," explained the waiter.

"I wasn't sure I was going to like Bernardo's food," Francesca confided in a low voice as she demolished three more shrimp in rapid succession, "but it really is delicious. What else is there?"

The answer came at once in the form of bite-sized pieces of salmon steak. We both tasted and Francesca gasped in delight. "I've never had salmon that good! What is on it?" The waiter explained that it was nasturtium butter and suggested we try the chickweed salad that was going the rounds in tiny bowls. Bernardo himself was circulating, recommending, advising, and acknowledging compliments with a modest dip of his head. He came over to us. "Have you tried the scallops yet?"

He waved the waiter to us. Small scallops from the Adriatic were added to simmering butter, vinegar, cream, and chopped shallots, he told us. Shredded leaves of wood sorrel were added, cooked quickly, then the scallops were put on a plate and more sorrel sprinkled over them. Eaten with a toothpick, they had a rich taste yet allowed the slight prickle of lemon to come through. We agreed they were superb.

"Do you have to go far afield to find all your herbs and plants?" I asked him.

He smiled a gentle smile. "No, indeed. Let me tell you a story. My friend Jean-Georges Vongerichten, who is as fanatical on this subject as I am, was lured to Manhattan to be head chef at the Trump Tower. Wandering through Central Park, he found no fewer than twenty-five edible plants and flowers. So you see, wherever you are, you can find them in your own backyard."

"But you can't collect them all year," protested Francesca. "Don't different ones bloom only at certain times?"

"That's true," said Bernardo. "Spring is, of course, the time to pick most of them but they can be freeze-dried and used throughout the year." He stopped another waiter. "Taste these. We call them *sambucus*." They looked like golden corn fritters and were scrumptious. "I make them from elderberries."

He excused himself to greet a newcomer who, judging from their conversation, was another chef. Pellegrini hailed him and they embraced, evidently old friends. "Pellegrini knows a lot of people," I commented. "He has many big businesses," Francesca said. "He supplies products to most of the restaurants in the area and even further away."

As more and more people arrived, the flow of antipasti

increased. Tapas and meze are considered the equivalents of antipasto in other countries but there is a difference—in Italy, the antipasto is considered to be restaurant food and is not eaten in the home except perhaps on special family feast days.

Small triangles of pizza—that culinary symbol of Italy—came round, bringing a fresh aroma of hot tomatoes and spices. In America and England, nutritionists rightly protest the fast-food pizza, piled high with saturated fat, sugar, and sodium. In Italy, pizza is a well-balanced meal: a complex carbohydrate (the dough), dressed with vegetables (onions, tomatoes, and peppers), a little protein (anchovies, ham, sausage), and some unsaturated fat (olive oil). Bernardo had added rampion and pimprenelle in this case, said the waiter, two plants that had been known for centuries for their herbal properties. Yet another tray came sailing along, its carrier informing us that it was mushroom pizza flavored with hyssop. This is a widely found plant that in Biblical days was the symbol of purification from sin. It had long been used as a disinfectant on wounds, the waiter told us, before it was discovered that the mold that produces penicillin grows on hyssop leaves.

We sampled *fritelli,* two voluptuous puffs of dough enclosing tender leaves of artichoke, which I reminded Francesca is really a flower. Tiny sausages followed, deliciously flavored with basil, garlic, and orange peel. Several thinly sliced cheeses were squeezed together in a breadless sandwich, attractive as each cheese was a different color: blue, green, yellow, and white.

A familiar face joined us. It was Giacomo, owner-chef of the Capodimonte where we had had the first dinner. He seemed bigger than ever in the crowded room, his beard seemed fuller, and he was bursting with good humor. "I wouldn't be here in this coffee shop," he told us in his booming voice, "if it weren't

for Pellegrini's birthday." He moved on, spreading more humorously critical comments on Bernardo and his "bits of grass"
as he called the edible plants and flowers.

Francesca moved closer to me. "I suppose this food is all
right, isn't it?" she murmured.

"Of course it is. What do you mean?" Then I realized that
she was not referring to the dangers of Bernardo's plants and
flowers. "No," I said firmly. "This isn't the kind of place where
there would be any murder attempts." She looked dubious and
I caught a whiff of her suspicion but pushed it away. "We're all
eating the same food," I said confidently.

Some kind of disturbance was occurring at the door. "It's
Ottavio," said Francesca in a breathy voice, promptly forgetting
my potentially perilous position. It was indeed the terror of the
kitchen at the Palazzo Astoria. Lank hair flopping, a cigarette
dangling from his mouth, he was managing to cause a com-
motion in his first thirty seconds through the door.

"Don't know why I'm here," I could hear him saying pet-
ulantly. "My kitchen crew needs somebody to use a whip on
them all the time, otherwise the place falls apart."

He was obviously a good customer of Pellegrini, who went
to thank him for coming. "Give me a drink," Ottavio barked,
waving away a tray of delectables. "No, I don't want any of that
flower stuff—birds have been shitting all over it."

"Ola!" Bernardo called out, going to him with an out-
stretched hand. "Ottavio! Glad you could come!"

"Not staying." He ignored Bernardo's hand. "What do
you have to do to get a drink here, for God's sake?"

Bernardo took care of that promptly. He was apparently
familiar with Ottavio's hedgehog mannerisms and his own in-
nate gentility made him tolerant of them. Two women hurried

over and Ottavio put an arm around each. Francesca looked on hungrily. "Go on over," I needled her. "You already met him. Ingratiate yourself."

She watched him, being her haughtiest. "I'll wait."

"Neither of those two women is competition for you."

"True," she agreed, eying them disdainfully.

"I'll circulate," I told her. "You're on your own—temporarily."

She gave me her condescending Cleopatra nod and I chatted for a while with Vanessa, Bernardo's wife. She was supportive of his enthusiasm for edible plants and flowers but not as expert as Bernardo.

"He is out at five o'clock some mornings," she said. "Some plants and flowers need to be picked just after the morning dew has left them." We talked about the various steps that her husband believed to be essential before cooking. "Flowers have to have their pistils and stamens removed and only the petals from the flowers are used," she told me. "Bernardo is meticulous too about how plants and flowers are prepared. Some must be chopped with a sharp knife, others need to be torn, some can only be used whole. Some need to be macerated in water, others must be dry. Many must be used the same day they are picked."

She beckoned to a waiter passing by with a tray of succulent-looking slices of terrine with tiny purple, white, and yellow flower petals sprinkled on top. "Have you eaten one of these yet?" I confessed that I hadn't and she explained that the slices were herb and flower cheese terrine. I tasted one and it was superb. "It is a terrine made with cream cheese, provolone, and parmesan cheese," she said. "The parmesan must be absolutely fresh—Bernardo uses only it only when made and eaten the same day. The flowers are called *viola tricolor*—in English you call them pansies. They are mixed in with the cream cheese and more flowers are laid on top." They had a most unusual flavor, hard to identify and almost, but not quite, a minty after-taste.

The birthday boy, Silvio Pellegrini, had worked his way through the still-thickening crowd. His smooth, well-fed face had a prickle of perspiration and he had a glass of champagne in his hand which was surely not the first. He caught sight of me and approached.

"Ah, amico mio, are you enjoying yourself with all these wonderful people?"

Ottavio's biting comments about somebody's wife were raising shouts of critical disagreement but I wasn't going to spoil Pellegrini's birthday by pointing out that "wonderful" might not apply universally. Instead, I told him that I was having a great time.

"Some of Bernardo's plant and flower antipasti are really excellent," I added. "Do you supply him with any of those?"

"No, he forages for those himself. Before dawn some times," he said with a smile. "A very dedicated man."

"It's good of him to throw this birthday party," I said.

"Oh, several chefs in the region do this—taking it in turns. They are all my very good customers." He looked around, making sure that no one was in earshot. Some were but the noise level was spreading like a blanket. Satisfied, he went on, "Have you thought any more about the buffalo incident?"

I hesitated, then told him of my encounter in the duomo at Modena. His eyes widened. "Extraordinary! Then perhaps it was you that the buffalo were intended to trample!"

"Can't imagine why."

He looked at me slyly, tapping the side of his nose in that

typically Italian gesture that implies secrecy. "The chefs," he said, "that must be the reason."

I tried to look as if I didn't understand. He continued, taking a different tack. "I examined the few charred remains of the fireworks. No clues there—you can buy them anywhere. I could find nothing else in the area."

"Have you told the police?" I asked casually.

He looked away. "No. It would not be good for my business."

"Is there anyone who might want to kill you?"

He smiled, slightly uneasily. "Several, I suppose. A man in my position has enemies in business—that is inevitable."

"But none specifically?"

He shrugged. "I am involved now in negotiations to buy some rice fields and that is causing some anger but no, not murder."

"It's a puzzle," I said, trying to draw him into further references to the chefs, but he moved on to another topic. "It is a shame you did not get to see my cheese factories," he said.

"I'd like to see them very much."

"Good. What about tomorrow?"

We agreed upon the details and he pushed back into the throng, receiving claps on the back from the men and kisses from the women. I spied a tray of what appeared to be a close relative of Mexican tostadas. The mashed beans were mixed with olives and avocado slices and the waiter told me that the leaves and petals were borage and lilac.

The lawyer, Tomasso Rinaldo, and his wife, Clara, struggled out of the crowd. Clara was a tall, coppery-haired woman who might have been a singer, for she had a strong, well-modulated voice. "How goes the quest?" Tomasso wanted to know with a conspiratorial wink.

RAI, the Italian television network, must have run a program on my mission. Everybody seemed to know about it. "My quest at the moment is to get a refill on this excellent champagne," I replied. It was an Italian version of champagne, I knew, and as such not strictly entitled to be called champagne, which must come from the Champagne region of France. But Italians (and some winegrowers in other countries) poo-poo such trivialities and are belligerent in defense of their right to produce sparkling wines which they feel should be judged on their merits and not according to where they are produced.

My decoy worked. As a lawyer and as an Italian, Tomasso was bound to contest champagne's determination to remain unique. He did. "This is Prosecco from Conegliano. Just as good as champagne—maybe better. Here, let me get you another." Italians have no qualms about waving, shouting, pointing, and all the other gauche things that Anglo-Saxons studiously avoid. Tomasso did all three and I had a fresh glass of champagne in my hand before you could say Gina Lollobrigida. I should have known, though, that as a lawyer, he would not be sidetracked.

"Our host tonight, Bernardo, is a most resourceful and original chef, don't you think?" I agreed that he was. "But then, so is Giacomo," he resumed. "It is impossible to imagine a difficulty that Giacomo could not overcome."

If he wanted to play that game, so would I. "Whereas Ottavio shows unmistakeable flashes of originality," I said.

Tomasso did not seem inclined to go along with that. Did his lip curl? I glanced at his wife. "What do you think of Ottavio?" I asked. "All the women seem to adore him." Did her glance flicker from my face to Tomasso's too quickly, as if this was a topic she did not care to delve into?

If she was going to answer, she was saved by the cantankerous voice of the temperamental chef himself. "Got to go. God knows what they'll be up to in that kitchen of mine. Hopeless lot. Don't know why I don't fire them all and start again." Like a good host, Bernardo protested such an early departure but Ottavio shook his locks of lank hair. "I'd be going anyway," he said. "Wouldn't want to stay for that camel soup of yours."

I looked to Tomasso and Clara for some exposition of that remark. Both smiled. "It means bread soaked in water," Clara said. "Children put it on their window sills at Christmas to feed the camels of the three wise men." She seemed pleased to have been able to change the subject, and Tomasso took her roughly by the elbow and propelled her into a group of people who he said were waving to them.

Several others came and chatted with me, then, just as Francesca rejoined me, we were asked to sit down for dinner. "You're looking sad," I told her, untruthfully. "You didn't have a chance to tell Ottavio how much you admire his pasta?"

"No, and now he's gone." She looked at the table, the great chef forgotten. "Doesn't this look wonderful?"

It did. In one way, this was better for my supposedly secret mission. I would be able to assess several different dishes prepared by Bernardo rather than those few courses that I would order. There was tagliatelle with olives, peppers stuffed with rice and flavored with garlic and anchovies, and gnocchi Romagnola, a creamy delicacy that melted in the mouth. The filling was ground beef with red wine, chopped tomato pulp, grated carrot, and parmesan cheese. There was also *cappelletti*, little hats, a popular pasta like ravioli stuffed with ground turkey, prosciutto, mortadella, chicken livers, and ricotta while Francesca went wild over the asparagus wrapped in prosciutto and then baked with melted butter and parmesan.

"Do you not like our wonderful food?" asked a female voice.

It was the sultry, dark-haired Elena Pellegrini, looking like an opera star with her ample figure and wearing an emerald-green dress that must have taken a while to get into. She beamed a high candlepower smile at me.

"It truly is wonderful," I agreed. "It would be difficult to pick out any favorites, it's all so good. I suppose many of the ingredients come from your husband's businesses?"

"Many of them, yes."

"But you probably don't have any interest in business?"

Her dark eyes flashed. "I am very interested. I help Silvio a lot. I could run the business better than he does. Mostly, though, I am busy with charity work. I am also on the board of the opera company, I am vice-president of the symphony orchestra association— I am active in many things."

We chatted further, then she was approached by a woman who wanted to know about a meeting of one of Elena's numerous activities. I returned to the food.

Bernardo was making full use of local ingredients, I noticed, and was not pressing too hard his beloved plants and flowers. Not that he had omitted these, for everyone admired the nasturtium fettucine and the cucumber salad with coriander flowers.

Main courses followed, small portions so that everyone could enjoy more than one. Pieces of swordfish steak were served sauteed and covered with flowers that a chef sitting across the table, a man I had not met before, told me was *Satureja*. It gave a piquant spicy flavor and we eventually worked out that it is known in English as savory. Another well-informed guest further down the table said it was the first herb planted by the colonists in America.

The parade of master cooking was unrelenting. *Moscardinetti*, baby octopus cooked in oil with garlic, rosemary, and tomatoes; *quartiretto*, leg of kid stuffed with spinach, eggs, and cheese; *rosettes di vitello*, which was so good I set up another hunt around the table for clues on how it was prepared. The chef remembered having it at the Cipriani Hotel in Venice, where he said it was a specialty. The secret of the sauce, he said, was chopped ox tongue with truffles, gruyère cheese, ham, and mushrooms.

Wine flowed in abundance, and I was pleased to note that Bernardo poured Gattinara among others. This was an old-time favorite of mine, but the quality had sadly dropped off in recent years and I was delighted to see it had bounced back resoundingly.

Desserts came and were sampled with cries of delight, but everyone was too replete to eat much of them. When we had said good-byes to everyone, congratulated Pellegini on his birthday once more, and complimented Bernardo on his magnificent cuisine, Francesca and I sank thankfully into the comfortable seats of the limousine.

"Want to come in for a nightcap?" I asked her, but she rolled her eyes agonizingly.

"I have a lot of work to do tomorrow," she said. "It will be a good opportunity while you are sampling all those wonderful cheeses with Signor Pellegrini."

"Work?"

"Paperwork. In the office."

"All right," I said. "I'll call you later in the day."

"The minibar in your room has Fernet Branca. Best cure in the world for over eating and overdrinking."

"I'll remember that if I ever do either one."

She gave me a look which softened into a smile as the limo stopped, and she left me a purring "Ciao."

CHAPTER NINE

The tour through the Pellegrini cheese factories was an indelible series of mental images: some ancient equipment in dark, echoing chambers with condensation trickling down the walls, and others sparkling new vessels and pipes with temperature indicators, time recorders, and flashing lights in red, white, and green. One minute, we were in the Middle Ages and the next we were on a 2010 science fiction movie set.

Women in white aprons and blue shirts operated machines, men in clean smocks peered through Ferrari glasses at dials and gauges and an occasional inspector walked by with a clipboard, a phone clipped to the waistband, a stopwatch in the hand, and an inquiring expression.

Old and new merged without conflict, the fifteenth century blurred into the twenty-first, and everybody looked professional and efficient in the steamy atmosphere permeated with the almost overpowering smell of sour cheese.

"Some areas are old," explained Pellegrini. "I know we should update them and we will, but as long as they continue to be efficient, we keep them. Some processes in cheese-making are just not suitable to mechanization and still need the human touch." I told him my knowledge of cheese-making was a couple of decades old and asked him to refresh my memory.

"Casein is a protein present in the milk of all mammals. When an acidic substance is added to it, it coagulates and ferments. Man's early attempts at cheese-making used rennet and the process ended there—it was a very sour cheese by today's standards."

"Isn't rennet something that comes from wild animals?"

"Yes, it's their gastric juice and it is extremely potent; one part of rennet will ferment five million parts of milk. The kind we use now though is a chemical substitute—a single enzyme called rennin. Look," he said, pointing, "they are adding some here."

A row of copper cauldrons gleamed soft warm tints, and two workers were emptying a tub of thick white liquid into the warm milk. We walked over a slippery floor to the next building where the curds were being lifted out of wooden vats in large canvas scoops. "This is another operation we will be modernizing soon," Pellegrini said. "Depending on what type of cheese is being made, there can be two or sometimes three operations like this. A stiffness, an elasticity develops—you can see it beginning." As the mechanical paddles stirred, the pasty mass was thickening noticeably. "When it is firm enough, the temperature is lowered and the slabs removed. Treatment from then on varies with the kind of cheese."

"How many kinds do you make?"

"Mozzarella is our biggest product." He smiled. "Thanks to pizza, which is the biggest consumer. Also we make parmesan, and that's thanks to spaghetti. Can you imagine eating a plate of spaghetti without a waiter asking you how much parmesan you want grated onto it? Provolone and caciovallo are our other main products."

We walked on through more buildings, each handling one of the different types of cheese. "Drying can take a month, maturing can take up to a year," Pellegrini was saying, but I was wondering how the workers could stand the smell. It seemed overpowering to me.

On his belt, a phone buzzed and he answered it briefly. "I must go back to the house for a few moments," he said to me after he hung up. "You were particularly interested in seeing how the buffalo are milked, weren't you?"

"Yes, but go ahead with your business in the house."

"I must do it from the phone there, I have some papers—" He called over a fair-haired youngish man with a pleasant smile. "This is Gunther, he is from Austria. He will take you through the rest of the operations here." He turned to Gunther. "I'll meet you in the packing shed for provolone in about fifteen minutes and I can take the signor to the milking area from there."

"Cheese is like wine—it does not travel well," Gunther said as we walked through the packing shed. "You can see that there are several lines, each using a different packing material. You see, cheeses which continue to mature are wrapped in waxed paper and stored in wooden boxes. This way, the cheese can breathe after it has left the cellar. Other cheeses stop maturing as soon as they are taken out of the cellar and they have to be wrapped in plastic to preserve their humidity."

"What about this smaller line here?" I asked. "Aren't those soft cheeses?"

"Yes, and they require different packing too. Some are wrapped in leaves, some real, some synthetic. Others travel on a bed of straw." He smiled at my expression. "Yes, even today this is still a popular method of packing certain of the more expensive soft cheeses. You'll find it amusing that health regulations of the European Union have been altered so that artificial straw can be used in some instances."

A further packing line was located near a massive spool taller than a man. It turned slowly, unrolling a wide sheet of aluminum foil. "That's for full sealing," said Gunther. "Some other soft cheeses are so sensitive, they must be dipped in liquid plastic."

The powerful smell was everywhere and Gunther told me of a nearby village with a cheese factory where an electrical failure occurred. Every operation was paralyzed, and the smell from the storage warehouses, no longer temperature controlled, was so powerful that the village had to be evacuated. Electrical repair teams then went in wearing gas masks.

There was no sign of Pellegrini as we emerged into the sunlight, so I took the opportunity to ask Gunther if mozzarella was the only cheese made from buffalo milk. "No, there are two others: provatura and provole. We make them both, too, but they have to be consumed within a day or two. They do not pack or travel well, so they are consumed locally." He cast an anxious glance around. Almost half an hour had passed and I said, "Look, you must have to get back. I'll walk back to the farmhouse, Signor Pellegrini must still be there." Gunther protested, but I insisted and enjoyed the relatively clear air of the hundred yard walk.

I knocked at the door of the farmhouse but there was no answer. I went in and called Pellegrini's name but all was quiet. As I closed the door behind me, I noticed the robust aroma of coffee. It must come from that elaborate piece of Italian engineering on the table just inside the door and I instinctively looked there.

The chrome-plated monster was quietly oozing steam but the big pot was gone.

I looked around the big room and the first thing that caught my eye was a trail of brown stains on the light-colored matting. They spread in a zigzag pattern and I followed them to find a dozen pieces of shattered china, apparently a coffee cup and saucer. Just beyond them was an overturned chair and the coffee pot, its contents a brown pool rapidly soaking into the floor covering.

Alarmed now, I called Pellegrini's name but all I could hear was the trickle of water from the giant waterwheel in the pond at the end of the room. The trail I had followed lined up that way and I walked tentatively forward.

Then I saw Pellegrini.

He was floating on his back in the shallow pond.

A loud scream came from behind me. An elderly, gray-haired woman with a large sack in one hand stood in the side doorway. She looked from me to Pellegrini and her face was contorted. She screamed again, pointed at me, then turned and ran.

CHAPTER TEN

Captain Cataldo of the *Carabiniere* looked as if he had just come from a dress rehearsal at La Scala. Thigh boots shone as if they got an hour's polishing every day. The black uniform with red piping was immaculate, and the hat with its high-swept brim and spray of feathers would have brought admiration from Hedda Hopper or Carmen Miranda. A sword clanked in a metal scabbard—not a feature seen in the police of very many countries. He introduced himself. His deep voice was beautifully modulated as if he took regular singing lessons.

He had an impossibly handsome face, a fuller version of Victor Mature, and his strong Roman nose was perfect for looking down at people—a posture made easier by his two or three inches over six feet in height.

I had pulled Pellegrini's body closer to the edge of the pool after getting over the shock of finding him floating. Making sure he was dead was not difficult even though I knew it must have occurred within the last half hour. I was sure that the woman who was either the cook or the housekeeper and the person who had found me looking down at the body had rushed off to call the police, but I had phoned Francesca, thankful that she was in the office today.

"Pellegrini is dead," I told her. "Don't ask questions. Yes, I'm still here at his house. Just call the police to come here, then come yourself—now, immediately."

"Dead!" she repeated, but it was the automatic reaction of 99 percent of the population. The one word was her only conventional comment. *"Pronto!"* she said crisply. "I'll be there right away."

She wasn't here yet, though, and this imperious captain was giving me a rough time. I told him the story up to the minute I had walked in here as we stood by the pool. Two of his men had pulled Pellegrini's body out of the water and were examining it.

"Thirty minutes," he said thoughtfully.

"Yes. Gunther can confirm that," I told him.

"You were touring the cheese factory," he said as if he found that a suspicious act.

"Yes."

"Why? What is your interest in cheese?"

It was at that moment that the door burst open and Francesca rushed in. She was wearing dark purple slacks and a tight black sweater—her office working clothes presumably—and I was never so glad to see someone in my life.

She threw me a quick glance and dashed into Captain Cataldo's arms.

My mouth probably fell open as they chattered in rapid-fire Italian, and then the captain turned to me. "So, you are here working for Mr. Desmond Lansdown?"

I had caught the name in their conversation but little else, it had been so fast.

I started to explain but Francesca took over. I did not object in the least—somehow it all sounded better when she said it. When she was finished, she said to me, "The captain knew Desmond while he was making *Don Juan* here. They became very good friends."

I nodded, relieved. Cataldo's look toward me eased slightly. I recalled Lansdown's comment in his fax to the effect that Francesca would be useful, as she knew a lot of influential people. "So what happened?" she asked briskly, as if taking charge of the investigation. I recapped and Cataldo listened attentively, although I had already given him an outline. Just as I finished, the police doctor came in and Cataldo took him over to the two men examining Pellegrini's body.

He rejoined us and said, "I shall, of course, phone Signor Desmond and ask him to confirm your story."

"Good," I told him. "I'll feel better if you do. By the way," I added, "he's in Spain."

"Spain?" he said, surprised. "He is not acting the life of El Cid, is he?"

When I told him whose life Lansdown was acting, Cataldo said, "Ah, King Richard with the heart of a lion, well, the English equivalent of El Cid. Where in Spain is he, do you know?"

"He gave me a phone number where he could be reached." I took the phone number out of my wallet and wrote it on the back of my card. He nodded, turned the card over casually and his face hardened. " 'The Gourmet Detective'," he read. "You did not tell me you are a detective."

That title is always getting me into trouble. It's too late to change it now, though, and I hastened to explain to him. "I'm not really, it's just a name somebody gave me once and it was good for business so I kept using it. I don't do any detecting in the sense you mean. I hunt for rare food ingredients, advise restaurants and producers on where to locate substitute or replacement foods—that kind of thing."

"And precisely what are you doing here in Italy? Desmond Lansdown is a world-famous actor—why does he employ you?"

Sam Spade or Mike Shayne would have given him a hoity-toity answer about their mission being confidential and tossed out some smart-alec remark like "Who's Desmond Lansdown?" but as I had found Pellegrini's dead body under circumstances which were decidedly suspicious, I decided honesty was the preferred policy. I told him about the three chefs and also my cover story as a journalist gathering information for Lansdown's eating guide.

Cataldo nodded slightly. "Ah, yes, I remember he has a famous restaurant in London."

"And others in New York and Miami," added Francesca.

He grunted then resumed his interrogation of me, asking some questions that were new and interspersing them with questions covering the same ground again. He was interested in the dinner of the evening before, and Francesca, explaining that she was there with me, loaded him with names and details.

"Bernardo Mantegna, eh?" he said thoughtfully. "He served plants and flowers in the food, did he?"

"Yes. That's his specialty."

"He is one of your three chefs," he nodded. He resumed his questions, and when a suitable pause in the interrogation came along, I took the opportunity to tell him of the two attempts on me. He listened, his smartly manicured eyebrows coming together in astonishment. "At first, you thought the charge of the buffalo was an attempt on Signor Pellegrini?"

"He did, although neither of us was sure."

"Then the attack in the tower of the duomo convinced you that you were the intended victim?"

"It seemed to suggest that."

"Tell me again exactly how it happened—this monk with a knife."

A strong element of skepticism was implicit when the question was put that way but I told him. "You saw no one else?" he asked.

I agreed.

"So you have no idea why he did not complete his task of assassination?"

"No," I said.

"You saw nothing to indicate what he may have seen that caused him to run away?"

"Nothing. I was baffled but obviously relieved."

He gave me a reproving look. "You should have reported these attempts to us."

"Well, Signor Pellegrini didn't want to report the buffalo charge and my story sounded so weak. I mean, a monk with a knife . . . would you have believed it?"

The police doctor came to us, drew Cataldo aside, and they talked in low tones. Cataldo nodded in response to the doctor's question and the captain rejoined us.

"The doctor must take the body to the forensic laboratory for further examination."

"Any idea how he died?" asked Francesca. Cataldo might not have answered me but he said to her, "Signor Pellegrini has a small contusion behind one ear. It may have been caused by a blow from the waterwheel."

"In that case," said Francesca quickly, "he must have been in the pool already. How did he get there?"

He smiled at her affectionately. "Perhaps I will hire you as an assistant detective." He pointed to the trail of coffee across the floor, the overturned chair, the coffee pot, and the broken china of the cup and saucer. "If I do, your first assignment will be to tell me what this means."

"A fight?" she offered, screwing up her eyes in concentration.

"Possibly," he said slowly. "We will see what other marks are on the body. May I see your hands, signor?" He examined them carefully, especially the knuckles. He nodded, satisfied, and snapped out an order to one of the men by the body. "An analysis of the coffee remains will tell us if something in it caused Signor Pellegrini to lose control and fall into the pool," he told us.

A man and two women came in, one of the women carrying heavy camera equipment and the man a tiny tape recorder. The reversal of roles did not seem to be affecting either of them. Cataldo had a few words with them, and I noticed that they treated him deferentially. He evidently had a high standing in the police organization.

"I'll want to talk to you tomorrow," he said. "When I have more information. In the meantime, you can go if you wish. After I have spoken to Signor Lansdown." He went out of the room. Francesca and I sat and watched the police experts, prowling, examining, searching, photographing, exchanging comments.

"I'm glad you're here," I told Francesca. She smiled then became serious.

"You didn't tell me you're a detective," she said accusingly.

"I'm not. Like I told the captain, someone nicknamed me that and the name has stuck. It has been useful for business so I have kept it. I'm really a food-finder, that's as near as I get to detecting."

"Were you a chef?" she asked.

"I was an apprentice chef at Kettner's, a famous restaurant

in London, then I joined the White Funnel Line as a chef on cruise ships. After several cruises, I worked out a way to stop at various port cities and work in a restaurant for a few months then catch the next cruise ship to another port. That way, I was able to study the cooking in a number of countries."

"You went all over the world?"

"Most of it. I worked ashore in Sydney, Singapore, Beirut, Athens, Lisbon, Miami, Santiago, San Francisco, and a lot of others."

"Then what?" she asked.

"I had had enough traveling so I got a job in London, hunting for rare food ingredients, advising on substitutes for foods that became expensive or hard to get. Eventually, I went on my own. I had a few successes and a columnist in a London newspaper wrote an article on me. She was the one who called me the Gourmet Detective."

She had been listening attentively. She said, "So you haven't had any cases like this one—with a murder, I mean?"

"Oh, I have. In the last few years, I've had more than I would like. Food has become big business. The products have much more value, so with the rewards higher, the risks are much greater."

She smiled. "So you have become a detective after all!"

"Not my idea," I assured her. "I'm not the violent type. The trouble is that a knowledge of food is sometimes necessary to the solving of a crime."

I gave her some brief details of the case that had brought me together with Scotland Yard. "It looked like fish poisoning at first but then it got nasty. Then there was a case in New York concerning a valuable spice from the Orient, and last year I was in France, on a simple case involving a vineyard. Simple! That's what I thought, but I was nearly killed a couple of times."

"Wonderful!" she said, applauding prettily.

"It wasn't. It was terrifying, I—"

"I meant you," she said sweetly.

"I've been lucky—and in this case, it's lucky you know Cataldo," I added.

"Poof!" she said dismissively. "I know a lot of people. He knows more than I do and many more know him."

"His uniform is spectacular."

"Italy has five police forces, did you know that?" she asked.

"No, I didn't."

"Each has a different uniform."

"Which one of the five uniforms does Cataldo wear?"

"None of them." We laughed, then she remembered that a body was just yards away and she covered her mouth with her hand in a little girl gesture.

When the captain returned, he beckoned to me with a wave that belonged in *Tosca*. "He wishes to speak to you," he said, and I followed him to a room that was a business office-cum-study.

"What the hell is going on there?" shouted the familiar Cockney voice. "No, you don't need to answer that, Cataldo told me. Terrible business—you'd better stick around there for a few days till he gets the situation sorted out."

"I may have to," I said. "As I found the body, Cataldo won't want me to leave just yet."

"Francesca helping you out okay?"

"She's wonderful. I'd hate to be involved in this without her here."

"She's a fine girl. Knows everybody."

"So I have found."

"Listen," he said. "I played Sherlock Holmes once. You probably saw the film."

"I—er, think I must have missed that one."

"It came around on video too," he insisted.

"I don't remember seeing—I mean, I'm sure I would remember if I had seen it. Perhaps I was out of the country at the time."

"It played everywhere. They dubbed me in twenty-nine languages . . . well, anyway, I learned a thing or two about detecting, and what you've got to do . . . " I listened as instructed. After all, he was paying me. "I think you'll find this advice helpful," he concluded.

"I'm sure I will," I said, although I was having trouble fitting the Hound of the Baskervilles into the setting of an Italian cheese factory.

Maybe he would add danger money if I told him the rest . . . I told him.

"A buffalo stampede?" he said aghast. "Then a monk with a knife? Never heard anything like it. Are you sure? Haven't been hitting that grappa too hard, have you? No? well, you'd better be careful."

I assured him that I had no higher priority.

"Keep me informed," he said. "I've got to get back and kill a few more Arabs."

He hung up. I replaced the phone reflecting that at this end, death was more permanent.

CHAPTER ELEVEN

I don't think it's safe for you to go out alone any more," Francesca said reprovingly. She was particularly lovely when she had that serious look.

"Are you going to be my bodyguard?"

"I can get a gun from Carlo," she said offhandedly.

"Who's Carlo? The local gun dealer?"

"Carlo Cataldo."

"Oh, the captain—but do you know how to use a gun?"

"You release the safety catch and pull the trigger." She made it sound easier than unhooking a bra.

We were having a light meal in a trattoria. Francesca had gone to school with the daughter of the proprietor and his industrious wife and chef. It had been a short day but a traumatic one. Here in the village of Fontanelice about ten miles southeast of Bologna, the sudden death of Silvio Pellegrini was a remote event, hard to believe it had happened.

Plenty of cars and numerous Vespas—those buzzing motorized scooters—filled the main street of the village, looking for parking places. A large, open-fronted hall was packed with slot machines, video games, and teenagers. A line waited impatiently in front of a movie theater, and cafes had a lot of business. Two snarling dogs circled each other, seeking every excuse to avoid a fight despite the cluster of onlookers calling for blood. In an alley, some small boys were playing soccer beneath strings of drying shirts, blouses, and underwear that hung limp in the still air. Men lounged, smoking, talking. Women leaned out of windows.

We were both eating pepperoni *ripieno*, red and green peppers with onion and anchovies. It is a simple starter, satisfying but not filling, tasty but not obtrusive. Crusty Italian bread rolls redolent with garlic accompanied the dish, and we were drinking the house Chianti. This is yet another wine which gained tremendous popularity only to have the market flooded with inferior product and severely damage Chianti's reputation. It has begun to fight its way back, and the quality of this house variety was proof that the fight was being won.

"I am sure you know the story of Chianti," Francesca said.

"I think I heard it once but I have forgotten it. Tell me again."

"All right whenever I do my guide duty, I tell it."

"Guide duty?"

"Yes, when I don't have any film work, I'm with the escort agency. We also conduct guided tours. When things are slow there—"

"Surely that never happens?"

"The tours slow down out of season. The escort business is always in demand."

"I'm sure it is," I murmured.

"Plus the interpreting and doing jobs like this one for Desmond and you."

"You have a busy schedule."

"I do, and when I am guiding tours, I tell the story of Chianti."

I did not interrupt this time and she smiled delightfully and went on. "The story starts with the Baron Ricasoli early in the nineteenth century. He was very ugly and very cross-eyed, poor man, but he was argumentative and stubborn—not at all likeable. Even so, he was clever and became prime minister for a time. He married a young woman called Anna Bonaccorsi and was extremely jealous of her. So much so that at a ball in Florence, when a young man danced with her several times, her husband, the Iron Baron as he was called, immediately took her out to their coach.

Instead of going to their family home nearby, they drove through the snow to Brolio, his family castle. It was a grim and gloomy place, empty for many years. The baron kept his wife there all the rest of their lives."

"It's a sad story," I agreed. "But what about"—I raised my glass—"Chianti?"

"I'm coming to that. The baron's hobby was experimenting with different types of wine and he tried something very experimental—he mixed black grapes, Sangiovese, with white grapes, Malvasia. He allowed this mixture to ferment twice. Others in the region tasted it and copied it and it became famous."

"And that was called Chianti."

"Right. One of the best Chiantis today is the Ricasoli and the best and most expensive variety is still called the Brolio Castle."

"A terrific story," I admitted.

"The baron preserved the sanctity of his family, kept his wife's name unsullied, maintained his own honor, made a fortune, and gave generations after him much pleasure."

"Everybody came out fine except his wife," I reminded her.

"Sometimes honor is more important than happiness," Francesca said primly.

"I'm not sure I'll drink to that but I will drink to your knowledge as a tour guide."

We did and confirmed that the Chianti really was as good as the earlier sips had promised. This one had not spent eight years in an oak cask like some of its more privileged relatives, but Francesca said four grapes go into the blend that makes Chianti today, and this one certainly extracted the maximum from them.

Francesca put her glass down. "I don't understand," she said, chin at a determined angle. "Just when you had decided that the buffalo stampede was an attack on Signor Pellegrini *pam!*—you are attacked in the duomo. So now it is you that someone wants to kill. Then Signor Pellegrini is found dead— *pum!*—it is not you!"

Her eyes glowed with a passionate intensity. It was almost enough to make me wish I was still in danger.

"Perhaps Pellegrini's death was an accident," I reminded her. "Maybe he had a heart attack or a stroke."

"The buffalo and the duomo?" she questioned.

"Then both must have been attacks on me."

She regarded me gravely. "No connection?"

"None."

"Hm," she pondered. "No, I don't like coincidence."

This was getting to be a tough trade-off, be a target for a killer so I could get Francesca's sympathy. "The question why is the same, though," I pointed out. "Who would want to kill me because I'm seeking a chef?"

She finished the peppers and looked impatiently towards the kitchen for the main course. Her gaze switched back to me. "Are you?"

"Of course I am. Even the chefs know it."

"Perhaps there is something else?"

"Certainly not . . ."

There was a glitter in those beautiful almond-shaped eyes that made my disclaimer fade away. "Someone thinks I am here for some other reason, is that what you mean?"

She nodded. "Doesn't it sound reasonable?"

"First of all, let me tell you that there is no other reason. I did use the cover story of collecting information for an eating guide, that's true. But my mission here—the job that Desmond sent me to do—really is to advise which of the three chefs he should choose for his new restaurant in London."

She looked deep into my eyes. "I believe you." She took the last bread roll and bit into it. "But someone else may suspect more."

Mama came in from the kitchen with two heaping plates of beef in Barolo. The red wine of Barolo, deep and strong in color, flavor, and aroma is the perfect medium for the long cooking of the cubes of shin of beef. We might have gone along with the conventional advice that says when a dish is cooked with wine, that same wine should be drunk with the meal but Mama had already told us they had used the last of the Barolo in the stew.

Food is almost always good in Italy and this was no exception. Foods look, smell, and taste as they should. All of them are honest, there is no subterfuge. Everything is eaten fresh—frozen and canned goods are rarely used in restaurants. It is true that the best French meal is better than the best Italian meal but in that rarified culinary atmosphere, the comparison is largely academic. Italy offers more good meals at any other level.

When we stopped eating to drink Chianti, I said, "You

may be right. It makes sense. The problem is I can't imagine who suspects and what it is."

"Nor can I," Francesca said, returning hungrily to the stew. "We'll see what Carlo has to say tomorrow. He will have some ideas. He is a very clever policeman."

"Have you known him long?"

She nodded. "Yes, many years." She took another large mouthful of stew and added, "My cousin is married to his sister."

In Italy, everyone seems to be related to everyone else. Families are large and especially in villages and small towns— for Italy is dominantly rural—family connections through marriage spread endlessly.

"When do we see him tomorrow?"

"Ten o'clock at the *Questura*."

"This is my first contact with Italian police. You said there are five police forces. Which branch is Cataldo with?"

She called for more bread as she answered my question. "The *Carabiniere* deal with serious crimes and are attached to the armed forces. The *Vigili Urbani* handle minor crimes and take care of traffic control. The *Polizia Ferroviaria* take care of crime on the railways and the *Polizia Stradale* are the highway police. Carlo belongs to the *Questurini*, the *Pubblica Sicurezza*—you would call it national security, I suppose. They investigate crimes."

"I'm impressed. How do you know so much about the police?"

"It is necessary in the escort business."

"You have to know who to bribe, you mean?"

Her eyes danced. "*Corruzione!* Corruption! What a terrible thing to suggest!"

"I thought you were kidding when you told me you were with the escort service."

"Oh, no. We really do supply escorts. It's all very high class, of course."

"Of course," I agreed solemnly.

"This beef in Barolo is very good, isn't it?" she asked demurely.

That redirection of the conversation kept us off that topic, although I made one attempt to return to it. She was a strong-willed girl though, and once she had made up her mind not to discuss the escort business, she held to it.

A pear soaked in wine was Francesca's choice for dessert and I opted for some fresh strawberries. Cappuccino completed the meal, and as we walked out into the warm night air, Francesca said suddenly, "I believe you—about only being here to find a chef, I mean."

"Good."

"Do you believe me?" she asked innocently.

"About your escort agency being high class? Yes, I do."

She giggled. Almost any other response would have told me something.

Police stations in most countries tend to be very much the same. I don't want to sound as if I have been in a lot of them but the ones I have do not show much variance. The Questura, headquarters of the Questurini, was a prominent four-story building with crenellated stone trim above all the windows, several large flags, and a pair of smartly uniformed police on guard duty in front. Not as smart as Captain Cataldo, but that would be a real feat, as well as not being a recommended route to advancement.

We were conducted through passages and corridors lit by

barely adequate bulbs. Men and women in uniform were hurrying to and fro, computer screens glowed proudly as they presented thousands of statistics, and the phone bill must have been horrendous. Cataldo's office, as I might have expected, was almost plush. If anyone in the building had a better office, he was the general or its police equivalent.

The floor was carpeted, a glass-fronted cabinet was filled with law books, and a large framed photo of Cataldo in full dress uniform dominated one wall. He was not a shy man, but then one of the surrounding photos showed him with the Pope, and another with the man who had been the last prime minister, so maybe Cataldo had no reason to be shy.

He greeted us cordially. He wore the same oufit as yesterday but the decorative hat was on a rack above the red-piped black jacket. His impeccable white shirt was his only condescension to informality, and he apologized for not being fully dressed. He moved aside a photograph of himself mounted on a magnificent black horse so that he could spread his elbows on the leather-topped desk.

"We have much information since yesterday," he said in a tone just short of a boast. "I will tell you of it because I think you can help." His glance went from me to Francesca and back. "First, the examination of Signor Pellegrini shows that he died from drowning. The contusion behind his ear evidently rendered him unconscious—he could have been hit by the waterwheel. There are no other signs on the body. His heart and other organs are in normal condition. He did not suffer a heart attack or a stroke."

He moved his elbows closer together and raised his head to survey us.

"Did you check the contents of his stomach?" I asked, not sure whether he was going to continue or not.

"Yes, there was nothing in the coffee."

"I had thought that perhaps something he ate at the birth-day party—"

"That was the night before."

"Yes but some edible substances that upset the stomach can take twelve to twenty-four hours to take effect."

"Edible substances, you say. Can you clarify that?"

I nodded. "I can. I think you've already considered it, though. The plants and flowers used by Bernardo Mantegna in his cooking."

He took his elbows off the desk, leaned back, and beamed at Francesca.

"You have a clever man for a client this time, *cara mia*. He knows about poisons—and what else, I wonder?"

"I didn't say he was poisoned," I objected heatedly. "It's an obvious suspicion, that's all."

He waved a placating hand. "One of the reasons you are here is because you know about food. Oh, Signor Desmond spoke very well of you, and Scotland Yard also holds you in high regard."

"You've spoken to the Yard? Already?"

He was almost purring with pleasure now. "*Certezza!* We do not grow grass under our feet here!" His mood changed. "There is one disturbing factor. When I took upon myself to tell the sad news to Signora Pellegrini of the death of her hus-band, I found that her doctor was with her. She is hallucinating and vomiting."

Francesca looked at me, her face puzzled.

"You already told me you had a suspicion about Bernardo's plants and flowers," Cataldo said to me. "Is not hallucination a symptom caused by some of these?"

"Some, yes, but I am sure that Bernardo would not be using any likely to be harmful or dangerous."

"I spoke to Signor Pellegrini's lawyer and friend this morning," said Cataldo. "Tomasso Rinaldo. He was not in his office and I had to call him at home. He was not feeling well. I am awaiting a report from his doctor." He leaned forward to fix us with a stern look. "Did you eat anything at that party?"

"Everything," Francesca said promptly.

"Yes, I remember that you always had a large appetite," Cataldo agreed.

"Including a lot of foods with plants and flowers in them. My English client here"—she flashed me a mischievous glance—"introduced me to some I did not know."

"I ate a lot of them too," I said. "I suppose it's possible that just one plant or flower was poisonous and was only eaten by Pellegrini, his wife, and Tomasso."

"You both feel well?"

We concurred that we felt fine.

"So how could three people get sick—and one so sick that he died?" Francesca wondered.

Captain Cataldo sighed deeply. "I see I have a lot of work ahead of me. I will start with you two. Before this day is out, I want a list, as near as you recall it, of everything you ate that evening. I will try to match it up with the same information from everyone else. I have asked Bernardo for a list of every plant and flower he used. You all drank only prosecco, I believe?"

"I didn't see anyone drinking anything else," I said and Francesca nodded.

"And you, signor, you will write out for me your professional opinion as to the characteristics of every plant and flower used at that party."

"I will. I can tell you now, though, that the most common reaction to a dangerous plant or flower is hallucinations. One explanation of Signor Pellegrini's death fits in here—perhaps he ingested something that caused him to hallucinate. He was dizzy, fell, dropped the coffee pot, knocked over the chair, broke the cup and saucer, staggered, and fell in the pool."

"And the waterwheel hit him behind the ear rendering him unconscious so that he drowned." Cataldo finished the grim scenario.

"One other thing you need to ask everyone who was at that party," I said to Cataldo.

He might be a peacock but he listened. "Yes?" he said alertly.

"Ask about allergies and medication. There was an instance in the U.S.A. a couple of years ago where otherwise harmless vegetables caused death when taken with Prozac, a common antidepressant. Many people died before the Food and Drug Administration investigators were able to tie the two together."

Captain Cataldo blew out his cheeks. "Very well. I will remember that."

"We will leave," said Francesca. "Let you get back to your work."

It was not the way an interrogation usually ended. In my limited experience, the detective reluctantly allowed the suspects to go, but I suppose that when your cousin is married to the detective's sister, you can change the rules.

CHAPTER TWELVE

How did Desmond take the news? I forgot to ask you yesterday."

Francesca and I were having an early lunch after leaving Cataldo's office, and she asked the question as the waitress was bringing us two plates of spaghetti.

"He told me of his role as Sherlock Holmes and gave me some tips as to how to solve the crime."

She gave a short laugh and said, "That sounds like Desmond. Did he appoint me as your Dr. Watson?"

"No, but I'm sure he would have if he had thought of it."

The spaghetti was perfectly al dente and we were having it the simplest way: *alla prestianara*, seasoned only with garlic and olive oil. The restaurant was O Forno, a place with a good reputation for reliable local cooking. "If it is good, you can put it in your eating guide," Francesca said.

She was expertly wrapping spaghetti strands round her fork while keeping it vertical and spinning it on the way to her mouth. In my business, I meet a lot of women with hearty appetites but Francesca was up near the top of the list. "You know the secret of eating spaghetti?" she asked me.

"No, what is it?"

"It was told to me by Sophia Loren on the set once. You have to imagine you're a vacuum cleaner, she said."

We were near Ravenna and close enough to the coast that

the catches of the day were among the offerings. We both chose for the main course the *sorpresa di mare,* the surprise of the sea, which today contained clams, langoustines, sole, scallops, octopus, and monkfish sprinkled with pine nuts, almonds, parsley, garlic, white wine, and olive oil. This was baked under a pastry crust then upturned on to the plate with the pastry crisp and golden brown. Pinot Grigio is another Italian wine that has become so popular that some of the vineyards producing it have let their standards slip in increasing their volume. The bottle we were sharing carried the Burti label and was one of the more dependable products.

"It was nice of Carlo to say we could help with his investigation, wasn't it?" said Francesca between mouthfuls of food and appreciative oohs and ahs.

"I don't think he put it quite like that."

"Well, that's what he meant," she said in that definitive, feminine way that bars all further debate.

"Okay," I said. "You know him better than I do. Meanwhile, let's work on our lists. As soon as you've finished that spaghetti," I added. Three more spins of the fork and she had finished. I took a little longer, then we compiled our lists, able to remind each another of plants or flowers that the other had forgotten. As we looked them over, she nodded. "That's all I can remember. I'll see Carlo gets them."

"So what do we do next?" she demanded. "Who do we— what's that lovely English word? I know—harass!" She gave it the American pronunciation with a firm emphasis on the second syllable. It sounds much more virile and disturbing that way.

"One thing I want to do," I said, disregarding her flawed approach to investigation, "is visit some rice fields."

She put down her fork—a sure sign that I had her attention. "Rice?"

"Pellegrini told me that he wanted to buy some rice fields. It sounded as if the owners were resisting him. That could be a motive. Besides, I've wanted to see an Italian rice field ever since that Anna Magnani movie."

"You may be disappointed. She doesn't work there any more." She resumed eating but during the next break, she asked, "Do you think any of the chefs are involved?"

"I wondered about that. Didn't someone tell me that all three of our chefs have financial interests outside their restaurants?"

"I am sure they do. Why?'

"I wonder if Pellegrini was involved with them in any of those?"

"Want me to find out?"

"Can you do that?" I asked in surprise.

"No è problema," she said dismissively. "My cousin is married to an accountant. He works for all the big banks."

We finished the fish and agreed on its excellence. The waiter had brought us another bottle of Pinot Grigio, and as we drank that, Francesca said, "Carlo wants us to come to Signor Pellegrini's funeral."

"He does? Both of us? I didn't really know him that well "

"The Anglo-Saxon attitude to funerals is different. You are so serious, so somber about them. Here, they are an occasion for people to get together, eat and drink—and mourn their friend too, of course. But many come who are perhaps not his friend. They come nevertheless. Everyone talks about the dead person. Some say good things, some say bad. Everyone has a wonderful time."

"Like the Irish."

"The Irish?" said Francesca. "They do this? Like us?"

"Yes. It's called a wake. They all enjoy it, get drunk . . ."

"The proper way to mourn."

"So why does the captain want us to come?" I persisted.

"I think he has a motive," she said in a lowered voice, enjoying the flavor of conspiracy. "All the people involved will be there. Maybe he expects one of them to get drunk enough to say something incriminating."

"Funny place to solve a crime," I mused. "Still, you're right, we might learn something. We'll accept his invitation."

"I don't think that's what it is," she said, emptying her glass. "It's more like an order."

Francesca had an appointment with a woman who wanted to engage the services of her escort bureau at a coming convention in Cremona. Francesca did not offer any details of the services, and I didn't ask. She was reluctant to have me go alone when I told her that I was going to Bernardo's restaurant, but I told her to keep her appointment and assured her that she could not help me anyway as she had no gun yet. She giggled and gave me a peck on the cheek.

I had two reasons for my visit. One was to talk to Bernardo about his plants and flowers, the other was to see his kitchen and assess how he operated it. The timing was good, for it was about an hour before opening for lunch. It was convenient too, for Bernardo was in the kitchen directing operations, busy but willing to talk to me at the same time.

His tonsure, his clipped beard, and his sad eyes gave him a

serious demeanor normally, but the death of Pellegrini made him even more austere. "I have been through the list of every flower and every plant that I used in the food for that party," he said vehemently. "Not one of them was harmful—they couldn't have been!"

"You are the expert," I told him "but a man has died and it's better to face some of these questions now."

He stopped chopping radicchio and said earnestly, "Very well. What questions?"

"Plants that look alike, for example. One is harmless, the other is dangerous. Take jasmine. I know the Arabian variety is used widely but the Carolina variety—which looks very similar—is poisonous."

"I know the difference," Bernardo said simply. "I know too that certain food combinations can affect certain individuals—there was a woman who got violently ill whenever she ate vanilla and orange in the same meal. There are other food combinations that have been reported as harmful—beetroot and rhubarb for instance. Salmon and strawberries are another. But these incidents are rare," he went on, becoming more ardent, "and they only affect something like one person in several hundred thousand. They are no more common when the food intake includes flowers and plants than in everyday foods."

I nodded sympathetically. "I agree. Tomatoes, coffee, sugarcane, pears, spinach, almonds, strawberries—all contain toxins and are potentially harmful. But people eat them every day—and still they can be dangerous in large quantities or to people with rare allergies."

"Exactly. I would like to use sunflowers, the seeds are delicious and the petals and the buds are very tasty. I don't use them, though, as they cause allergic reactions in some people."

Bernardo was cooling down as he realized I was on his side.

"Still," I went on, "we have this unfortunate circumstance of Signor Pellegrini's death, and questions will continue to be asked."

"And I will give answers," he said earnestly. "I know that there is the suspicion that I may have picked a toxic flower and mixed it in with the others. There are so many of these. Azaleas, buttercups, marigolds, oleanders, rhododendrons—all are poisonous. Anyone who wants to kill a—" He paused as he realized where this was taking him. "But I have made a life study of plants and flowers and I know which are dangerous . . ."

I picked up on his previous words. "You were about to say that anyone who wants to kill a person can readily do so with a plant or a flower."

He became more animated than I had seen him. "I didn't kill Signor Pellegrini. I had no reason to do so."

"But someone may have—and they could have done it by putting a hallucinatory flower or plant into the food."

"It would have to be someone with a certain knowledge . . ."

"Like another chef?"

Several reactions to that question flitted across his face, which was more responsive now and no longer the clerical mask of innocence. "I—I am not suggesting that." Further thoughts were occurring to him. He said, "That would mean deliberately throwing suspicion on me."

I tried to look as if I had not already thought of that. He flicked his short beard with a finger. "You seem to know something about plants," he hurried on to say. "You must know that many are hallucinatory but have no other effect."

"Yes, I know that."

"So how could a murderer know that Silvio, in an hallu-cinated state, would fall into the waterwheel pool and drown?"

I gave him a sage look, cocked my head on one side, and looked pensive.

"Then there are other plants or flowers that are halluci-natory in the immediate early stages and then become deadly," I pointed out.

"The police would find them in Pellegrini's stomach."

I gave him an infinitesimal head movement meaning "Yes, the police would." I had, in fact, considered that very problem and both those points, getting nowhere with them.

I knew something he didn't though—namely that the po-lice lab had not found any substance in Pellegrini's stomach that should not be there. How did that help? I asked myself and got no answer there either.

"The police will come up with something very soon, I'm sure," I told him. When all else fails, a platitude is soothing. "Captain Cataldo appears to be a very efficient officer."

"He has a good record for solving crimes," said Bernardo. That made the score 1–1 in platitudes.

"If you want to go ahead and prepare for lunch, please do," I said. "Do you mind if I watch?"

"For your report?" he asked blandly.

I gave him a meaningless smile. Everybody else seemed to know, there was no reason that Bernardo shouldn't know too. He went off to chop some turkeys.

This is a popular meat in Italy and not at all limited to feast days as it is in the U.S.A. and Britain. Bernardo was separating some of them—the breasts, which would have slices of pro-sciutto and mozzarella laid on them; the legs, which would be boned and filled with forcemeat and then braised; and the wings, which would be baked in sauce. He was removing the livers, for to some connoisseurs, these are more prized than chicken livers. He was also removing the head, the feet, the kidneys, and the gizzard for one of the classic garnishes such as *financière*.

He was setting aside the giblets, which are of special importance as they are popular in a number of ways: fried in butter, fricasseed, boiled with vegetables, in a ragu (the Italian version of a ragout), browned with chipolata sausages, or boiled farmhouse style, perhaps in a strong red Italian wine. His staff worked industriously and expertly. Unlike the mercurial Ottavio, Bernardo clearly saw no need to stand over them with a whip—his tongue.

I thought of Ottavio's complaint that his kitchen fell apart when he was not there, which I disbelieved completely. I contrived to take a look at Bernardo's meat grinders. That much-favored Italian dish, *polpettone,* contains a mixture of ground meats—beef, veal, and pork. The meat grinders used are difficult to keep clean, and they are a good indication of a kitchen's condition. Bernardo had four grinders, the fourth for ham, and all gleamed clean metal.

I looked at the stock pots, but there was no indication that these were reused and topped up—another kitchen economy. I noticed that raw meat and poultry were separate from other foods, avoiding cross-contamination. Similarly, raw meat was kept well away from cooked foods. All in all, the place got high marks, and after looking through the storage, I thanked Bernardo and went back to my hotel.

Italian hotels are fond of a very large room key that discourages the guest from taking it with them. Always eager to adopt new technology, they were among the first in Europe to introduce

electronic cards as door openers, but too many complaints resulted and the large key made a comeback. Consequently, I had
to go to the desk to claim mine, and the woman at the desk
pulled out a note along with the key.

"You have had two phone calls, 'urgent,' it says."

"Did they leave a name?"

She looked at the note. "They will call again at four
o'clock."

Above the desk, clocks displayed the time in a dozen cities
from New York to Tokyo. When I found the one that said
"Bologna," it showed five minutes to four. As I entered the
room, the phone rang and I picked it up.

"It's Brother Angelo," said the voice.

CHAPTER THIRTEEN

You have got one hell of a nerve!" I yelled angrily.

"Don't hang up—"

"Why should I listen to you? The last time I did, you tried to kill me!"

"No, I didn't—"

"Does the Vatican know you carry a knife?" I demanded.

"I want to explain—"

"Surely a knife is not standard equipment for Dominican monks, is it?"

"I wasn't going to use it." The voice was the same but more hesitant, even nervous.

"Not to kill me maybe but to force me over the parapet. Isn't that breaking at least one of the Ten Commandments?"

"That was not my intention either. You must listen to me—" The voice went up and, angry as I was, I noticed that the accent on the English words was less noticeable now. There was still that Italian inflection but it sounded different. "I want you to meet me and I'll explain everything."

"Meet you! You must think I'm crazy! First, you phone me, tell me you're a Dominican monk, say you have important information about a murder, ask me to meet you then you try to kill me in two different ways. Neither of them works so now you want to try again!"

"You'll understand if you'll only listen to me." His tone was almost pleading.

"Go ahead then, explain."

"Not on the phone. It's too dangerous."

I couldn't believe him. "You think this is dangerous? What about cathedrals? What about bell tower platforms and parapets? Now *they* are dangerous!"

"It is much more important to talk now." There was a slight tremor in his voice.

"Important to who?" I demanded. My grammar always suffers when I am under stress.

"To me."

"I take back what I said about you thinking I'm crazy! You must be the one who's crazy! You mean you want me to meet you?"

"Yes."

"When?" I asked, knowing that I had not the least intention of doing any such thing.

"This evening."

I laughed. "After dark, I suppose?"

"No, about seven."

"You really are crazy—"

"Anywhere—I'll meet you anywhere." His voice quivered slightly. He was certainly a good actor, but I had no desire to play the corpse in one of his melodramas.

"Not in a cathedral," I said, recalling Thomas à Becket.

"Anywhere," he repeated.

"Give me one good reason why I should," I suggested, just digging for clues but still firm about avoiding the murderous Brother Angelo at all costs.

"I can tell you about Pellegrini and the three chefs."

That stopped me in midbreath.

"What about them?" I asked the question before I could stop myself.

"Not on the telephone, I told you. Where can we meet? Anywhere . . ."

"All right," I found myself saying, leaving my better judgment laying there in fragments. "In front of the Questura."

I heard a swift gasp. "The police headquarters! There are guards in front!"

"I know. They can guard me."

Silence. That's stymied him, I thought. He won't go for that.

"All right," he said abruptly. "Seven o'clock."

He hung up. I stood there, looking stupidly at the dead phone in my hand.

In many of the detective stories I've read, when the investigator goes to keep a dubious rendezvous with a suspicious character, he shows up very early to look over the area. I was there by five o'clock, standing across the street and studying the Questura building.

Somewhere inside, Captain Cataldo was probably pondering the Pellegrini case, reviewing evidence, and studying forensic reports. I tried to remember the view from his office window. Did it look this way? If he saw me talking to a figure in the robes of a Dominican monk, he'd be down in a flash. It was not likely that the person I was going to meet would be wearing that disguise again, though. Maybe he would be a mailman this time. Instinctively, I looked for mailmen but none were in sight. All I could see were the two guards in front of the building. I didn't want to be too paranoid but I did watch them for a minute or two. They passed the inspection.

The passersby all looked harmless. Nobody was loitering. No one stood with a face behind a newspaper. A man and a woman got out of a taxi and went into the building. A *furgoncini* passed me—these three-wheeled bicycles are still used for local, light deliveries. A big blue bus stopped, not at its marked stopping place because that was filled with cars. I watched passengers get off, and they all scurried in various directions. I watched passengers getting on and there was no one left behind. Nothing suspicious. No monks.

Two men stood in front of the Questura building, arguing but not loud enough for me to hear them from across the street. I didn't need to, for it was like watching a mime contest. The gestures used by Italians are known all over the world. They use them mainly to emphasize meanings or feelings but also to express a thought that is better not put into words.

One of the two across the street was now rubbing the back of one hand horizontally under his chin, to and fro. It means, I couldn't care less, nothing to do with me. The other tapped the side of his nose—a gesture that has been adopted by many other nations to imply secrecy or information withheld. The response to this was a closing of both eyes and a slight raising of the head. This means, I did all I could. It's out of my hands. I watched them use a whole repertoire of others. Some I recognized, some I didn't, and yet others probably passed unnoticed by my unaccustomed eye. Finally they went into the building, and I wondered how many of those gestures would be brought out in a courtroom to help seal the verdict of the jury.

I looked in all directions for a little while longer. There was no other sidewalk entertainment to match that, and all appeared peaceful and unthreatening. Fleetingly placated, I walked along to the corner and across the Piazza Verdi where I knew several restaurants could be found. Whatever I was going to face, I would face it on a full stomach. The Albergo Solferino was one of the few eating places that were open this early. It was near the Teatro Municipale and evidently catered to people working there and audiences before and after performances.

It was a pleasant place with an array of tempting antipasti just inside the door so that you had to walk past it to reach your table. Paintings and photos adorned the ocher walls, and I noticed that the same man was smiling and waving in many of the photos. "Our former mayor," explained the waiter when he handed me the menu. "He still eats here." Judging from the hammer and sickle flag fluttering prominently, all the photos were taken during the period when Bologna was the bastion of Communism in Italy.

The antipasto table proved to be irresistible and I sampled the green gnocchi filled with gorgonzola, some salmon mousse, a few garlic shrimp, and some mushrooms stuffed with truffles. The veal scallopine with fresh asparagus made an admirable main course and a bowl of fresh cherries completed the meal. A bottle of Sangiovese was smooth and ruby red—then I remembered that the name means the blood of Jove; I really didn't want any mentions of blood as I contemplated the coming encounter.

I had stretched out the meal with a cup of espresso and I returned to the Questura where I stood again, across the street and ten minutes early. Italian cities are slowly coming to life at seven o'clock but it is still too early for the crowds. Some were leaving offices and shops, and the flow of buses, cars, and taxis was thickening. In front of the Questura, all looked calm and peaceful. Long may it continue, I thought fervently.

At seven-fifteen. I was ready to conclude that it had all been some kind of hoax. I was taking one last look up and down the street before leaving my post when I saw him. The brown robes of a Dominican monk with the cowl pulled up around the head and face. He paused in front of one of the guards outside the Questura, then walked along until he was in front of the other. He stopped and surveyed the surroundings.

He made no move as he saw me approaching from across the street. I dodged a bus seeking a place to stop. A taxi blared its horn, then I reached the sidewalk. I stayed a few paces away from him. The nearer of the two guards was about the same distance.

"If you have something to say, say it," I invited.

He stood there immobile. His hands were hidden inside his robes and I kept a sharp eye on them. His face was a pale blur inside the cowl that was drawn well forward. The proximity of the guard seemed to intimidate him, which was just what I wanted. His head turned marginally in that direction then back to me. He came a few steps closer.

"I didn't try to kill you," he said. It was almost comical in the way he was trying to speak so I could hear him but keep his words from being heard by the guard.

"What did you want to do? Scare me away?"

"Of course not." He was very definite. It baffled me.

"Why then?"

"The buffalo were stampeded to kill Pellegrini. If they had killed you too, that would have made it look like an obvious accident. If they had killed Pellegrini only then any suspicion would have fallen on you."

Again I had that nagging feeling that the voice should be telling me something about its owner but I could not determine what it was. The accent was back, Italian surely . . . but something about it was not quite right.

"What about the incident at the duomo?"

"That was to make it look as if Pellegrini's death in his house was an accident. All the other attempts would appear to be against you."

"You mean Pellegrini's death was not an accident?" I raised my voice in incredulity at this revelation, and he glanced apprehensively at the guard but his eyes still looked straight ahead. "Who killed him?" I asked.

The cowl twitched and pasty features were partially revealed, but before I could see more a nervous convulsion went through the robed frame. He seemed to be looking past me and I turned. I had an ephemeral thought that it was the oldest trick in the book, but then I saw a black car with the window down and a face looking out directly at us.

I was about to dive for the pavement, having seen enough gangster movies to know about drive-by shootings but by then I was aware of "Brother Angelo" running past me on sandaled feet. I heard him gasp—it sounded like fear. My gaze swung to the car but the ugly snout of a weapon had not appeared. The face was still there though, and observing the robed figure racing towards a bus that had stopped by a rank of motorscooters as the only available place. He flung himself inside just as the door snapped shut.

The face moved back to me. I promptly made a dash into the Questura.

Captain Cataldo was out, I was told by a stern-faced woman police officer. Would I like to talk to someone else? I didn't think so. It would be too long an explanation. Suddenly, I remembered that I had in my pocket the list of everything I had eaten at Pellegrini's birthday party. I handed it over, asking that she be sure the captain received it.

She read it suspiciously, looked at me for clarification. "He asked me for it," I explained. She looked at it again and I realized that it did look like a shopping list. "It's for a case he's working on," I told her and when that got no reaction, I added, "A murder case." That worked. She put it in a huge official-looking envelope with a large red tassel attached which she used to wind around the large buttons.

When I asked if there was a back exit, her suspicions returned but I told her my car was out there. She said the front entrance was the only one for the public. I was wondering how long I could hang around before being arrested for loitering in a police station when a group came along. Two men were uniformed and three more were in plain clothes. Two of the latter were handcuffed together. They went outside and I followed, staying as close as I could. The two handcuffed men seemed remarkably friendly and chatted away to one another.

I walked along with them, smiling at the nearest to make it look as if I was with them. He looked puzzled, as if trying to place me, and then smiled back. We went to the next block and up the steps of a large building with massive columns. The words chopped in stone on the front proclaimed it to be the law courts. We all went inside.

I had to lose my protectors then, but I talked with a lady at a desk and stretched out my request to talk to Captain Cataldo, making a show of not understanding her directions to a building on the next block. The long Italian lunch from noon to four o'clock meant that many of the hard-working defenders of the law working here were only now leaving their offices. I scanned all the faces within my vision then mingled with a bunch of chattering men and women leaving. The taxi queue was short and the brief wait uneventful.

CHAPTER FOURTEEN

How was your business meeting yesterday?" I asked Francesca. "Successful, I hope?"

It was the following morning and we were in the limo heading for the church where the funeral service was to be held. I had spent a quiet evening and eaten in the hotel dining room, surrounded by German tourists. A change in rooms was the only precaution I had taken, though I had considered changing hotels.

"Yes," Francesca said. "The woman wanted three girls."

I wanted to ask the obvious question but did not. Francesca smiled sweetly and asked, "How was your visit to San Pietro? By the way, don't you think that's a good name for a restaurant owned by a chef they call the hermit?"

"I didn't learn much. Bernardo is convinced that none of the food he served that night could have been harmful."

"How does he account for three people having hallucinations from it?" she wanted to know.

"You would make a good interrogator," I told her. "A swift, direct query like that."

"So how does he?"

"He can't. I am looking forward to hearing what Captain Cataldo has to say today. He was going to run the tests over again and make absolutely sure that there was nothing harmful in Pellegrini's stomach."

I looked out of the window casually. "The rest of the day

was more informative. I had another meeting with Brother Angelo."

Her eyes widened. "He didn't try to kill you again, did he?"

I told her the whole story. She listened with parted lips. "He said he wasn't trying to kill you before? Just make it look as if you were the victim so that when Signor Pellegrini died, it would not look like murder?"

"Right."

"So Signor Pellegrini was murdered?"

"If we believe Brother Angelo."

"But how?"

"Like I told you—he didn't get that far. He didn't tell me how or who. This car stopped and a man was leaning out, staring at him. Brother Angelo—or whoever he is—seemed to be terrified and ran for the bus."

"Did the car follow him?"

"I think so, but I couldn't be sure."

"You didn't recognize the man in the car, I don't suppose?"

"Never saw him before, but I think I'd know him if I saw him again."

Francesca shook her head in despair. "I am not letting you go anywhere alone any more. You can't even go to a cathedral or a police headquarters without getting into trouble."

"There's no point in risking your life too."

"I'll have a gun today." She screwed up her eyes; it was supposed to give her a ferocious look. "Carlo is bringing me one."

"At a funeral?"

"Why not?"

"I'm probably the one who should be carrying it."

"You're a foreigner. Better not."

I was relieved to hear her say that. I hate guns and never carry one, even when a case gets dangerous—which is rare. I recalled my view of this assignment as having "no risks at all" when I had first talked to Desmond Lansdown. How wrong I was.

The ceremony was an elaborate one, and the big church in Bologna was nearly full. Elena, Pellegrini's wife, sobbed throughout, and the monsignor conducting the service spoke eloquently of the deceased's benevolence and many donations to charity. I saw many familiar faces—Tomasso, the silvery-haired friend and lawyer, supported Pellegrini's wife, and on the other side, the lawyer's wife, Clara, was dry-eyed but stone-faced. Giacomo and Bernardo were there, though on opposite sides of the aisle. I could see no sign of Ottavio or Captain Cataldo.

The coach that took Pellegrini's body to the cemetery was the most magnificent vehicle I had ever seen. Massive and with enormous wheels, the outside was decorated with angels, saints, cherubs, and harps. The coffin was almost as elaborate, and the bearers, six of them, were resplendent in black tail-coated suits and towering shiny black hats.

Some gray clouds flitted across the sky, giving a clichéd grimness to the scene during the burial. Elena was still weeping and so were other women, evidently relatives.

Half an hour later, the scene in the banquet room at the Hotel Excelsior could not have been more different. True, there were no balloons and no jazz band but hardly any other feature was lacking from a festive affair. People seemed animated and even more talkative than usual. Drinks were being dispensed and the air was crackling with bonhomie and good humor.

"Italians really know how to celebrate an occasion, don't they?" I commented.

Francesca nodded, surveying the chattering crowd eagerly pressing around the buffet tables. "The sad part is over—the service in the church and the burial. Now we remind ourselves that life goes on. It sounds heartless to some foreigners, I know, but we are saying 'It is a shame he is dead, but we celebrate the fact that we are still alive'."

Before I could respond, she grabbed my arm. "Look, he's here!"

It was the tyrannical master of the Palazzo Astoria, the scourge of the kitchen—Ottavio Battista. He looked scruffier than ever and his hair was even more unruly. He came within earshot and we could hear him saying. "What a place to have a reception! Worst food in town!"

Despite his appearance and his manners, he had a small crowd around him and Francesca looked on starry-eyed. One of his admirers asked him a question and he snapped, "I'm not sorry he's dead—maybe I won't have to pay back all that money I owed him." His adoring fans were lapping it up and squealed in delight when he said, "Oh, God, here comes Bernardo! Let's move on, he's going to say something pious."

I shook Francesca by the elbow, breaking the spell. "Shall we try the buffet?"

We surveyed the tables. Despite Ottavio's criticism, the Excelsior was one of the best hotels in the region. Contrary to many other countries, hotel restaurants in Italy offer a very high standard of food and this looked as if it was maintaining the standard.

Francesca studied them dubiously. "None of them has flowers, right?"

"Stop spreading propaganda about Bernardo's food. It is innocent until it is proved guilty."

"Italy still has the Napoleonic Code, didn't you know? Guilty till proven innocent is the law here."

"Anyway, I don't see any flowers. The shrimp look good."

They were butterflied and served with a spicy dipping sauce, strong on the red chilies. Crab on jicama wedges was even better, a fresh tomato sauce with plenty of lime juice in it making it lively on the tongue. We made our way over to the drinks table where white-uniformed bartenders were a chorus of flashing hands and bubbling liquids. Francesca had a Campari and soda, I had a gin and tonic. She spied a friend and went to chat. I was back at the buffet tables when a voice hailed me from behind.

It was Tomasso Rinaldo, the silvery-haired lawyer. "Have you recovered?" I asked.

He held out his glass. Its contents were clear and a few bubbles were rising.

"Mineral water," he said. "Yes, I feel fine now but the doctor suggested I eat and drink carefully for a few days."

"What do you think caused it?" I asked.

"H'm," he pondered. "Well, I can't say it was a poisonous plant or flower. I just don't know. It didn't affect me until several hours later."

"Did you have hallucinations?"

"Yes and when I tried to sleep, I had the wildest dreams."

"Sounds like a mild dose of—whatever it was."

"Fortunately for me," he agreed. "I have been asking around to see who else was affected. You had no problems?"

"None at all."

"So far Elena Pellegrini seems to be the only other

one," he mused. "Strange, that. She apparently had the symptoms worse than I did. She was strongly hallucinated and disoriented."

We both sampled the squares of focaccia, the Italian cornmeal bread, spread with mozzarella, prosciutto, and chopped olives, pronounced them excellent, and went back for more.

"I certainly hope it wasn't a dangerous plant or flower that caused poor Silvio's death," said Tomasso Rinaldo. "Bernardo is fanatical about that stuff—it's obvious he wouldn't kill anyone with it."

I sipped some gin and tonic and looked thoughtful. "Doesn't seem very likely that anyone actually killed Pellegrini anyway, does it? Some kind of bizarre accident is a more probable answer, surely?"

He nibbled on another focaccia. "Certainly."

"Although if someone did want to kill him, using a poisonous flower would be an easy way to do it and at the same time, push suspicion onto Bernardo."

"I can't think who it would be." He finished his mineral water. "Oh, he has some business rivals and competitors but I can't believe any of them would do anything like this. The man did have a knack for getting people angry at him, though. He has been wanting me to bring a lawsuit against a big landowner here for weeks."

"Not enough motive for murder there though, surely?"

"Not in my opinion."

"What kind of action was it?"

"Ah." He looked away then shrugged. "Can't do any harm to tell you now. It was a breach of contract. Silvio wanted to buy some rice fields, and he believed that the owner had given him a verbal promise to sell."

"That's something I want to see, the rice fields," I told him. "Hope I can do it while I am here."

He brandished his glass. "Have to get some more of this, keep me healthy."

He left me and I wandered, having a few desultory conversations. In one corner of the big room, I heard what sounded like singing and I strolled in that direction. Anita, the wife of Giacomo, was playing a guitar and accompanying herself as she sang what sounded like a very bawdy song. Guests were moving nearer so they could hear. Giacomo himself was in a small group and talking spiritedly. I edged closer to listen.

"It is a shame that Bolognese cuisine, the finest in Europe, has to have clowns like these," he was saying. "One of them behaves like a spoiled child, all tantrums and nasty remarks. The other cooks with flowers and plants—food isn't good enough for him!" That brought a laugh and he went on, his beard waggling as he talked. "The good name that our cooking has—our great reputation that has been amassed over the centuries—what is going to happen to these if egotistical prima donnas like these two continue to wreak havoc in this way?"

His booming voice was attracting more listeners, who came with full glasses and ready laughter. "Poison both of them, Giacomo!" shouted someone at the back, while another wit called out a suggestion that would require the assistance of a local noblewoman who claimed to be a descendant of Lucrezia Borgia.

Anita was playing louder now, seemingly in an attempt to drown out her husband, and her lyrics were getting more ribald. Francesca drifted back to me. She was dressed very demurely as befitted a funeral but spoiled that image at once. "Coarse bitch," she said, commenting on Anita.

"Have you tried these *salsiccie*?" she asked me. Tiny sausages with a wide variety of flavorings are an important part of any antipasto selection. These contained fennel and garlic, a very toothsome combination.

I told her of Tomasso's comments.

"No one would kill over a breach of contract, would they?"

"Hardly. Is the dashing captain here yet?"

She shook her head. "We'd have seen him." She had a point.

"How about the master chef? Talked to him yet?"

She pouted. "He's in a foul mood. Can't say a nice thing about—or to—anybody."

"Sounds like he's normal."

She raised a finger in a charming gesture—sometimes she had the mannerisms of a teenager. "I wanted to tell you, I just heard a strong rumor. It's about Giacomo. They say he's about to lose his third star in Michelin."

I whistled. "Whew, that's serious!"

She looked surprised. "Is it? Who cares about that as long as the food's still good?"

"Lots of people. It could have damaging consequences for his career."

As I said it, there was a stir in the room, a sudden shift in the timbre of the conversation. A majestic figure with a tall, plumed hat and swinging a black cloak had swept into the room.

Captain Cataldo had arrived.

CHAPTER FIFTEEN

The plumes on the hat were undoubtedly eagle feathers; I would not believe that the captain would wear any other. The uniform was similar to that he had worn in our last encounter, but this one had three rows of medals. The epaulettes had shiny silver emblems, and the most striking feature of all, the cloak, was big enough to make a tent for a platoon.

He made his way to Elena, the widow, first of all and was clearly consoling her, though he was too far away for us to hear. The monsignor who had conducted the service was next for him to talk to, and then he chatted with several relatives one after another. "I know he swaggers a lot," said Francesca, "but he is a very compassionate man."

I got Francesca and myself another drink and we had time to pay another visit to the buffet table before Captain Cataldo had fulfilled all his duties. He exchanged greetings with a few other people, then finally made his way over to us. Francesca hugged him, cloak and all.

"Is this your first Italian funeral?" he asked me.

"It is. Very illuminating, new viewpoints on the Italian character."

"The Anglo-Saxon funeral is a very depressing affair. I attended one once. It tried hard to match the dark skies and the rain which did not stop."

His handsome tanned face with its bold features and proud

Roman nose was even more impressive than I remembered it, perhaps accented by the magnificent outfit. I congratulated him on it and he preened. "I wear it for special occasions," he explained. "I have another—well, two—three if you count the full dress uniform—but this one is more suitable for a funeral."

He eyed me reflectively. "So, no more attempts on your life, I hope?"

Francesca and I traded glances. He was quick to interpret them correctly. "Better tell me," he ordered gravely.

I told him of the latest episode involving the murderous monk.

"So he claimed not to be trying to kill you or even frighten you . . ." He thought about that for a moment. "At least you showed good judgment in choosing a rendezvous." He permitted himself a slight smile. "In front of the Questura, near the guards—that was good."

"I didn't tell him about the assistant public prosecutor who was shot dead in front of that building a few weeks ago," said Francesca matter-of-factly.

"Probably different circumstances altogether," I maintained lamely.

"A drive-by shooting," she said.

Cataldo was tactful enough to change the direction of the conversation. "You say you think you would know the man if you saw him again?"

"I'm pretty sure. Now, what can you tell us?" I asked, hurrying to head off any more helpful comparisons from Francesca.

"Further analytical work has found absolutely nothing harmful in Signor Pellegrini's stomach. We have tested and double-tested samples of all the different plants and flowers in Bernardo's kitchen—nothing."

"Any other victims?"

"Another guest reported having severe internal pains that night. Our police doctor is conferring with the man's family doctor to see if the symptoms match. There may be no connection—we Italians have *crisi di fegato*—problems with the liver. It is a national complaint like you English have always had the gout, Jews are always constipated, and Americans all have stomach problems."

"So where does that leave you?" I asked.

He hitched his cloak in a swirl. It must have been designed to show to advantage in that maneuver. "I wonder how much credence we can place in this Brother Angelo's statement that Pellegrini's death was murder."

"He baffles me," I admitted. "I can't understand him at all."

"Tell me, from your experience in the food business, do you have knowledge of poisonous substances in food?"

"Some," I said. "Why do you ask?"

"Is there such a thing as an untraceable poison?"

"I'm sure you have already asked your forensic experts," I countered.

He grimaced. "They say there is no such substance, but then, like all experts, they don't want to admit there is something they don't know about."

"Experts always like to protect their rear. They will all say that they don't think there is an untraceable poison—but if there is, they have not run into it yet. Maybe in the future . . . who knows?"

"I hope this is not the future," said Cataldo gloomily. "I am just a policeman—I need more help than this!"

"We can help," chipped in Francesca, "but as I told you when I phoned, we may be in danger. We need to be able to protect ourselves."

"Yes, well," said Cataldo a little reluctantly, reaching inside that capacious cloak, "take this." He handed her a copy of *Oggi*, the popular magazine. It was folded two ways and secured with tape. "Don't open it here!" he told her in alarm and just in time. "There is a temporary license there too." She gave him a businesslike nod and stuffed it carelessly into her purse, though I noticed she was vigilant when clipping it shut.

"I received your list of the foods you ate. Very comprehensive," he said to me. He turned to Francesca. "I do not have yours yet. Let me have it quickly."

She gave him a mock curtsy. He sighed in equally mock exasperation and left us to go to the bar. Drinking on duty was evidently not prohibited by the Italian police rule book. Francesca patted her handbag affectionately. "You see how easy it was?"

"Too easy," I said. "Are you sure you can handle it?"

She gave me a scornful look and stalked off to the buffet table.

I was not alone for long. Anita, the guitar-playing, bawdy song–singing wife of Giacomo Ferrero, chef and owner of Capodimonte, appeared at my side and gave me a probing look. "Remember me?" she asked in a seductive voice.

"Very well," I said. "You sing beautifully."

She moved closer. She was a sultry woman, with jet black hair pulled back and a large mouth which she used to maximum effect. "I always wanted to be a singer," she said, "but so do many others in Italy. It's just as well perhaps." She smiled meaningfully. "Opera lyrics are dull. The ones I was singing today are better, don't you think?"

"I must admit that I haven't heard those particular ones sung at a funeral before."

"Did I shock you?"

"I was completely shocked," I said solemnly.

She laughed. It was an earthy, throaty laugh. Perhaps it was well she had not become an opera singer. "I have others that are much more shocking," she said, looking at me with big eyes. "I must sing some of them for you sometime."

"That would be . . ." I was trying to think of a better word than "interesting" when she said brightly, "I know—we'll go to Venice!"

"We will?"

Her eyes searched my face. "Have you ever been to Venice?"

"Once, many years ago."

"Then it is time for you to go again. It is such a romantic city. I know it well—I can be your guide." She looked upwards, thinking. "Yes, we will go this weekend."

Before I could comment, she was continuing. "You live in London?"

"Yes."

"An exciting city. I am looking forward to living there."

"Oh?" I said, very surprised. "You are going there?"

She surveyed the room, making head-to-toe studies of a couple of women nearby with disdain. "Why, yes," she said silkily, coming back to me. "You are going to recommend Giacomo for the job there, aren't you?" She gave me a full attention smile with that wide mouth. "But we can talk about that in Venice. I'll be in touch."

Francesca wound her way through the knots of people and rejoined me. "How did you and the vampire of Capodimonte get along?" she wanted to know.

"Anita? I was congratulating her on her singing."

"You obviously know nothing about music. What did she say?"

"Invited me to a weekend in Venice," I said casually.

"Sounds like her style. She has quite a reputation, did you know that?"

"I can believe it." I told her the substance of the conversation.

"Presumptious cow! Thinks she can seduce you so that you'll recommend her husband." She showed me her lovely Italian profile, chin raised. "She can't, can she?"

"The English are not bribeable."

"Ha!" she scoffed, then became suddenly serious. "Listen, Elena is coming over. I talked to her for a few minutes, and Carlo suggested she mingle. She's still teary-eyed. It will do her good. Here she comes now."

Elena looked very fetching in black with a veil, and she seemed to have her grief under control. I commiserated with her for a few moments. "Captain Cataldo has been most kind and sympathetic," she said in a soft voice. "Naturally, he was asking about Silvio's interest in opening a sales operation for edible plants and flowers. It's understandable—at least three of us ingested something dangerous. I'm lucky to be alive, Tomasso escaped, only poor Silvio . . ." she dissolved into sobs but quickly wiped them away with an embroidered handkerchief. "I'm sorry—it's just so difficult to accept."

"I understand that you took a study course in edible plants and flowers," I said, not wanting to upset her further but curious to hear what she had to say about this.

"I did, yes. Silvio asked me to—I was going to be a botanist, you know, until I met Silvio and we were married."

"I didn't know that. So you already had an interest in the subject?"

"Yes. Rice was another product that I gathered information on for Silvio."

"Why rice?" Francesca asked innocently.

"It's one of the most important commodities in the food business in Italy. Silvio wanted to know all about it. He has a large share of the cheese market, he had visions of being just as powerful in rice. He was a very meticulous man—he needed to gather masses of data on a subject before making a decision about it."

We could hear Ottavio's whining voice complaining about the antipasti, the drinks, and the crowd and declaring that he was leaving. Funerals were boring anyway, he added, and Elena gave a nervous half-smile as if excusing him. A man who introduced himself as Elena's cousin came along and said he wanted to take her away to talk to another member of the family. Elena and Francesca embraced as if they were bosom friends and Elena left.

"Rice keeps turning up in conversations," I said. "Aside from having an interest in seeing it harvested, as I mentioned, maybe we should go have a look at this place that Pellegrini wanted to buy."

"Sure," said Francesca readily. "We can go tomorrow. It's not far."

Cataldo approached, a highly visible presence with his regal stature and imposing uniform. "I have to go back to the office," he told us. "What are your plans? What dangerous situation do you plan on entering next?" he asked me and Francesca answered promptly. "We're going to the Dorigo Farms near Gremolana."

Cataldo frowned, perplexed. "Why are you going there?"

Francesca explained. Cataldo kept frowning. Finally, he shrugged. "Very well. Need I add, 'be careful'? You seem to be a lightning rod for attracting hazards."

"I'll be safe," I told him. "I have an armed bodyguard."

Somehow that assurance did not seem to placate him.

CHAPTER SIXTEEN

The almost impossibly bright green stretched out as far as the eye could see in every direction. The endless rows of rice plants were two feet high and tightly squeezed together, so that they seemed like a vast green blanket covering the earth. Only an occasional levee broke the green monotony—low banks of packed earth to prevent water draining off. In the distance, silvery silos with conical tops squatted in groups, waiting to be filled, and just beyond, long metal-roofed buildings contained the equipment that prepared the rice for packing and shipping.

Our guide was a young woman of about Francesca's age. Our party was eight in number. Two were Canadians from the wheat belt, curious to compare the similar processes used for mankind's two most important grains. A serious German couple with an interest in everything, and two Austrians who had run out of cathedrals to visit, made up the total as we rolled along an access road in a large Jeep-type vehicle extended to accomodate more seats.

"There is only one species of rice," the efficient young woman told us, first in English and then in German, "but there are over eight thousand varieties. Some produce long-grain rice, some medium-grain, and some short-grain. There are many aromatic and scented varieties, while others are bred to suit specific local conditions."

"Does this kind of rice grow any higher?" one of the Austrians asked.

"It will be fully grown in another week or so," said our guide. "It will have grown to about three feet by then. Some varieties in other parts of the world grow over six feet tall."

Many of the rice fields were flooded, and a Canadian asked why. The guide explained that the main purpose of the standing water was to drown out the weeds that deprive the rice plants of sunlight and air. These fields were the rice paddies that are the typical image of rice growing. "Looking for Anna Magnani wading through the water?" Francesca murmured.

Huge flocks of birds came sweeping down like flying clouds, their raucous calls drowning out even the vehicle's engine. "They live on the ripe grain," explained our guide. "Their migratory habits are dictated by our planting cycle."

The tour of the extensive fields completed, we were taken through the large buildings we had seen earlier where the grinding, milling, and sieving were done. The hull was removed first, said our guide, showing us a line of red-painted machines with shiny metal pipes and funnels. This produces brown rice, she told us, and this can be eaten, but the brown-colored bran layers contain oil which causes the rice to spoil rapidly. She took us past batteries of brightly painted blue milling machines which polish the grains and produce the pearly white appearance that everyone finds familiar.

One of the big buildings was arranged as a museum, displaying antique equipment and large colored boards describing different rice varieties. That led into another building fitted out as a cafeteria. A hum of conversation came from the area for employees, and there was a pleasing smell of cooking food. We were invited to eat in the visitors' area and the meal was, not surprisingly, rice dishes and risottos.

All were Lombardy dishes, as a menu clarified. There was *ris e erba savia*, rice boiled in consomme with onion and sage; *ris e lovertis*, rice boiled in consomme to which is added at the last minute, hops browned in butter and lots of grated parmesan cheese; *ris e erborin*, rice cooked in consomme with parsley; and *risotto con el rane*, which caused me to ask Francesca, "Isn't *rane* frog?"

She conferred with an attendant and then said to me, "We should have guessed. All these flooded fields means there are thousands of frogs."

"So the easiest way to keep down the frog population is to eat them."

Francesca nodded. "Yes. They boil the frogs, pound the meat into a pulp, and add it to the rice with butter, oil, garlic, and onion."

We ate small quantities of several risottos, sampling and comparing. The long tables and benches were sufficient to accomodate a much larger number of visitors but it was, as Francesca pointed out, a little too early in the season. A very ordinary Soave was served—this being another of those Italian wines that is produced in response to a familiarity with the name so that quality has sadly deteriorated.

"What's the matter?" Francesca asked suddenly.

I didn't answer at once. I was staring across the cafeteria. "Over there," I said, "putting his tray onto the pile. Now he's heading for the door."

She followed my line of sight. "Who is he?" Then she said quickly, "The man in the car? When you talked to Brother Angelo in front of the Questura?"

"Yes. I'm sure it's him."

She looked from him to me. "What are we going to do?"

"Do you have that gun Cataldo gave you?"

She patted her purse affectionately. "Of course."

"Better give it to me."

"You hate guns, remember? I'll keep it for the time being."

She was a willful girl as I knew by now, so I didn't argue. "Come on. We'll follow him."

We watched as he walked across the open space in front of the cafeteria building. He was easy to spot, a short stocky fellow with a slight roll to his walk. He had black hair and a squat, flat face.

"He's going to one of those vehicles," Francesca said. A row of trucks, bulldozers, scrapers, and similar wheeled equipment stood there, and the man took a key from his pocket. He stopped at a yellow six-wheeler with a folding contraption on the front. He was going to get in, then he changed his mind and went to inspect the back tires.

"We're parked near enough," I said quickly. "We can get your car and follow him."

We had come in Francesca's Fiat and she nodded. "All right. Let's hurry."

We pulled out of the parking lot and she drove slowly along the front rank from where we could see the collection of utility vehicles. He was still there, examining a tire, then, seemingly satisfied, he opened the door and climbed in. He drove off along a well-used track, apparently across the wide-open spaces of the rice paddies.

"Don't go yet," I warned. "We can watch him from here and he can't see us."

In a couple of minutes, his destination was clear. Two huts sat in isolation some distance away and the yellow six-wheeler slowed and turned towards them.

The man got out and went to one of the huts. He opened the door and stood, looking inside. He was much too far away for us to hear but he was having a conversation with someone in the hut. It was apparently heated, for he was waving his arms and gesticulating.

"Can you see who he's talking to?" Francesca asked.

"No. We'll have to get closer."

"We can't—he'll see us." While I said it, I was studying the huts. "But if you drive ahead, we'll be able to stop where the other hut blocks his view. We'll be able to keep an eye on him but he won't be able to see the car."

She drove and stopped. "Let's leave the car here," she suggested. "If we walk along this track, we'll be closer, and from that angle we might be able to see who he's talking to."

I wondered if Desmond Lansdown had known what an adventurous assistant he was handing me. Still, it made sense from an investigative point of view and we walked about thirty yards. The rice plants were higher here and we only had to crouch slightly to be out of sight. The man was still talking and moving his hands, then he went inside.

We stood there, seemingly alone in the universe. The unbelievably green plants surrounded us, reaching to the horizon in every direction. Insects buzzed around us. The air was hot now that it was early afternoon, and it was very humid.

"We should get closer still," murmured Francesca.

"I suppose we could wade," I said but my tone must have been dubious because she did not respond. The soil between the rows of rice plants was soft and yielding. Pulling a foot out of it made a sucking sound as if the earth were reluctant to let us go.

"What's that?" demanded Francesca.

I listened. "I don't hear anything," I said, but then I did. It was a hum, louder than the insects. It increased to a steady drone then got louder still. "Look!" cried Francesca, pointing.

A speck was visible in the sky. Then it was a big dot and moving so fast that it solidified into two horizontal lines, and in seconds it was identifiable as a plane. It was not high, which was why it looked to be moving so fast. It rapidly became a shape, a biplane with a strangely tall fuselage.

It was heading straight for us

The nose dipped and we stared as if hypnotized, nowhere to run, nowhere to hide. I had the uncomfortable feeling of déja vu but could not place it, and the aircraft thundering at us filled the sky.

A spray of white fumes spurted out from the bottom of the strange aircraft and then they enveloped us as the plane roared overhead. We both fell to the ground, coughing and gasping, trying to roll away from the choking canopy of gas.

We must have lost track of time, trying to scramble out of the fumes because here it came again. The spray was settling slowly, and as we strained to get our heads into clear air, we had a terrifying view of the aerial demon streaking towards us. Then another asphyxiating cloud swept over us and the water did not matter, as we both went splashing calf-deep in our attempts to find a place to breathe.

"Where's the car?" Francesca gasped. In the panic and confusion, we did not know which way to look. Unwillingly, we looked upward. The plane was banking tightly, turning for another run at us quickly before we could decide where to hide.

Francesca flung her arms around me in fear and I held her tightly. There was no escape. The biplane grew bigger and bigger as it dipped and came at us.

A peculiar yammering sound replaced the roar of the engine, an irregular stuttering, then the engine stopped altogether. One wing drooped limply, like that of a wounded bird. One terrifying moment it seemed as though it was going to hit us, then it veered away and hit the water with an almighty splash.

I pulled Francesca to where the fumes seemed to be thinner. We staggered out of the suffocating white clouds. They were settling now, and though still spluttering we seemed to be unharmed. Francesca certainly was. "Let's have a look at the pilot," were her first words.

We stumbled to the plane. It looked smaller now that it was grounded and helpless. The deep fuselage was due to a tank that was built into the underside and contained the chemicals.

"They always explode in the movies," I warned her, but her experience in the make-believe world of films made her contemptuous of such a risk.

She tried to pull the door open but it had jammed, perhaps with the impact. The aircraft was nose-down at about a thirty-degree angle out of the rice paddy. There was the soft hiss of a dying hydraulic system then all was quiet. We grabbed the door handle together and heaved. It was still stuck. "Once more," I said. We pulled mightily and it flew open.

We looked in the cockpit. It was empty.

Francesca and I stared at each other. She tried to climb inside, but there was no step. I had her put her foot in my clasped hands and I heaved her up. I stretched as high as I could to see. Not only was there no pilot, but there was no control column and no rudder bar. Only three instruments adorned the small panel and they had no indicator needles—they were strictly recorders. We both reached the same conclusion as we said in unison, "It's robot controlled!"

Francesca slid out of the cockpit with an agile push and a twist. "So that's what the man was doing in the hut," I said.

"You think so?"

"Look!" I pointed to the hut. A large antenna poked out of the roof.

"You know what I think?" Francesca asked and didn't wait for an answer. "I think we were set up. I think that man wanted you to see him. He wanted us to follow him out here where we would be—what do you call them—sitting ducks."

"He must still be in there," I said. "But wait a minute—where's that vehicle he was driving?"

The deep bellow of a powerful engine came in answer, shattering the silence of the rice fields. The menacing bulk of the big yellow vehicle was racing at us, and we turned to run. It changed direction to head us off.

We stopped and Francesca seized my hand. We were cut off from her car and the yellow monster loomed larger.

CHAPTER SEVENTEEN

The plane!" I shouted. "Come on!"

I pulled at Francesca's hand and we struggled across the rice fields, tripping over the rows of plants, squelching through the ankle-deep water. The howl of the yellow vehicle grew louder. I pulled harder. "Come on! We've got to get to the plane!"

The bellowing six-wheeler was almost touching us. It pushed a mass of warm air over us then came water splashing in great gouts, but we scrambled to the plane, flung ourselves against it, and our pursuer raced by, swerving away at the last second. We could see now the ease with which it negotiated the water and the rice plant rows. Its wheels were sprung independently, and it swayed and rolled but stayed on course.

Wet and gasping, we slid around to the other side of the plane so as to put it between us and our enemy. We could hear a groaning, screeching sound and Francesca and I exchanged puzzled glances. We slithered along the airplane's fuselage so as to be able to see what was causing the sound.

The mechanism on the front of the vehicle was unfolding. We could hear metallic crunching as it slotted into position. Two steel arms, articulated and hinged so they could reach in any direction, reached out as if feeling for us. On the ends of the arms were giant claws with metal fingers which flexed as if relishing the idea of crushing us in their grasp. The motor roared, then the machine rolled towards us, picking up speed.

We were nearly knocked to the ground as the impact slammed the airplane back. For a moment, it seemed about to tilt over and fall on us but it settled into the swampy ground in a different position, tail higher now. Gears screamed as if in anger at our resistance, then the groping metal arms reached out and gripped the fuselage of the robot plane, lifting it into the air.

The intent of the driver was obvious. Unable to reach us when we were using the plane as cover, he was going to lift it and drop it on us. We could not have held on to the plane if we had wanted—there were no projections to grab, no hand-holds. I could see Francesca's eyes opening wide in terror as our protective shield rose before our eyes.

One wing, already partly severed, snapped and fell near us, hitting the mud with a soggy thud and flinging up a great brown wave. It must have blocked the driver's view momentarily. We dodged aside and we had our closest view yet of the driver's compartment. All we could see was a dim outline of a figure, any details hidden by the dark tinted glass all around to screen out the Italian sun. The arms swiveled as if human and rammed the remains of the plane down on us.

The breaking of the one wing was our savior, for we had already moved to avoid it and now we just had time to move again. Another wave of muddy water hit us, leaving us drenched and defenseless. The yellow monster was moving on us again, still holding the aircraft in its claws.

As it did so, white clouds of gas started to spurt out, sweeping around the vehicle. In seconds, it was enveloping it.

"The chemical tank has burst!" I gasped in relief and Francesca hung on to my arm.

We stood, helpless and exposed, but the spray was spreading around the front of the yellow six-wheeler. I did not know if it was penetrating the cab, but it was certainly obscuring the driver's vision. "Let's go!" I shouted. We hesitated for a moment. In all the excitement, we had become disoriented and neither of us knew where the car was. Francesca had the presence of mind to look for the two huts and then she pointed. "The car's there!"

We ran.

It started at the first touch. Francesca spun the wheels, flinging up large puffs of dust, then we were racing along the road. I looked back. A billowing screen of white vapor hid the front of the yellow vehicle.

"Shall we find Signor Dorigo and tell him his hospitality needs improvement?" Francesca called out as she rammed the pedal to the floor.

"Yes!" I shouted back. "But not now. Keep driving."

"My hotel will refuse to let me in looking like this," I complained.

"Let's go to my apartment. We can get cleaned up there."

Her apartment was like many in the larger towns in Northern Italy. It was in an old building that looked grim and forbidding outside. Entrance was through large wrought-iron gates but then the entire complexion changed. The inner courtyard was dense with flowers and shrubs, a riot of early summer colors. The stairways were narrow and dark and the elevator tiny and creaky, but Francesca's apartment was a delight. High ceilings and old furniture were blended with an occasional modern piece. The floor was Tuscan tile, rusty red, with worn but serviceable Persian carpets. Tall windows let in beams of yellow sunlight and one gave a view of the busy street below.

She insisted I shower first and handed me a blue bathrobe. "I'll clean up your clothes as soon as I come out," she said. When she did emerge, she was wearing a white version of the same robe. Her lustrous black hair was piled high and her face was scrubbed fresh and clean. She had put on the merest touch of makeup and her smile was warm as she came towards me.

She stood close. I could sense the heat of her body from the shower. "Do you think those dirty clothes of yours would wait for a while?" she asked softly.

I put my hands on her waist and drew her closer. Then we were kissing, gently at first, then with mounting passion. I kissed her cheeks, her eyes, her nose, then her neck. She pulled a half step away from me and I was about to ask her what was wrong when her robe fell open. I eased it off her shoulders. It slipped to the floor.

The heat of her body was not entirely due to the shower, I realized. . . .

"An exciting day." Francesca said languorously as, much later, we sprawled on a large settee, still in one blue and one white robe although we had exchanged.

"The most exciting I have had in a long time," I told her. "This morning was very exciting too."

Her lips quivered but she kept a straight face. "I had forgotten about that, yes, do you think Carlo will believe us?"

"I wonder. I haven't been the victim of such imaginative attempts at murder for some time."

"I suppose I should tell him."

She disengaged herself and left me to sprawl alone. I could hear her on the phone in the next room. Her rapid-fire Italian was like a musical machine gun. She paused occasionally when

Cataldo was evidently asking her questions. Finally, she came back and sat beside me.

"He has started a hunt for the driver of the vehicle. He wants us to go in, sign a statement, and show you a photograph."

"A photograph? Is that what he said?"

"Yes. Why?"

"I thought he would be showing me a lot of them and expect me to pick out the one."

"That's right," she said thoughtfully.

"When does he want to see us?"

"He wasn't precise."

"If he needs to know timing, won't it seem odd that two or three hours elapsed before you called to report?"

"I shall be vague on times."

"Vague! You? Never!"

She raised her chin haughtily and showed me that lovely profile. "I can be anything I want."

"And what do you want to be right now?"

"I want to be late going to the Questura," she said, moving closer and turning those big, almond-shaped eyes to me.

Captain Cataldo did not ask for specific timing of our adventures. As he conducted the interview with his usual efficiency, I presumed it was out of discretion rather than any neglect of duty. He must have seen that he had a reason to be discreet, for Francesca had a glow of satisfaction about her like an aura. If she had been a cat, she would have been purring. Her light gray pantsuit might have come straight from an Armani runway and her black hair was more lustrous than ever.

We went through the statements he had prepared and

signed them. A solitary photograph lay on his desk facedown, and I was consumed with curiosity. At last, he turned it over and held it out to me.

"That's the man," I said promptly. The dark Sicilian features in the broad face, wide-nosed and bushy-browed, left me in no doubt.

"You said you were not able to see him in the vehicle," said Cataldo.

"I saw him clearly in the car in front of this building when I met Brother Angelo. I saw him in the cafeteria at the Dorigo Farms. I saw him when we followed him outside."

"I didn't see him in the car, of course but I saw him all the other times," Francesca chipped in. "That is definitely the man who tried to kill us."

Cataldo handed us prepared forms in which we confirmed his identity. We signed them and Cataldo clipped the photograph to them.

"Do you know who he is?" Francesca wanted to know.

"Yes," he said and pushed a button. A uniformed woman came in and took the forms and the photograph.

"Thank you for coming in," Cataldo said. Francesca waited for him to answer her question. When he stood up in a movement of dismissal, she said impatiently, "Come on, Carlo, who is he?"

"I'll know more when I see you again," he said impassively. Then a flicker passed across his face. "I hope the next time, you will not have such a colorful report to make."

"We'll take a bus back," said Francesca, as we left the Questura. "Have you taken a bus since you've been here? They're fun."

I told her I hadn't, and thought once more how delightful were her switches of mood and how she liked the simple things as well as the sophisticated ones.

The bus was crowded and we had to stand, jammed against each other. "Let's go to a nightclub tonight," she shouted in my ear. "We need to break the monotony!"

She had that pseudowicked glitter in her eyes so I asked blandly, "Are night clubs open this early in the evening?'

We all swayed with the bus as it wove through the traffic and she pressed against me.

"No, but they will be in a few hours."

CHAPTER EIGHTEEN

The stroboscopic purple sign outside said "Fica" and I asked Francesca what it meant. She just giggled and we went inside past a uniform that welcomed her by name.

The throb of music set up reverberations in every nerve in my body and Francesca hugged my arm. "This may be more dangerous than the rice fields!" she warned.

The outfit she wore looked dangerous enough. A dazzling cobalt-blue blouse was almost see-through, and the tightest and briefest of black miniskirts had the look of wet leather. Her black pumps had the highest of heels and sheer black stockings showed her shapely legs.

Flashing lights sent exploring beams into the dark recesses of the cavernous place while managing not to reveal anything. Faces gleamed pale for milliseconds and reflections bounced off mirrors and bottles, but the interior remained dim and mysterious. Ethereal effects came when the haze of cigarette smoke drifted into the flickering lights. Neon strips on the walls glowed in luminescent colors.

"I think we're safe here," I said. "Nobody will see us." I had to repeat the statement as the first one was lost in the throbbing beat.

"You'll soon become used to it," she said soothingly.

A waiter materialized out of the gloom. He had the advantage of being dressed all in black and only the whites of his eyes gave him away. He showed us to a table, although we had to navigate the final landing operation by fumbling until we our hands encountered chair backs. Francesca ordered a vodka martini and I asked for a scotch and soda.

Francesca was right. My vision did adjust and I could see now that the place was nearly full. Some couples were dancing to the insistent beat, shadowy figures were table-hopping, and in fact, one hopped to our table. He gave Francesca a peck on each cheek, put his drink down on the table, and pulled a chair close. She introduced me. His name was Aldo and he was with a scandal magazine, she told me. He was dismayed. "No, sweetie, we are a sociopolitical journal."

She put on her hauteur. "The only time you've ever been political was when you wrote that piece on the under secretary for trade who was caught in a brothel with three Asian women."

"We also mentioned his defense," Aldo protested. "Remember he said he was concluding a commercial deal with Japan?" he asked with a sly grin.

"Commercius interruptus." Francesca giggled. "Wasn't that what you called it?"

"It all sells magazines." Aldo shrugged modestly.

"So whose names are selling the next issue?" demanded Francesca with that marvellous talent she had for merging boldness with naiveté.

"Promise to buy a copy?"

"No," she said, "but I'll read it in the hairdresser's."

"Anything connected with Pellegrini's murder gets coverage," offered Aldo.

"Photographs!" Francesca said scornfully. "The grieving widow . . . scenes in his cheese factory . . . his handsome son who is at school in Switzerland . . . what do they tell? Nothing."

"Well," drawled Aldo, "everybody connected in any way will get their fair share of attention in the next couple of weeks. We don't have much else in the way of juicy scandal—excuse me, sociopolitical comment—just now. Have to fill space."

"Everybody?" queried Francesca keenly. "Everybody who?"

Aldo drank again and said, "No point in looking around from this table. Can't see a thing, but I'll tell you this . . . a lot of the characters concerned come in here."

Francesca leaned forward eagerly. "Who, for instance?"

"Clara Rinaldo, for one."

The wife of Pellegrini's lawyer! "Who with?" Francesca wanted to know.

"I can't say, but I doubt they are discussing cooking methods."

"Chefs?" gasped Francesca.

"My lips are sealed." Aldo grinned. "Read the paper."

"I will, but tell me now."

"Okay," said Aldo, "I'll tell you about Giacomo Ferrero. He's losing one of his three stars."

"That's not what I meant. Anyway, it's not news," Francesca said disparagingly. "I heard that last week. What we want to know is, who is taking it away from him?"

"Oh, the committee I suppose—"

"Committee my *asino*—oh, pardon me," she said, turning in my direction.

"That's all right, I was absent at that week's Italian lesson."

She smiled and turned back to the journalist. "Aldo, don't be obtuse! You know perfectly well decisions aren't made by committees. They might be in some countries but not Italy. Now, come on, who was it?"

"I can't tell you."

"Why not?" she demanded.

"I never speak ill of the dead."

"Aldo, you always speak ill of the dead. They are the only ones who can't defend themselves." Then the import of his answer caused her eyes to widen—at least, as far as I could see in the near darkness. "You mean Silvio Pellegrini?"

Aldo grinned and sipped at the drink in his hand. He said nothing. Francesca looked at me. Her big luminous eyes shone as if to say "How about that?"

"Are you reporting that story?" I asked him.

"Not unless some aspect much more lurid emerges," he said, still grinning.

"Aldo, you know something more lurid!" Francesca hurled the accusation at him like a spear.

He put on a straight face. "Now what makes you think—"

"Don't try to fool me, I know you!"

He leaned forward. "And you can know me better if you play your cards right."

She ignored that. "Tell us. What is it?"

"You're not a stringer for *Foro di Vista*, are you?"

"That's another scandal magazine," Francesca said for my benefit. "No, I promise you won't see it anywhere else—well, not through us anyway."

Aldo took another drink, perhaps trying to decide. Then he emptied his glass and motioned to our left. "Take a look inside the last booth." He slapped his glass on the table, gave us a catlike grin, and disappeared into the void.

I was peering in the direction he had indicated and Francesca said, "There's a row of curtained booths along that wall. For couples that want privacy."

"How do we get a look inside?"

"Not a voyeur, are you?"

"This is a serious investigation," I told her severely.

"I know. I ruined a skirt, a blouse, pantyhose, a pair of shoes, my nails, and a new hairdo already. It's very serious."

"Put them on my bill. Now, that last booth, how do we—"

"Give me a ten-thousand lire note."

I reached for my wallet. "Better make it twenty," she said.

She took it and pushed her chair back. "Come on."

I followed her and she watched the waiters, picking one she obviously knew. She whispered in his ear, at least a whisper to compete with the music. He took the bill, crinkled it to assess its value in the darkness, and nodded, saying something to her. She took my hand and we moved close to the last booth.

Black curtains enclosed it and a square board was above it. The waiter rapped three times on the board, and after a moment a voice within uttered something we could not hear.

The waiter motioned to Francesca, telling her to be ready. The waiter twitched aside the curtain and poked his head in, being deliberately careless in leaving one side open wider than the other. Francesca peered into one side of the booth, waving frantically to me to look in the other side.

It was over very quickly. Francesca said a word of thanks to the waiter and we returned to our table. "Did you see your side?" she hissed anxiously.

"Yes," I told her.

"Well?" She banged her fist on the back of my wrist. "Who was it?"

"Giacomo Ferrero."

Her mouth opened in astonishment, showing her white teeth.

"Did you see?" I asked.

"Yes." She looked away deliberately.

I banged a fist on her wrist just as she pulled it away, laughing.

"Well, come on! Who was it?"

"What makes you think there was anyone else in there?" she asked innocently.

"In that kind of booth? Tell me or I'll—"

"Please! No violence! It was Elena Pellegrini."

There was a moment of silence. It was silence between us at least. The music had found a new and more penetrating beat. I ordered another round of drinks. "We need these," I told Francesca, "as shock absorbers."

It took her only a split second to grasp the meaning of the English words and I continued. "A widow's grief lasts longer in England."

"In Italy too," she said. "In opera at least."

"Whereas here in real life . . . we had better tell the captain, hadn't we? Or maybe he doesn't listen to gossip?"

"He probably knows already," she said, indifferent.

"How?" I asked in surprise.

"He stations one of his people here whenever he has an important case. This is an ideal place to pick up rumors."

"Do you know who it is?" Automatically, I looked around in the gloom.

"He uses someone different each time. Sometimes it's a customer, sometimes a waiter. Sometimes it's a man, sometimes a woman, and other times . . . half and half." She gave me an amused smile. "Gossip and scandal are part of the Italian way of life."

"Yes, Italians love intrigue, don't they?"

"We learned it from the masters: Machiavelli, Cellini, Cagliostro, Casanova . . ."

I shook my head. "A police force making use of gossip! Extraordinary!"

"When is it gossip and when is it an important clue?" Francesca asked.

The drinks arrived. She drank and then said, "Many Italian men have mistresses. No Italian woman does. Most of these mistresses are the wives of other men."

"Go on," I urged. "I have the feeling you're leading up to a point."

"Well, don't you see? The funny thing is that it's only recently that men have been getting uneasy about this. It's taken them all this time to work out that the situation is mathematically impossible."

I thought about it. "You're right," I said, and she gave me a superior smile.

"Still," I added, "we'd better tell Cataldo."

She sipped and nodded pensively. "Pellegrini's wife and Giacomo Ferrero together . . . that does suggest a motive, doesn't it?"

"The eternal triangle? Yes, it does. I wonder, too, if it fits in with Brother Angelo's statement about 'Pellegrini and the three chefs'?"

"I don't trust that Brother Angelo," Francesca said, and there was that look of steely determination on her face. "I don't care if he is a monk."

"I'm sure he isn't. The bishop would have tossed him out

by now. Threatening people with a knife and almost pushing them off parapets cannot in any way be part of routine monastic training."

"You take things like that personally, don't you?" she chuckled. Then her expression changed. She was staring past me, towards the door. "It can't be!"

Entering the Fica was a daunting experience, as I had found out already. It was like stumbling into a dark cave with no idea if the next step would find ground under it. Now that our vision had adjusted, it was amusing to watch others come in, fumbling for a chair or a table, staggering as if sightless.

The couple coming in now were just as cautious and uncertain. They came close to our table, obviously not seeing us. We could see them, though, which was the reason for Francesca's astonishment.

They were Ottavio Battista, the enfant terrible of Italian gastronomy, and Vanessa Mantegna, the wife of Bernardo, chef-owner of the San Pietro and the wizard of plant and flower cookery.

CHAPTER NINETEEN

It was three o'clock when we left, and in the taxi we dissected the night's findings, pondering over the unexpected couplings taking place—and being observed—in the nightclub.

"The demure Vanessa, seemingly devoted wife and partner of Bernardo, plant and flower chef, seen in the Fica with the demon king of the kitchen, Ottavio!" I said. "Does that have any significance as far as the puzzle of the three chefs is concerned? I can't see how. It's just a marital infidelity and nothing more, isn't it? A sort of romantic culinary triangle?"

"Maybe," Francesca said, musing.

"Now the words of Brother Angelo—"

"I don't believe a word he says." She was blunt and uncompromising.

"I know you don't, but some things he said might have been true. 'I can tell you about Pellegrini and the three chefs.' That's what he said."

"But he didn't tell you."

"True—his life was in danger."

"Are you sure of that?" she asked darkly.

"Clearly, you have taken a dislike to this cleric you have never met."

"He tried to kill you."

"Yes, but—"

"And he's no more a cleric than he is pope."

"It seems likely—"

She sighed in deep exasperation. "There you are then." Her tone changed. "Now Giacomo Ferrero and Elena Pellegrini, that's different."

"A different bowl of minestrone altogether," I agreed. "Another of the three chefs and the grieving widow of a man who may have been murdered . . ."

"There's motive written all over that," Francesca said decisively.

"There certainly is." I fumbled over my next words, trying to put them the right way. "You have a lot of . . . affairs in Italy, don't you?'

"We are a very passionate people."

The taxi swung around a corner and Francesca put out a hand to steady herself. It fell on mine. I left it there. So did she.

"Many of Italy's most famous men have dedicated churches to their mistresses. Did you know that?' she asked me in a neutral tone.

"No, I didn't." I thought for a moment. "Nor can I think of any other country where that could happen."

"Raffaello—you call him Raphael—is most famous for his many paintings of the Madonna. You know of him, of course?'

"Yes, I've seen some of them—in Washington, in the Louvre, in Munich."

"He used his mistresses as models for all of them. Most are portraits of La Fornarina, the baker's daughter."

"I didn't know that," I admitted. "But you still don't have divorce, do you?"

"And never will."

"So that encourages infidelity in marriage, doesn't it?"

"Oh, yes, but divorce is worse. It would endanger the family structure—and in Italy, the family is the structure of life, the basis of everything."

"So," I said, squeezing her hand, "infidelity could be a more powerful motive for murder than I think."

She squeezed back. "We say in Emilia Romagna that food is a more powerful motive than sex."

"When you say 'we', do you include yourself?"

"I—oh, here we are." The taxi pulled to a stop in front of her apartment. I looked at it longingly but she leaned over, seemed to hesitate, then gave me a quick kiss on the cheek and said, "I'll see you tomorrow."

With a flash of long legs swinging out the taxi door, she was striding across the pavement and I was giving the taxi driver the name of the Ambasciatore Imperiale Hotel.

At that time of the morning, the lobby of the Ambasciatore Imperiale was quiet. I retrieved my key and went up to my room. I closed the room door behind me and flicked the light switch.

I was not alone.

Brother Angelo sprawled facedown on the floor.

He was in the same brown robes and his back was stained in blood from the knife protruding from it. I recognized the knife at once—I had last seen it pointed at me on the top parapet of Modena cathedral.

It was a shattering moment and yet mitigated by the inevitability of the outcome. Brother Angelo had shown every sign of being terrified by the man whose face he had seen in the car outside the Questura. He obviously feared being killed because of something he knew. The fact that that same man was a killer was in no doubt after his murderous attempts on Francesca and me with the crop-spraying robot plane and the six-wheeled behemoth.

Then the thought struck me that both Brother Angelo and his killer had managed to enter my room. Was the killer still here? I opened the room door wide to facilitate a high-speed exit. As a weapon, I could see nothing that I could take with me on my search. My eye went back to the knife at least twice but I could not envision myself pulling it out of the body. I took a large ceramic lamp as the best weapon to hand.

The bathroom and the small adjacent lounge were empty. I breathed heavily with relief, put back the lamp, then hastily closed the door and put on the chain. Then I picked up the phone and called Francesca. She sounded wide awake.

"I thought you might call," she said breathily. "Do you want me to come there?"

"Yes," I said, "very much, I—"

"I'll be there in ten minutes—"

"Wait! Don't hang up—listen, bring Cataldo with you."

There was a silence.

When she spoke, her voice was glacial. "I certainly will not and I'm disappointed that—"

"Listen!" I implored. "Brother Angelo's here and—"

"What?" She spat out the word and I had to jump in to stem a flow of what were surely going to be scatological words in Italian with which I had no familiarity.

"Listen ! *Listen!* He's dead!"

"Dead?" It was inevitable that even a girl as fast on the uptake as Francesca should repeat it.

"He has a knife in his back, the same one he threatened me with."

"There? In your room?" Her voice was little more than a whisper now.

"Yes. I opened the door, came in, and there he was."

"All right." Not for the first time, I appreciated her lightning-quick acceptance of a situation. Her voice was normal as she said, "I'll call Carlo and then I'll be right over."

I hung up and prowled around the room. I stopped and examined the half of the face that I could see. It was more than I had been able to glimpse in front of the Questura. He looked to be in his late thirties or maybe a little older, a pale complexion, a large nose, and a long chin.

The window was sealed and I was on the tenth floor. I searched the room but could find nothing. I looked in the bedroom and the bathroom with a similar result.

I could not go out of the room and I could not stay in it but nevertheless I had to stay. Sitting quietly in a chair looking at a recently murdered corpse is a very difficult thing to do. Not that I wanted to keep looking at it, but it was there wherever I looked. I went over the room again a couple of times but still found nothing of any interest. I touched the back of one of Brother Angelo's outflung hands very cautiously. It was still warm.

A few more torturing minutes and there was a rap at the door. I opened it and Francesca threw herself into my arms. She gave a little cry as, over my shoulder, she caught sight of the body. She untangled herself and stared down, fascinated. She had hastily put on dark brown slacks and a loose yellow sweater and she looked adorable. She had put on only a minimum of makeup and her eyes looked enormous as she stared at Brother Angelo.

"So that's him."

She was still staring as a heavy banging on the door announced the arrival of the dashing captain of the Questurini, Carlo Cataldo. He gave us each a brief look then went over to kneel by the body. He spent some minutes examining it without touching anything.

"Was the door open when you came in?" His question encompassed us both.

"I wasn't here. I had gone home," Francesca said.

"It was locked," I said.

"The body was just like this?"

"I didn't touch anything—oh, except for that lamp—I took it with me to make sure there was no one in the bathroom or bedroom."

He checked all the rooms, finding nothing. "The night manager will be up here in a few minutes," he said. "You two had better wait in the lobby."

We sat at a table at the entrance to the bar, open to the lobby sufficiently that we felt reasonably safe. A night waiter brought us cups of espresso. There was not much to say and we didn't say it. A murder can really stifle conversation. People started to come in, a few in uniform, most of them not. They all headed for the banks of elevators and they all pushed ten. My room must have been like the Marx brothers' stateroom in *A Night at the Opera*.

Captain Cataldo joined us after some time. He called for an espresso and lit a cigarette. He was wearing the same uniform as always but without the plumed hat. He did not look in the least tired. He asked questions relentlessly and his memory seemed encyclopedic.

"Is this the same man you saw in the duomo at Modena?"

"It looks like him, but I'm only going by the robes and the knife. I didn't see his face."

"The same man you talked with in front of the Questura?"

"I got only a glimpse of his face. I couldn't swear to it but it looks like the same man."

"Now that you have seen his face, do you recognize him?"

"No. I never saw him before."

He sipped his espresso. "I try not to jump to conclusions but we may have a line on his killer," he said.

"So soon?"

He puffed a couple of times on his cigarette, pensive. "I have talked to Signor Dorigo and he is very unhappy at your amateur investigating."

"Would he prefer an official investigation? It sounds like he may have something to hide."

"We will find out. I want you to come with me to the Dorigo Farms. One of the workers there is missing. I asked if the man could program the robot spray plane and drive the vehicles. He can."

"That's your man," I said. "If he tried to kill us, a hundred to one he's the one who killed Brother Angelo."

"We have some other information, Carlo," Francesca told him and recounted our evening at the nightclub. He nodded. "Your man there will be telling you all this when you go into the Questura this morning," Francesca went on briskly, "but we wanted to be sure you knew." He nodded again. It was hard to tell whether he had a man there or whether he found the information useful.

"I'll pick you up at ten o'clock," He motioned to me first. "You"—and to Francesca—"then you."

"*This* morning?" she said.

"Yes. It is now nearly four o'clock. You had better get some sleep." To me, he added, "The night manager is having your belongings transferred to another room. This is your third, I believe." I wanted to comment that the hotel had six hundred others but refrained.

"Did you drive here?" he asked Francesca and she nodded. "Then I'll see you at ten." He strode back to the elevator, boots thudding on the marble floor.

Francesca gave me a quick kiss. "You're a man who makes life exciting, aren't you?" Then she was gone.

CHAPTER TWENTY

S o you are the two who wrecked my Caproni and my Yaki-moto!"

Antonio Dorigo spat out the words. Captain Cataldo looked at us affably and waited for us to answer.

"Is the Caproni the crop-spraying plane?" I asked innocently.

Dorigo glared.

"And the Yakimoto the big six-wheeled vehicle? Or is it the other way around?"

Dorigo gave a jerk of a nod. He looked about to boil over, a short pudgy man with little hair and a round, fat but disagreeable face. We sat in his office at his farm location, a couple of buildings away from the cafeteria where I had spotted the face I recognized—the event that had started it all.

"We didn't wreck them." Francesca said coldly. "The man who works for you tried to kill us with them." She sat back in the uncomfortable chair, crossed her elegant legs, and stared right back at him.

"That's rubbish!" Dorigo snapped. "Why would he want to do that?"

"Exactly what we are here to find out," said Cataldo amiably.

"What were you doing on my land?" asked Dorigo unpleasantly.

"We were taking your tour," said Francesca, lolling in the chair like a Medici princess.

"The tour doesn't go through the rice fields," Dorigo said.

"After the tour, we went into the cafeteria and we saw a man who had been involved in a previous murder attempt and followed him," I told him. It was not the full story but an explanation of the events involving Brother Angelo could get complicated and I didn't want Dorigo to have any opportunities for diversion.

"Spezzano tried to kill somebody?" Dorigo put a hefty dose of disbelief into the question.

"So you know who it was?" Cataldo slid in the question like a well-greased stiletto.

Dorigo muttered some kind of accord.

"Spezzano is the man you told me about over the phone?" Cataldo was still smooth and friendly.

"The man who is missing."

"And why do you assume that he is the same man who was responsible for the—ah, accidents with the two pieces of equipment?"

Dorigo glared at him. "It seems obvious, doesn't it?"

"Not to me," said Cataldo.

Dorigo looked from me to Cataldo to Francesca, frustrated. "Spezzano is an ex-convict. You probably suspect him every time a crime is committed and he is anywhere in the vicinity."

"So he ran away." Cataldo was slowly defusing the volatile Dorigo.

"A clear sign of guilt," said Francesca, icily. "Dropping airplanes on us and then trying to run us into the ground with yellow monsters! No wonder he disappeared!"

Dorigo glared, turning to Cataldo, but the captain declined to comment on Francesca's lofty disdain of legal procedure. Instead, he said, "Luigi Spezzano, that is his name, isn't it?" Dorigo grunted agreement.

Cataldo nodded. "His record is not good. Armed robbery, causing bodily harm, assault with a deadly weapon. Did you know this when you hired him?"

"I have hired ex-convicts before," said Dorigo, his belligerent attitude ebbing.

"Under the Rehabilitation and Retraining Program?"

Dorigo nodded.

"You receive a rebate on each salary you pay to any person under this scheme, don't you?"

"I like to help people whenever I can," said Dorigo virtuously, "including those who are trying to get a new start in life."

"How long had he been working for you?"

"About three months."

"He knew how to operate all the equipment?"

"He was still learning."

Just as well, I thought. If he had not banked the biplane too tightly, it might not have stalled and crashed. The noise from Francesca was a loud, scornful grunt at Dorigo's claim of his charitable efforts at the regeneration of convicts.

But Dorigo's resistance was weakening. He did not threaten Francesca and me with a lawsuit, and Cataldo, having softened him up, moved on to more relevant questioning.

"Do you intend to sell your rice fields, Signor Dorigo?"

He shrugged. "Most businessmen sell things when the price is right."

"Did you intend to sell to Signor Pellegrini?"

His pudgy face showed some of his earlier pugnacity but he controlled it.

"He made legal offers. I refused them."

"Was there animosity between you?"

He was about to deny it when he realized that his previous attitude would make any denial preposterous. "Yes, some," he admitted, "but I had no reason to kill him."

Cataldo continued to question him but when it was clear that he was not going to get any further useful information, he thanked Dorigo politely and we left.

In the car going back to town, Francesca said, "Thanks, Carlo. I'm glad we don't have to buy him a new airplane."

"Other than that, we didn't learn much as far as the investigation is concerned, did we?" I said.

"We are not entirely empty-handed." Cataldo replied. We waited for some amplification. To break the silence, I asked, "How did you know the man was an ex-convict?"

"When I talked to Dorigo on the phone yesterday evening and told him we were coming out today to talk to him, he gave me the name of one of his men who had disappeared. I ran an immediate check."

Francesca and I waited again for some elucidation but Cataldo merely looked at us with the merest hint of a smile on his face.

At our request, the police car dropped us at the Capodimonte. I wanted to take another look at the place and this time visit the kitchens. It was early for lunch but Francesca put on her most charming smile and the maître d' remembered us from the earlier visit. He became very eager to please and gave us an excellent table.

"He probably wants to see Giacomo get the job in London so that he can take over here," she said shrewdly.

After consultation with the sommelier—who, if he recognized us, made no comment—I chose a Terlano from the wine-growing region west of Bolzano. This is the Alto Adige, the German-speaking part of Italy which was under Austrian rule until the end of World War I and called by Germans the South Tyrol. These wines are not readily found, as most of them are exported to Germany. They need to be drunk young and resemble a good Riesling. Francesca had suggested a light white as it was lunch. She opened her purse and took out some sheets of paper. She smoothed them out between glasses.

"My cousin finally got me the information on the three chefs," she said, sounding exasperated that he had taken so long.

"He did an extraordinarily rapid job, I think. If you paid for that information in London, it would still take a week or more."

"He is my cousin," she said peremptorily. I assumed that meant the poor fellow didn't stand a chance.

She studied the sheets. "First, Giacomo Ferrero . . . he is half-owner of a vegetable distribution chain, he has stock in a company with a fleet of delivery trucks, and . . . let's see, what else? Ah, his other holdings are in Italtel, the telephone company, IBM Italia, Alitalia airlines, and some government bonds. Next, there is Ottavio. He owns half a hair-dressing salon—"

"Pity he never goes there himself," I commented, but she went on unheeding.

"He has part, about a third, it looks like, of a bakery, and, h'm, about two-thirds of a garage."

"A garage?" I queried.

She shook her head. "Doesn't mean anything. It's run by

his brother. Ottavio just has money in it. Then we have Bernardo, the plant and flower chef. He has been very cautious in his investments. They're mostly blue chip and some bonds in the city of Bologna."

She set most of the sheets aside.

"It doesn't tell us much," I said, disappointed.

"No," she agreed, but there was a tone in the one word that invited me to ask her, "Go on, what else?"

She curved her lips in a satisfied smile. "Where the three chefs have their money is not helpful but what is helpful"—she tapped the sheets still in front of her—"are these. They tell us where Pellegrini had *his* money."

"I remember at the funeral when Ottavio said he wasn't sorry that Pellegrini was dead because now he might not have to pay back the money he owed him."

"I remember that too," Francesca said. "But it's not just Ottavio, look." She pushed the sheets over to me.

"Bernardo too—good heavens, Giacomo as well! All three owed him money!"

"Like my cousin Enrico said, though, it's not surprising. See, Signor Pellegrini has financed several restaurants over the years. Some have paid him off, some still owe him."

I looked again. "All three of our chefs still owe him."

"Enrico says it's common for a supplier to help support his customers financially. By keeping the restaurant in business, he makes sure he keeps a customer."

"True enough. Then the question arises, is any one of these debts worth killing for?"

She looked thoughtful. "No, I suppose not. Wait! What if there was another motive too?"

"Such as . . . ? Ah, some marital infidelity perhaps?"

She looked amused. "Is that what you call it in English? Yes, very polite. I was thinking of that. You remember last night at the Fica."

"Yes, there was some straying going on there. I wonder how many other of the people involved in this might be straying too?"

She was mentally ticking off names in her mind and examining possible pairings. I gave her something else to think about.

"Or what about all three chefs together?"

She laughed gaily. "Impossible! Those three!" Then her expression became more serious. "You can't be suggesting that Ottavio, Bernardo, and Giacomo would plot together—no, no." But I could see that she was considering it.

"It's an improbable conspiracy, I admit."

"It is," she agreed, "very improbable. Still . . ." her voice trailed away. "I wonder if Carlo has thought of it."

"We'll ask him. Meantime, I want to ask you, have you dried out the gun?"

"Yes, I put it in the oven."

"I hope you—"

"Of course I took the bullets out first. I dried them too, with a hairdryer."

She was a resourceful girl and I congratulated her on it. "Did you dry out your phone too?"

"It was ruined. I had to get another."

"So once again, we are armed and dangerous."

"You don't expect to need a gun here at the Capodimonte, do you?" Her eyes were widening.

"No, I have enough money to pay for the meal."

————

Yet another way of rating a restaurant is to sample its midday menu. As prices are lower, attendances possibly less, and customers not as demanding, there can be a tendency to lower standards.

There was no sign of the bearded, burly, and boisterous Giacomo but we overheard a patron ask for him and be told that he was picking up some produce on his way. Most of the clientele were tourists and the staff was handling them with speed and efficiency.

For a starter, Francesca ordered *garmucia,* a vegetable soup with broad beans, peas, artichoke hearts, and asparagus tips. I had a soup that was one I had never encountered before, a specialty of the Garfagnana district of Tuscany. It was called *infarinata,* a reference to the maize flour that thickens it to the consistency of a porridge. White beans, bacon, and black cabbage were the main ingredients, and it was rich and creamy, almost like a polenta.

"I feel adventurous today," Francesca said. "Haven't had these for ages." *Lumache di San Giovanni* was the menu name and it was snails cooked with chili peppers and tomatoes. I had the *quaglie rincartata.* That was something I had not eaten in ages: quails baked in bread dough. It was a specialty of Orvieto, said the waiter, and reflected the home town of the sous-chef whose creation it was.

"So the renowned Giacomo gives his sous-chefs opportunity to express themselves, does he?" I asked, and the waiter said that he was very supportive in the kitchen and encouraged his staff. Another point in Giacomo's favor, I noted. The wine was fresh and lively. It was well able to stand up to the snails and the quails.

It was a meal that cramped conversation, especially discussion of murderous monks, untraceable poisons, and deadly airplanes. We agreed on a *café correto* to complete the meal. This is an espresso which contains a generous splash of a favorite liqueur. Francesca selected amaretto, the almond-flavored drink that is very popular in Italy and I ordered *aurum*, which is gold in color and orange flavored.

That was when Giacomo arrived. The maître d' must have told him we were there, for when he came into the restaurant, he came straight to our table. His greeting was effusive and he was concerned that we had enjoyed our meal. He beamed when we assured him that we had.

"Professionalism. That is the secret," he said in his deep booming voice. "Every single act in the kitchen is important. Nothing can be overlooked."

"We didn't see your kitchen on our previous visit," I said. "May we do so now?"

"But of course! Please come this way."

The kitchen counters were white-tiled. When a drop of sauce was spilled, a hand was there to wipe it away. Giacomo waved a proud hand to show it to us.

"When I was a poor boy in Milan, I got my first glimpse of a restaurant kitchen at the age of thirteen. I thought I had died and gone to heaven. The sparkling white jackets, the tall hats, the delicious smell of food—I knew there and then that was what I wanted to be, a chef."

"You started to work in a kitchen at that age?" asked Francesca.

"Yes, and I have never done anything else. Nor have I regretted a second of it. I am here every day the restaurant is open. I am involved in the buying and preparation of all the ingredients."

He took us to stand at the side of a sous-chef preparing a sauce. "This is the way it is done," he said. "Whisk, taste, add, whisk, taste, and on and on till it is exactly right. To do better than your competitors, you have to work harder and better than they do." He took a spoon and tasted, nodding to the young chef who gave us both tastes too. It was a sauce for veal, tantalizingly flavored. "The kitchen of a restaurant is a place for hard workers with a desire for precision," he went on. "It is no place for prima donnas." He rolled his eyes, leaving us in no doubt as to whom he was referring.

We continued on the tour. He made no effort to impress us, but it was an impressive demonstration nevertheless and Giacomo knew it. "Perfect food and flawless service," he said without arrogance.

We strolled around further. It was hard to find any fault, and he beamed still wider when I told him so. He escorted us back to our table and before we had said farewells, the wine waiter came with our fortified coffees. It was another example of the fine service.

"Naturally, he's going out of his way to please you," Francesca said.

"Of course but you can't fake a kitchen like that even if you know someone is coming."

We were taking our last sips of coffee when Francesca's purse began to buzz. She took out her phone and answered. I could hear deep male tones at the other end of the line. She snapped it off.

"Carlo wants to see us in his office."

"Now?"

"The way he said it was *now!*"

CHAPTER TWENTY-ONE

Captain Cataldo looked grim. His manner was cold as he greeted us, and we were barely seated when he fired his first barrage.

"If there is anything you want to tell me about this case, now is the time to tell it," he said, his voice harsh.

"I've told you everything that's relevant," I said.

"Relevant, ah, I see. So what have you not told me because you didn't think it was relevant?"

"I haven't kept anything from you," I insisted. "I've told you the truth."

"The truth! Well, now——"

"Carlo," said Francesca in her sweetest tones. "Will you tell us what your problem is?"

He leaned back and surveyed us. "Very well. We have established that Brother Angelo was not a member of any monastic order. Furthermore, under his monastic robes, Brother Angelo was wearing a suit made in London. His shirt too was made there and so were his shoes. Our forensic expert in dentistry identifies Brother Angelo's teeth as exhibiting signs of work done in the English style."

His mood was mellowing just a little, probably because he noted my discomfiture. "Do you have any comment on this?" he demanded.

"No, I don't."

"You and I will go see him," said Cataldo.

The morgue in the back of the Questura building was not as forbidding as it might have been. It was attached to the police hospital and looked much like one of the wards there. Cataldo insisted on Francesca staying in his office even though she wheedled and cajoled to be included. He led the way with his long, official stride, and we went through the hospital to a long room with white-tiled floors and walls and the smell of disinfectant.

The body had already been wheeled out to await our inspection. Cataldo nodded to the white-uniformed attendant who whipped aside the sheet. It revealed a pale-faced man in his late thirties or early forties. He had a longish nose and a pronounced chin.

"He is the man I found on the floor of my room in the hotel," I confirmed.

"Was that the first time you saw him?"

"I have told you of the encounters in the duomo and in front of the Questura," I said, "but on both occasions, he was wearing brown robes and the cowl was pulled forward so as to obscure the face. He might be the same man but I could not swear to it."

The attendant replaced the sheet as Cataldo took me back to his office.

Francesca was waiting impatiently. "Well?" she asked.

Cataldo took his place behind the desk. He motioned for the two of us to sit but it was me he addressed.

"This man looks English, wears English clothes and shoes, has been treated by English dentists. He may have tried to kill you twice. He apparently wanted to give you information. Yet you say you don't know him."

"There are lots of Englishmen I don't know."

"You realize that you are the only person who claims to have seen this man before, don't you?"

"The nun whom he told to send me up to the bell tower might remember him," I suggested. "The guards on duty that day might remember him."

"The guards recall seeing a monk, but they are not uncommon. We have not been able to trace the nun." He pointed a finger at me. "He spoke to you, both on the phone and in person. Didn't you recognize his voice as being English?"

"His accent varied—I mean, it wasn't consistent. But I didn't assume he was English."

"Did he have a passport?" Francesca wanted to know.

He paused as if deciding whether to include her in the interrogation. He evidently concluded it would be impossible to keep her out of it. "Not on his person. Nor have we been able to find out where he has been living here."

"You have checked the hotels?"

Again Cataldo paused then said, "We tried that. He would have had to show his passport in order to register. None of them recognize him and none of them has an unclaimed passport."

"You think he arrived recently?" Francesca was not going to be left out.

"Forensic are sure of it due to his lack of tan. Within the last week or so."

"What about Immigration?"

At this point, most policemen would have told her to mind her own business and stay out of the investigation, but the family connection was probably too strong.

Cataldo said, "They have checked all single men arriving from England during the past week. Most are here on business and easy to trace. One eludes us so far. Of course, he could be staying with a family. His name, incidentally, is Hamilton. We have not been able to locate him yet." He fixed me with an inquiring look. "Does that name mean anything to you?"

"Hamilton? No, nobody I can think of."

He leaned back and studied us both, then turned his attention back to me. "Can it be that you and Signor Desmond are trying some trick here?"

"Absolutely not!" I said vigorously. "I certainly am not, nor do I know of any trick. I don't believe Lansdown is involved in any such thing either."

"Do you agree that this looks very strange?" Cataldo asked, marginally less aggressive.

"I do. It looks very strange."

"Do you think it is possible that Signor Desmond sent this man here for some purpose connected with your mission for him?"

"Checking on me, you mean? I doubt it. Even if he had, all this monk's robes disguise and the knife and so on? No. I don't believe it."

"What about the Ambasciatore Imperiale Hotel?" asked Francesca. "How did he get into the room?"

"I had a man look into that. The night clerk left the lobby briefly, he says. He admits to two or three times so it could have been more. The key could easily have been taken."

"By Brother Angelo," I said swiftly. "Who would be above suspicion. The person who killed him could have been following him."

"Another possibility is that the killer was really waiting for you but the chance to eliminate Brother Angelo was too good to let pass. Killing him in your room put you under suspicion and would neutralize you until the killer could find another chance for an attempt on you."

"That's an unpleasant possibility," I complained.

Cataldo shrugged.

"Have your forensic people come up with any new thoughts on untraceable poisons?" I asked.

"How can they trace a poison that is untraceable? That is their position."

"I suppose you know about Pellegrini's wife studying plants and flowers?"

"Tell me," he invited. I told him of my conversation with Elena Pellegrini. He nodded. "Unfortunately, that does not add anything to theories about untraceable poisons." Then he surprised me.

"Modern criminology originated in Italy, did you know that?"

He rapped out the question and I caught a glimpse of Francesca's puzzled look, which was probably mirrored in mine.

"No, I didn't know that," I said obediently.

He shifted his position to a more comfortable one. "An eighteenth-century lawyer named Cesare Beccaria did not agree with the opinion of the time, namely that only the circumstances surrounding a criminal case were of importance. He had an original approach—he believed that the crime itself was of primary importance. His book, *Crimes and Punishment*, was the foundation of a new approach to crime and the law."

"Fascinating," I murmured, wondering what this had to do with me.

Francesca was listening attentively but I could see she was just as curious.

"Beccaria founded what is today called the Classical School of Criminology. A hundred years later, three other Italian lawyers, Enrico Ferri, Cesare Lombroso, and Rafaele Garofalo, established what is now called the Positive School of Criminology—this moved attention from the crime to the criminal. The work of these four men formed the basic principles of American and British criminology today."

Cataldo was regarding the two of us with an expression bordering on smug. We waited for him to continue. He obliged.

"Sometimes it is good to be guided by the past, don't you agree?"

I nodded. Francesca made a tiny sound.

"Criminal cases—particularly murder cases—differ and need different methods. This is an occasion when we must concentrate on the criminal."

He was getting to the point at last. "I think I see what you're saying," I told him. "The circumstances surrounding this case are confusing the issue."

"Precisely," he said, slapping a hand on his desk.

"Carlo," said Francesca an accusatory tone. "Do you know who the murderer is?"

"There is no doubt that the ex-convict, Spezzano, killed Brother Angelo, as we must call this mysterious Englishman until we know more."

"You think he's working for someone else?"

"Someone who suspects our friend here, the Gourmet Detective, of knowing something vital. I think he will continue to try to silence him."

I didn't like the sound of this, and Francesca flashed me a worried glance.

"That is why," Cataldo went on, "I am going to switch full attention to this criminal."

"Good," I said, relieved. "You'll provide me with some protection too, right?"

Cataldo shook his head. "Oh, no, that would not help solve the case. We are fortunate that our man is so determined. Our best chance is to encourage him so that we can catch him in the act."

So much for a case that I had decided would be easy . . . a real pleasure, I had told myself, with no risks involved at all.

"You will not be in jeopardy for long, though," said Cataldo, reassuringly.

"Why won't he?" demanded Francesca, her voice sharp.

"You have heard of Italvin, the famous wine fair? It is held every year, near Verona. The day after tomorrow, they are having their Guest Day. Everybody who is anybody will be present. I want you both to be there. That will make it very convenient for me—"

"Convenient for you to do what?" Francesca asked suspiciously.

"Why, to conclude this case, of course."

I grumbled all the way in the taxi ride back to my hotel. "Who would have thought a simple matter of picking one chef out of three could turn out to be so dangerous? I feel like a goat pegged out waiting for the tiger to show up—a hungry tiger, at that."

Francesca was sympathetic. "I still have my gun."

"Great. You'll be able to shoot this guy after he's killed me."

"I know Carlo. He isn't abandoning you. He doesn't want to put an obvious guard on you, but he'll have police watching. I can guarantee that."

"Can you? After having a knife jabbed at me, almost being pushed over a parapet, nearly being choked by poison gas, having an airplane dropped on me, being run down by a six-wheeled truck, and finding a man stabbed in my room—can you really guarantee anything?"

She patted my hand. It was pleasant but not as much re-assurance as I wanted. What did I want though? To get out of here and back to safe old London, I supposed. The captain was not going to allow that, though. I had to stay here and face—face what?

When we stopped at my hotel, Francesca asked, "Want me to come up and console you?" Her eyes were big and inviting, but I shook my head. "Thanks, but I'm going to do some solitary thinking."

"You promise no brooding?"

"No, just thinking."

Where on earth did the three chefs fit into all this? That was the main thought that I wrestled with and it soon had me on my back and both shoulders pinned down. The wild idea of the three great rivals being in a conspiracy together came back to me. It was a fascinating possibility, and the fact that it was so unlikely gave it a paradoxical importance.

I opened the minibar and took out a bottle of Asti Spu-mante. I keep a few of those handy in my office in London as I find that they are conducive to thought. Perhaps it was because the bottles shipped to England contain a sweeter brand, tailored to the English taste. This one was the Bertolo Brut, Gran Riserva, and deliciously dry, but it was doing nothing for my thought processes.

I watched a *telenovela* on the hundred-channel TV. That is the name the Italians use for soap opera and it was no better than that in other countries except for some melodramatic touches borrowed from *Tosca*.

I tried to think of whom I might know called Hamilton but that was in vain. Then I tried to think of what I might know that I did not realize I knew. It seemed to be the main reason for my being in danger. By the time the Asti Spumante bottle was empty, I had concluded that there was no way to know what I didn't know.

I wished I had accepted Francesca's offer now but she would have affected my concentration, such as it was. The best answer was to feed the brain cells, I decided. It was early for dinner in Italy, but large hotels have become accustomed to the strange desires of foreigners and open their restaurants early even if the trattorias and the independent restaurants stay with the later hour.

As I was not evaluating the kitchen or the cuisine here, I opted for some dishes typical of the country. I had the minestrone first. Typical is perhaps a wrong description of this popular soup for it varies from town to town, from kitchen to kitchen, and from one season to another. It can be different every day too.

The minestrone of Milan is the most famous and this one was in that style. It contained celery, carrots, and onions as these are available all year around. Then it had garlic, Swiss chard, potato, zucchini, cabbage leaves, lima beans, and tomatoes. Other versions add rice, still others add pasta. In Genoa, they leave out the tomatoes and the lima beans but add split peas, spinach, and kidney beans. The Florence way of preparing it is to flavor it with *soffrito,* a sauce of finely chopped pork, red peppers, chicken giblets, and tomato sauce. Around the rest of Italy, the variations continue as some contain eggplant, others mushrooms, and yet others broccoli or cauliflower. Italians prefer the meatless minestrone. Some chefs serve without seasoning, relying on the long-cooked flavor of the vegetables. When used, oregano, basil, and bay leaves are the seasonings of choice.

For the pasta course, I elected to have the *tortelli di zucca,* a specialty of Mantua in which the squares of pasta are filled with puree of pumpkin. This is not a dish commonly found, so I was glad of the opportunity to enjoy this different pasta.

Osso buco is world-renowned, and its peasant origins were perfectly in line with the meal. The slices of shin of veal are cut so as to keep the marrow inside the bone, and if the dish does not sound authentically Italian, it is because its origins in the north of Italy stem from years of German occupation. In the case of osso buco, its venerable age is reponsible for the many variations in its preparation. After simmering in wine, some add tomato and some do not. All however, sprinkle the seasoning known as *gremolada* over it at the end. This is a mixture that varies widely, grated lemon peel being the only common ingredient. Parsley is used by most and so is garlic. The Milanese add crushed anchovy fillets.

Mashed potatoes and peas sound like a plebeian touch but again this is a Milanese habit and were served instead of pasta or rice, the other two accompaniments. It was a fine dish, the sauce thick and rich and the meat falling away from the bone.

To drink with this excellent meal, I asked for Sassiacaia, the rich red wine of Tuscany. It is one that has always been high on my list of favorites and yet, paradoxically, it does not rate a D.O.C. designation. This illegitimate status of one of Italy's greatest wines is due to its being made from Cabernet Sauvignon grapes, which are French. To the drinker of it, such despicable nationalism is to be ignored, though the fame of Sassicaia has spread so much in recent years that only an expense account like Desmond Lansdown's can handle it.

Such a meal could not be allowed to cloud my judgment, though, and I scanned my room very carefully before entering. A double check of doors and windows completed my security survey, though I did for a moment wish I had Francesca's gun . . . accompanied by its carrier. She had, after all, assured me that she knew how to release the safety catch and pull the trigger.

CHAPTER TWENTY-TWO

A stirring action-adventure movie with the Roman legions gleefully massacring thousands of barbarians kept me awake for at least half an hour. The other channels had variety shows, soccer games, blood-spattered news broadcasts, clever commercials, and numerous conflicts between cops and robbers. In fact, it was just like being at home—or anywhere else in the Western world.

I was reentering my room after breakfasting downstairs next morning when the phone rang. That silence that is not a silence hovered ominously until a bright female voice said that Mr. Desmond Lansdown wanted to speak to me. Noises in the background blended Spanish voices with heavy objects being moved. Finally the familiar Cockney tones came on the line.

"Listen," Lansdown said, his voice clear and strong. "I have something to tell you. I don't know if it will affect in any way what's going on down there, but I only just found out about it and thought you ought to know. First of all, though, what's new with the business about poor old Pellegrini?"

I debated whether I should tell him about the rice field episode or not. Deciding it might be worth a danger bonus, I gave him a condensed version. He whistled and the line reverberated. He was considerate enough to ask first if I was all right and then quickly ask about Francesca. "There's been another murder too," I added. He whistled again and I hurried on before he could ask questions. "Cataldo has a firm grip, though." I told him. "He seems confident and I think he's going to tie it all up very soon."

"Good! Now listen, what I want to tell you is this. You remember Nigel, worked for me?"

"I don't think I—oh, yes, he's the fellow who made the appointment for me to come and talk to you."

"Right. Well, I had to fire him. He was mixed up in some drug selling and I gave him the heave-ho—that was about a week ago. Reason I'm calling now is, I just heard that he used one of our phones to call around locating another job. I told you he was with me all the time we were making *Don Juan* there in Italy, didn't I?"

"I don't think so," I said slowly with an ominous sense of what was to come.

"He was a great help to me at that time. His mother was Italian so he speaks the language well. In fact, he did a good job all around," Lansdown was saying, "but, well, he got mixed up in a drug-peddling business there too. The Italian police picked him up and he swore to me he was innocent. He admitted smoking some but insisted he never did any dealing. I believed him. That's how I got to know Cataldo—he was tracking down that distribution ring. Well, Cataldo recommended a lawyer and Nigel was released."

The sense of foreboding persisted but I let him continue.

"When I fired him, he was really pissed off at me although I had more right to be. Having the same thing happen again told me he was probably guilty as hell the first time too. He told a few people he was going to get back at me and now I just heard that he had left for Italy where someone was going to help him. The point is, he may be just nasty enough to blab about our deal and the three chefs. So I wanted to warn you—"

I had to interrupt him there. "Was his last name Hamilton?"

"Yes, it is. Nigel Hamilton."

My end of the line was silent just long enough for him to call out, "Are you still there? Hello!"

"I'm still here. I told you a minute ago that someone else had been murdered. That was Nigel."

It was his turn for a few seconds of astonished silence. "Good God!"

"He was wearing monk's robes and—"

"He enjoyed playing at acting," Lansdown said sadly. "He liked dressing up. I got him a few roles as an extra but why on earth—"

That explains the Italian-accented English, I thought, and why it was not consistent. I told him what I knew. He studded my account with gasps and grunts at the right moments. "So Cataldo thinks he can catch the killer by keeping watch on you," he said at the end. "I'm sure he's right," he added. "He's a clever fellow. Matter of fact, I used that technique in the third of those Sherlock Holmes movies I made—or was it the fourth?" Then he came to the point that had clearly been bothering him all this time. He had shown enough consideration to hold it in until now.

"So everybody knows I'm looking for a chef, do they?"

"As far as I know, no one is aware that it's you. But the word is out that a prominent chef in this region will be offered a big job in London."

It was inevitable that he should ask the next question.

"So what's the connection between my wanting a chef and all this skullduggery?"

"We haven't uncovered the whole answer to that yet.

We're close though." I felt that my contribution as a tethered goat justified the "we."

A little more chitchat concluded the conversation. I said I would give Cataldo the number where Lansdown could be reached in Spain. The captain might call him, needing some further verification, I told Lansdown, Nigel's body having been found in my room. I didn't want to alarm him further, so I said nothing about the three chefs all having motives for killing Pellegrini.

After hanging up, I felt like going downstairs for another breakfast, but I pushed aside procrastination and called Cataldo. He recalled the incident involving Lansdown's assistant, but had never met him personally. He said he would call Spain at once.

Until I talked to Cataldo again, I didn't want to make any moves in the investigation. Instead, I could make some progress in Lansdown's project to hire a chef. I called Francesca.

It took a minute or two, the call apparently being routed through several electronic channels before I heard her voice. I told her of my conversation with Lansdown

"I never did trust that monk," she said decisively. "I met Nigel once or twice when he was here. Didn't like him much either."

"What about lunch?" I asked her. I could be decisive too.

She was surprised when I told her I wanted to go back to Ottavio's restaurant, the Palazzo Astoria. I told her I needed to see how the chef and his kitchen coped with the reduced demands of serving lunch.

Italy has a great many varying regional styles of cooking, and although Italians are largely loyal to their own district, it is a popular practice for restaurants to give periodic prominence to others. Today, Ottavio was featuring modern Roman dishes, and the place had one table left when we arrived. The temperamental chef himself was nowhere in sight, probably behind the scenes terrorizing his staff.

Francesca started with the *carciofi alla giudia*, tender fried baby artichokes. I reminded her that they are really thistles, but she just pouted and said she didn't care. She had enjoyed it before and knew that it was the only form in which the entire artichoke can be eaten. Rome has the reputation of having more ways of preparing pasta than anywhere else in Italy, and I had one I was not familiar with: *fettucine alla Romana*. The egg pasta ribbons are prepared with tomatoes, chopped ham, mushrooms, and chicken giblets. Fettucine originated in Rome and has been made world-famous by Alfredo.

Lazio is the region containing Rome and along with its northern neighbor, Umbria, is famous for its game dishes. One reason is that huge flocks of migratory birds use the area as a stop on their twice-a-year flight between the Alpine North and the sunny South. They stay for a month to feed on olives and juniper berries and fatten themselves up for the remainder of their long flight. The abundance of such fine bird food has resulted in the raising of game in this area too. Guinea fowl, hare, pheasants, partridge, pigeons, quail, and thrushes are all found on menus.

I picked the woodcock, *beccaccia*, on the menu, as I consider it the best of all winged game. It yields the most meat, as only the gizzard has to be removed. This was roasted with bastings of brandy and then finished *salmis* style by being cut into pieces and served with buttered mushrooms and white truffles.

Francesca studied it with a little envy so I had to give her some. She had ordered the *abbacchio*, milk-fed baby lamb that has never tasted grass. It is usually spit-roasted, but Francesca was having it *brodettato*—cut into small chunks and cooked in a pan with garlic, olive oil, white wine, egg yolks, and lemon peel. Rosemary is agreed to be the essential seasoning. It was delicious and melting in the mouth, close to being as good as my woodcock.

Like its French equivalent, Beaujolais, Valpolicella is an Italian red which can be chilled a few degrees so as to make it an ideal accompaniment to game. Sadly, it is a wine that has exceeded its own popularity and become the most plentiful red wine after Chianti. Consequently, much Valpolicella of indifferent quality is on the market—especially the export market. We were fortunate here though, because Ottavio had several bottles from the vineyard of Giuseppe Quintarelli, the maestro of Valpolicella. It had a velvety richness and yet remained dry and spicy with a surprising intensity.

"I think we should do more of this," declared Francesca, cleaning her plate. "It's not fair to make any hasty decisions."

"I agree. Now what about dessert?"

She clapped her hands with delight when she learned that Ottavio made *bocconotti*, a favorite of her childhood. The waiter brought a tray of them, tiny tarts with a filling of apricot jam, grated chocolate, grated lemon peel, sweetened with honey and then soaked in rum.

"As good as you remember?" I asked her.

"My mother didn't use rum—this way is better."

"Do you have to work this afternoon?"

"No. Why?"

"We could make plans for which other restaurants we want to visit again," I suggested.

"Fine. Let's do it at your hotel."

We did not spend the afternoon making plans. We spent it much more delightfully, and it was early evening when Francesca said lazily. "Where are we eating tonight?"

"You can't be hungry again!" I protested.

"Making love makes me hungry."

We were preparing ourselves to go out when the phone rang. "This is Antonio at the Ristorante Regina in Cittareale. May we invite you to dine at our establishment? It would be a shame if you returned to England without giving us an opportunity to be compared with the 'Three.' We have an excellent reputation."

I rolled my eyes at Francesca. I whispered to her. "The Regina in Cittareale. Inviting us to eat there. Do you know it?"

"Everybody says it's wonderful!" She was excited. "Let's go!"

"Very well," I said. "Could you accommodate us tonight?"

"Certainly. We look forward to seeing you."

Francesca was delighted. "I wonder how many other good restaurants would like to compete with the Big Three?" she wondered.

"So everybody knows." I said bitterly. "Everybody in Italy knows. Anyway, it isn't really fair," I protested. "We are leading them to believe that—"

"Fair! Poof!" she said, standing there in black bra and panties and looking regally wanton. "You Anglos have peculiar ideas about 'fair.' You have that saying, don't you. Never kick a man when he is down. That's crazy—it's the perfect time to kick him."

"I've always thought it strange that the Italian language has no word for *honor*," I retaliated. "Oh, I know you have the word *onore* but you use it to mean rank or distinction, not honor as we mean it."

"That's a terrible thing to say about my people," she said, wagging a finger at me.

It was only a wicked glint in her eye that prompted me to ask her, "Wasn't it Macchiavelli who complained that 'some men do not know how to be wicked in an honorable way'?"

"It might have been Casanova," she retorted, coming closer.

"No, it wasn't—"

By then she was close enough to put her arms around me and murmur, "We have a saying that there is some of Casanova in every man."

"You do?" I tried to say as her lips pressed against mine.

"Yes. That's just a part of it. The rest says 'including those you expect the least.' "

Consequently a couple of hours elapsed before we were finally ready to leave the Ambasciatore Imperiale. We were going out the door when the phone rang. It was Cataldo.

"I thought you would be relieved to hear that Spezzano was picked up at the Yugoslav border," he said without preamble.

"That's good news," I said, delighted. "Have you got anything out of him?"

"Not yet. I just heard a few minutes ago. But we will," he said ominously. "I'll keep you informed."

I told Francesca and we left, heading for the Ristorante Regina in nearby Cittareale in an ebullient mood.

CHAPTER TWENTY-THREE

Francesca's exertions had not tired her in the least. On the contrary, she was bubbling with gaiety, fizzing with excitement, and I told her so.

"You're more than *allegro,* you're *allegrissimo.*"

"I feel like Vesuvio!" she said, eyes sparkling.

"Good, but watch the road."

It was only a twenty-minute ride to Cittareale, a village northwest of Bologna. At the autostrada exit, some patchy fog, ghostly-white, hung over the damp ground. The waters of the River Po exert their powers over a vast area, even at this time of year. We went down a country road, past a few sprawling farmhouses. Francesca was driving slowly and over the sound of the engine, a dog barked loudly.

I pointed. "There! On the right!" A large sign for the restaurant sent us down a country road, and the building was there before us, situated in a wooded area with a large parking area surrounding it. We were able to park close, and we walked arm in arm through the twilight, for dusk was now falling rapidly.

The entrance to the restaurant was through a large sheltering portico with trelliswork and twisting vines. Perhaps it was our euphoric mood but we reached the large wooden double doors before I noticed that the place was almost in darkness. Simultaneously, Francesca said, "There weren't many cars in the parking lot. I wonder—"

There was a sound behind us and we turned to see the figure of a man in dark clothes emerging from the bushes.

"Go on in," he said in a voice that did not invite argument. As an additional persuasion, he took his right hand from his pocket. It contained a black and ugly shape that wasn't clear in the fading light, but I decided against the need for precise identification. We went in.

As I pushed the door open, I saw the sign that declared the restaurant open six days of the week. Today it was closed for business.

"Turn left." The voice was speaking Italian but it did not sound familiar. We went along a corridor with photographs on both walls then through swinging doors. We were in the kitchen.

Familiar stainless steel and copper shapes gleamed as the man snapped on a light. It illuminated only the section of the kitchen that we were in now. Fading into the darkness were tables and chopping blocks, racks of dishes and plates, and all the customary paraphernalia. The soothing smells of garlic and onion hung in the air despite the obvious signs of careful cleaning and ventilation.

I had thought we were safe with Cataldo's welcome news that Spezzano had been apprehended and that threat removed. It had led to an elation that had now burst like a collapsing soufflé. How could another assassin have been put on our trail so quickly?

"Yes, you're the one," the man said in a quiet voice. I could see him now. He was medium height, light, thinning hair, and in his forties. His face was grim and hard, and his complexion was pasty, as if he had lived several recent years indoors. His eyes were flinty and bore the look of one accustomed to a life of violence. He stared at Francesca. "Pity you had to be along too," he grunted then his expression changed. "Still," he said with a leer, "maybe we can enjoy ourselves after he's left us."

"We both have to leave," I told him though my mouth was a little dry. "We need to find a restaurant that's open."

I took a step and his right hand moved sharply. I had full confirmation of the nature of that black and ugly shape in it. It was a gun. I stopped.

"Who are you?" Francesca demanded contemptuously. "What do you want? If it's money, we—" She snapped her handbag open, stopped as he waggled the gun at her.

"In due course, I can get to that," he said with an unpleasant grin. "For now"—he looked meaningfully at me—"it's just orders. That's all, just orders."

"Orders from whom?" In Italian, the grammar was not in question. "At least, I deserve to know that." I did want to know, though the desire to keep him talking, to stall as long as I could, was more important.

He was not a believer in last requests. He ignored my question. "Over there." He motioned to the far end of the kitchen, wreathed in darkness. I obeyed quickly, the vague thought that the darkness might offer a hiding place. I obeyed so quickly in fact that it took him unawares. I hurried past the racks of dishes with the intention of separating myself from Francesca, keeping us apart so as to make it as difficult for him as I could. I was rounding the end of the bench when I saw ahead of me one of the wooden-slatted platforms that chefs place on the concrete floors to stand on while working.

"Slowly!" he said harshly.

I paused, put my hand on the corner of the bench top as I half turned. He was coming towards me and I moved my hand.

His eyes flickered to it, looking to see if I was reaching for something to use as a weapon. There was nothing there on the scrubbed wooden surface, and he grinned mirthlessly. Francesca stopped too, a few paces behind me.

He waved the automatic for me to go on towards the dark alcove. I could only presume that he had made some preparations there for our disposal, but I didn't want to speculate on what they might be.

I went on, trailing my hand on the bench top as I turned the corner, trusting that he was looking at my hand and not at the floor.

He kicked the edge of the slatted platform just as I had hoped and almost fell, saving himself only with a grab at the table with his left arm.

I might not have another chance. I had spotted a row of iron skillets on a rack above and I snatched the nearest and swung at him. It missed his head but hit him on the right bicep as he was pulling himself to his feet. His fingers instinctively let go of the automatic and it clattered to the floor. Francesca took a step forward to run and pick it up but he lunged for it. He dropped his hand flat on the gun, pinning it to the floor.

He was a cool customer. Where most would have scrambled to get a grip on the gun, he kept it there, his hand covering it while he sized up our relative positions. Francesca and I were seven or eight feet apart so he had to look from one to the other. An evil smile came over his face as he slowly fumbled to get the gun into his hand, keeping his eyes on us and not giving in to the temptation to look down at the gun.

I edged to my left, widening the space between Francesca and me, increasing the angle between us. He had to turn his head further now to look from one to the other, but as he did, he was palming the gun. He was having to do it with his left hand, and I had noticed that he had held it in his right before. Most people are one-handed and have a strong preference for the favored hand. Gambling on him being that way, I guessed that he would rather shoot me with his right hand, so I watched breathlessly as he scooped up the gun.

I took another step to the left. I had guessed correctly, he switched the gun to the other hand and as he did so I threw the skillet at him. Heavy iron skillets are not easy to throw and I had no time to wind up a swing. It sailed through the air in a lazy arc and he sneered as it dipped to fall on the concrete floor in front of him.

The sneer promptly disappeared as the skillet bounced once on its handle and rebounded to hit him on the shin. He winced but held on to the gun. In that half second, I had taken another step and banged against a bench. I glanced at it swiftly—there must be something there. A knife was what I hoped for, but I knew kitchens too well to really expect one. They are always kept in racks on the wall, where they are safer than left lying on a flat surface.

He was facing me across the end of the bench and the blow on the shinbone had not improved his temper. He muttered something I did not hear, but it sounded profane. He raised the gun and took aim. His manner was smoothly professional.

The crash of the gun was deafening in the confines of the kitchen. Echoes rolled from saucepans to stew pots and bounced down from the low ceiling. A stack of plates shivered and some glasses rattled in a dishwasher.

He stood staring at me, his expression threatening. The reverberations were still rolling when there was another explosion.

At the second shot, the man jerked visibly and his gun arm

sagged. His legs gave way and his mouth opened in almost comical incredulity. He crumpled to his knees and he was still staring
at me. His torso folded and he toppled forward to crash facedown on the concrete, the automatic still in his hand.

Francesca stood there, her hand still inside her bag. A whiff
of smoke spiraled up from it. Two patches of blood were spreading rapidly on the man's back and she looked down at them
scornfully. The look on her face was almost frightening. She
could probably have shot a whole platoon if her ammunition
had held out.

She looked ruefully at her handbag. There was a large rag-
ged hole in the bottom of it, the fiber edges still smoking.

"It's usual to take the gun out before firing it," I commented.

"There wasn't time," she said simply. She lifted the bag
and examined it. "I paid three hundred thousand lire for this."

"Maybe you can get it repaired."

She gave a choking laugh, dropped the bag, and threw
herself into my arms.

When Cataldo arrived, we had every light in the restaurant blazing. He looked at the body.

"You are running up a high death rate here," he commented.

"I was right to insist on having a gun, wasn't I, Carlo?"
Francesca asked pertly.

He grunted a grudging acquiescence.

"It was a good idea to give me a license too," she added.

He examined the body and then the gun. He sniffed my
hands and then Francesca's. We told him exactly what had happened and he listened without comment. The investigation team

started arriving in ones and twos and he nodded to them to go ahead. To us, he said, "Let's take a look down here," and we went in the direction of the dark alcove where we had been headed.

Two very large black plastic sacks and a garbage wagon on wheels were there, and Francesca gave a look, a shudder, and turned away. An older detective with years of experience written all over his face came up and said something to Cataldo in a low voice. The captain nodded thanks.

"One of my detectives recognized your assailant," he told us. "His name is Perruchio—he has a long criminal record." He glanced at Francesca. "Thanks to you, it won't get any longer."

"After your phone call, I thought we were safe," I said with a touch of acerbity.

"I did too," Cataldo admitted. "I didn't think a replacement for Spezzano could be found that quickly."

"Yes, that was a bad mistake, wasn't it?" I commented.

He looked at me quickly.

Francesca frowned. "Mistake? Whose mistake?"

"You already know, don't you?" I asked Cataldo.

He was studying me with a quizzical expression, cautiously assessing what he was going to say.

"Two ex-convicts and Desmond Lansdown's assistant. It's obvious now when you put those together," I said.

The vestige of a satisfied smile was beginning to spread over his face.

"But you don't have quite enough evidence," I suggested.

He smiled and his strong, bronzed face lit up.

"Between us, we can conclude this case!" His voice was triumphant.

Francesca looked from Cataldo to me and back again.

"Will you two tell me what you are talking about?"

CHAPTER TWENTY-FOUR

Italvin, as it is known, is the biggest wine fair in Italy and perhaps in Europe. It is the showcase of the wine industry and only open to persons in the trade, but it was child's play for a man with Cataldo's influence to get tickets for Francesca and me.

Situated in the gently rolling countryside south of Vicenza, five massive pavilions housed booths where over five hundred vineyards offered sample tasting of their wares. We signed in— Cataldo had arranged it all—and we were given large badges which identified us as representatives of some organization with several bewildering initials. Francesca glanced at them and nodded, satisfied that she could answer questions about our supposed status. We strolled down the first aisle, admiring the work that had gone into the display boards and backdrops. In one, rows of vines stood out in almost three-dimensional green against the brown soil, and a spectacular old castle converted into a mansion stood proudly on top of a hill. Some had only posters on the wall, some had racks of bottles and boards covered with colorful labels.

The banquet was to be at eight o'clock but Cataldo had asked us to be there early and suggested that we spend the time in the wine pavilions. It was a proposal not to be declined, and Francesca noted I was having a hard time controlling my salivation.

"You can't wait to do some tasting, can you?"

"It would be unfair to all these vintners who have spent so much time—"

"Let's try this one."

The Italian wine industry is the most baffling and infuriating in Europe. It can delight and excite but it can also exasperate and disappoint. Great names such as Soave, Frascati, and Verdicchio have been abused by overproduction, and this is a shame because the country has an infinite variety of climate, landscape, and soil. Over a thousand grape varieties mean a treasure trove of rare and original wine tastes—in theory. The planting of too many inferior but high-yielding clones has resulted in an ocean of cheap, cheerless mouthwash.

Signs of the tide turning are encouraging, though. Chianti has been brought back from the depths of mediocrity and investment in replanting, modern equipment, and the right clones continues to grow.

The Casa Vinicola Montello had a stand being run by the elderly Signor Montello himself, aided by his two sons and his daughter and a twenty-year-old grandson. Many of the stands here belonged to family-owned and operated vineyards, Francesca told me. Some had been forced to sell to the big-name producers but others like this one steadfastly continued the family tradition.

"Taste this," urged the daughter. It was a Mammolo, an ancient variety of red rarely encountered. She poured less than an inch into a large bulb-shaped glass that would hold half a liter. "It keeps in the bouquet for tasting purposes," she explained. It had a delicate perfume and a rare balance of lean elegance and almost smoky fruit. They were trying to develop a business in up-market reds, aware that they would have to sell at higher prices than they would get for table wines but the decision was influenced by their limited production.

"Let's find some whites," Francesca said and we stopped at La Pergola Giuliano Agricola. Like most booths, it consisted of a counter like a bar with various open bottles. Boxes and crates stood behind the bar ready to replenish the supply. Giuliano himself, stocky and a true son of the soil, was beaming with pleasure and pouring from his selection of Sauvignon, Pinot Bianco, Riesling Renano, Nebbiolo, Tocai Friulano, and Chardonnay. Francesca particularly liked the Pinot Bianco. "Let's find some more of that," she said.

It was no problem. We found many more—and then many more. We talked to vintners, some old and some young, some sedately traditional and some progressive, some optimistic and some pessimistic. One had sold his vineyard, gone into real estate development, then returned and bought the vineyard back. Another had been to California, marveled at the technological razzle-dazzle of Napa Valley, but come back to his drab cellars in the foothills of the Alps and continued to make wine just as before.

"It's as well they only give us a few milliliters of each wine to taste." Francesca commented.

"In total volume, we've only drunk about a bottle," I assured her.

Prices were not displayed anywhere. A prospective buyer could ask and negotiate but this noticeable lack of one aspect of commercialism at least was refreshing.

We tasted some Merlot, another wine that has suffered not only from overproduction but also from its high yield which has attracted "pirate" vineyards to produce blends with inferior wines, a practice that is illegal.

This wine has the recurrent problem of the intrusion of a blackberry flavor. A modest amount is essential to Merlot's rich mellowness, but just a little too much and the blackberries grab you by the taste buds. It is a popular wine in Italy as Italians rate it as the perfect accompaniment to robust pasta dishes.

A small drinking group had already emptied several bottles which a smiling young man hastily disposed of to make room for us. The group was bewailing the legal entanglements of the wine industry. "There are too many laws," the young man protested.

"That's not just the wine trade," interjected an older man. "It's the same everywhere you look in this country. Rules, regulations, statues, canons, decrees, acts, charters—only a lawyer could understand them and most of them don't. How could they? A lot of laws may be five hundred years old but others were passed only last week. They don't have time even to read all of them."

It was a comment I had heard repeated many times in Italy. The conclusion usually reached at the end of such discussions was that if all the laws were applied, the entire country would be paralyzed. Most of this assembly wanted to talk about the wine industry, though, and the strangulation effect of too many rules and regulations. "In the Middle Ages," contributed another, "table wines were flavored with herbs and spices. This is now illegal—it is prohibited by law—"

"Unless you are making vermouth," called out someone from the end of the bar. "Then you can salvage wines that couldn't be sold otherwise." There were rueful laughs at the truth of this. Wine producers in Italy particularly are angry because wines from a bad harvest are used in vermouth, which then becomes saleable.

On the next aisle, we ran into Bernardo, plant and flower chef *straordinario*, and his demure wife, Vanessa. He was a little more somber than even his usual eremitic self. He told us he was still concerned about the shadow cast over his style of cooking and his use of natural ingredients. "There have never been any dangerous products in my cooking," he stated firmly.

Out of the corner of my eye, I could see Francesca casting an occasional furtive glance at Vanessa, who looked shy and said little. I knew that Francesca was trying to reconcile this image with the woman we had seen slipping into the nightclub, Fica, with the brilliant but obnoxious Ottavio.

The big pavilions were crowded now, and the hum of discussions, arguments, claims, counterclaims, and customer comments both favorable and otherwise rose to the high raftered ceilings. The sharp clink of glass and the soft gurgle of wine added to the excitement of the occasion. As we walked past one deeply involved group, we were hailed by a familiar voice and face. It was Tomasso Rinaldo, the dapper lawyer.

After we had agreed on what a good time we were all having, Francesca pointed down the aisle. "I think they could use you there to defend the law. Some harsh words are being used."

Tomasso smoothed his smartly trimmed beard and waved a beautifully manicured hand in a conciliatory gesture. "The law comes in for some heavy criticism today," he admitted. "Everyone has an opinion on it—all find it either too weak or too strong."

"The wine business must be a minefield of legal problems." I said in commiseration. "The food business being not too far behind."

"True," he agreed. "We are having a discussion on labeling. Already we have to show if a wine contains sulfites. Some legislators want to force winemakers to show the percentage of sulfur dioxide on the label. That will mean changing winemaking methods to reduce the amount of it used."

"Which in turn will mean more chemical sprays in the vineyard and more complaints of damage to the health of the community," I added.

"All bad for the winemakers but good for the lawyers," said Francesca.

Tomasso looked rueful. "Not the way we want more accounts, I can assure you."

We left him trying to decide whether to stay with his present group or try the other. "The law is full of dilemmas," he told us, shaking his head.

Italians are fond of giving their wines extravagant names, and one stand pressed on us a taste of their *Sangue di Giuda*— the Blood of Judas. We felt betrayed by it. Francesca found some *Torre del Greco*—the Towers of Greece—but was disappointed when it was not as she remembered. We passed a group at one stand arguing heatedly over "big name" wines. "Customers buy big name wines because they feel secure with them," maintained a woman with a large hat. "But their reputations were gained by offering quality whereas today a big name means nothing more than that the wine has not been abused." A thin man with a face weathered by decades in a vineyard said, "I blame the European Community. They support the big producers and penalize the small vineyard trying for quality."

We came in near the end of a spirited debate on another stand over the relative merits of wood and glass for aging red wines but at least we were in time to enjoy the full flavor of their clean, well-balanced Montepulciano. Francesca looked at the large clock at the end of the hall. "We should be going in to the banquet room."

Her words gave me a tingling feeling. Cataldo was going to try to draw the final curtain and would no doubt do it with an operatic flourish. I had an uncomfortable memory of so many Italian operas that ended in bloodshed and death . . .

CHAPTER TWENTY-FIVE

The banquet room seemed small after the cavernous halls of the exhibition. Tables each seating six or eight people were set, but the couple of dozen people who were here already stood in groups, drinking wine served from the tables round the walls. We went over to one of these and found that they were pouring superior wines from some of the best vineyards.

I found myself examining the young man handing us two glasses of Principessa Gavi from the Banfi vineyard in Siena. He looked reliable and so was the wine. It was one of the cleanest, crispest, most refreshing white wines I had tasted, and Francesca agreed enthusiastically. After we had confirmed that opinion, I said, "Let's circulate. Do some investigating."

The group I joined was being lectured at by a man with a flowing mustache and a strong voice. "It should not be allowed to be displayed at an exhibition as serious and prestigious as this one," he was declaring. "It is an insult to the Italian wine industry." I raised my eyebrows at a red-haired woman standing nearby. "He's talking about Lambrusco," she whispered. "Professor Peralto from the wine institute."

"It is as near to undrinkable as a wine can get," the man continued. "Is that so surprising? Everything we know about Lambrusco tells us that. For instance, it can be drunk the day after it is bottled—now we all know that wine needs to age. Lambrusco is eight or nine percent alcohol—any good wine is at least twelve percent. It is slightly sparkling—but for how long? The bubbles die immediately. It is thin-bodied, sharp-tasting, and a sickly pink color that looks as if it came out of a laboratory. It is not rosé and it is not red—it is not even anywhere in between."

His verbal assault brought titters from his small audience then a voice called out, "Millions drink it—they must like it!"

The professor shook his head vigorously. "We nickname it Lambruscola. Does that not tell you something?"

"It's an insult to a good soft drink!" commented a woman supporter.

"Millions like it, you say." The professor pointed to the man who had made that remark. "They are people with uneducated tastes. Isn't it our responsibility to educate them?"

"Yours maybe," grunted someone. "You're the educator."

The professor leaped on the statement. "Exactly. I'm trying to do that now—educate people—and that means condemning the bad as well as praising the good."

A babble of voices drowned out the next words as several voluble Italians all started to speak at the same time. I wandered on, unable to resist a scrutinizing look at each waiter.

A deep voice hailed me and I found Giacomo pumping my hand. "My friend! I am glad to see you. Tell me, how goes the search?"

"I hope you mean the search for who killed Signor Pellegrini. That is the important one," I said in my most reproving tone.

"Of course, of course." His beard looked fuller than ever, and he seemed to have grown in all directions. He was just as ebullient as before, and my rebuke went right over his head. "I just saw Captain Cataldo coming in," he said. "Possibly, he has news."

"Let us hope so," I said piously. "I didn't expect anything like this when I came to Italy."

Giacomo shrugged his massive shoulders. "Italy is a blood-stained country. Our people are violent and their emotions are apt to boil over without warning. Husbands kill wives, wives kill mistresses, elder brothers kill men who defile their sisters, young lovers think they are Romeo and Juliet and die together." He sighed and his entire bulk shuddered. "More Italians have died in all these ways than in all this country's wars put together. Death is never far away for any Italian."

I nodded in understanding. It was permissible for him to say that, but as a foreigner I knew that my opinion was not worth a pinch of salt, so I said nothing on the subject. Instead, emboldened by this opportunity, I said to him, "Tell me, Giacomo, what is the truth behind this rumor that Signor Pellegrini was using his position to have one of your stars taken away?"

It caught him a little off-balance. "It may be true." He recovered quickly. "I hope that others will see me differently."

"What about Captain Cataldo?" I asked. "Will he see it differently?"

He laughed, throwing back his head. "Kill a man for a chef's star! Not enough motive there, my friend."

"Not alone," I agreed, getting braver. "Another rumor is floating about too, though. It says that you and Pellegrini's wife have been seen together."

If I was expecting a flash of guilt, I was to be disappointed. He laughed again, louder this time. "We have been together once. That was at the Fica nightclub. You know it?"

No hint of suspicion showed in his voice. He continued,

"That was at the widow's request. She wanted to discuss a rescheduling of the debt I owe."

"At a nightclub?"

He smiled widely. "She is an unusual woman."

An acquaintance came and took him away. Francesca rejoined me. "Did you learn anything?" she asked. "You were certainly amusing Giacomo."

I gave her the substance of our conversation. "So they didn't see us," she said, relieved. "Talking about money in a private booth at the Fica! Was he serious?"

"You think he was covering up?" I had not considered that. "Maybe I'm too naive."

She patted my cheek. "Everyone likes honest persons. On the other hand, deception is useful. There are times when it is necessary because of the evil nature of humanity. So the more you can gain the reputation of being truthful, the more effective you will find it when you want to be deceitful."

I chuckled at the shining eyes and eager parted lips as she expounded this bewildering theory. "Did anyone ever call you Signorina Macchiavelli?"

"Don't you laugh at me!" she warned, trying to keep a straight face. "Anyway, I have been sleuthing too. I talked to Vanessa Mantegna."

I knew Francesca had been bursting with curiosity about Vanessa's liaison with Ottavio in the nightclub. Was it tinged with envy?

"Bernardo's wife . . . good. Learn anything?"

"Yes, but let's have another glass of wine first."

"Another Gavi?" I suggested.

"It was very good. Let's see what else they've got, though."

We chose a Bianco de Pitigliano, the knowledgable waiter

telling us that this was from the Trebbiano grape grown in the volcanic soil in the south of Tuscany. It was dry and delicate, appetizing yet with a fruity acidity.

We moved away, out of earshot of the people around the busy bartender. "Go on," I urged, "tell me."

"Vanessa saw us, so she knew we had seen her with Ottavio. I didn't have to prod her much, she was anxious to explain herself. She says Ottavio has been after her for some time and she's always resisted."

"Until now."

"She says the reason she went to the Fica was to see what she could do to help Ottavio get the job in London."

"You mean Bernardo?"

"No, I mean Ottavio."

"Surely you didn't believe her?"

"I'm sure she was telling me the truth."

"What?" I protested. "After what you just told me about learning to be deceitful! I don't understand. She doesn't want her own husband to get the job?"

"I think Vanessa is basically an honest person," she said decisively. "Her reason for wanting Ottavio to get the job was so that Bernardo *wouldn't* get it. You see, she's been to London and would hate to live there. Bernardo doesn't know this, of course. Oh, he knows she doesn't like London but she doesn't want him to know that she kept him from getting the job."

I shook my head in bewilderment. "Women's minds are bizarre, aren't they?"

"Not a bit. They are perfectly logical."

"Vanessa didn't have to pay too high a price for this, did she?"

Francesca shook her head. " '*Virgo intacto*,' she assured me."

"You asked?"

"Of course," she said, looking surprised.

"Okay, you did a good sleuthing job."

We touched glasses.

"I did, didn't I?"

"Have you seen the captain?" I asked. "Giacomo said he was here."

"I haven't seen him yet. Who shall I harass next?"

"This white wine is making you aggressive. Finish the glass."

I supposed that Francesca was right about the triangle of Bernardo, Ottavio, and Vanessa. It wasn't really a triangle after all, just a straight line with a few curves in it. She had a lot of "street smarts" in her makeup and she was shrewd. The story might not make sense anywhere else, but we were in Italy.

There was something of a stir at the main door. It was easy to see why—the imposing figure of Captain Cataldo had entered and he stood looking imperiously around the room. He went to speak to a couple of the waiters and I supposed they were police. He left them and came in, whipping off his cloak with a majestic swirl. He made the gesture as if proclaiming that he was here and now all would be revealed.

CHAPTER TWENTY-SIX

He stopped to greet people and chat very briefly. He moved through the crowd with the easy confidence of a massive ice-breaker going through thin melting ice. It looked like casual progress, but it was planned. He stepped onto a dais and held up a hand for silence. Mussolini could not have commanded it more effectively.

"If you will take your places at the tables," he began in his rich voice, "I will tell you of current developments following from the unfortunate death of our friend, Signor Pellegrini. This sad event has had a far-reaching effect on our community, and you are all anxious to know the present status."

Everyone did as he ordered. Francesca and I found ourselves sitting with several people we did not know. There was no time for introductions, for Cataldo was continuing.

"The most perplexing part of the entire investigation has been the hunt for the poison that hallucinated Signor Pellegrini so that he fell into the pool. Our Forensic department tells me they know of no poison that does not leave a trace in the stomach. They have considered interacting substances, allergens, dangerous combinations—every possibility—and still have found nothing. Nothing to account for Signor Pellegrini, his wife, Signora Pellegrini, and Signor Rinaldo being the only ones to be poisoned. We have repeated all the tests and talked to experts in other countries, still to no avail."

The crowd was silent, hanging on his every word. He turned his head slowly, encompassing everyone there, enjoying his moment in the spotlight though it was obvious he enjoyed that position often.

"I was telling our English friend here" —he nodded in my direction— "of the Italian pioneers who founded modern criminology. I told him how the focus of investigation shifted from the circumstances surrounding the crime to the crime itself and then to the criminal. When I was not able to make progress in the search for an untraceable poison or learn how it was administered, I decided to follow Lombroso's technique. I concentrated on the criminal."

An electric silence filled the room. A plate clanked. Someone asked, "You mean you knew who the criminal was?"

Cataldo smiled complacently. "Not at that moment, no. It was not fully clear that there was a criminal. Signor Pellegrini could have hallucinated for some other reason and fallen into the pool. Except . . ."

The crowd waited for him and he obliged. "Except for the earlier attempt on Pellegrini's life."

A gasp floated from table to table, most not aware of this.

"A buffalo herd was stampeded and Pellegrini was almost killed. I have examined the location more than once. Only someone familiar with Signor Pellegrini and his habits could have known that he always stopped at that place."

When Cataldo resumed, he was speaking more slowly and enunciating even more carefully, His words began to take on more significance.

Cataldo shifted his stance slightly. It was the only movement in the room.

"Motive is, of course, a matter closely connected with the

criminal. Who gained from his death? We know that some of our regional personalities had business dealings with Signora Pellegrini."

"He means several chefs owed him money," whispered Francesca. "I wonder why he's being so tactful?"

"Another suffered injury to his career," added Cataldo, and glances flashed in Giacomo's direction. Little secrecy surrounded this incident and it was widely known that Pellegrini was blamed for Giacomo losing his third star.

"Are these reasons for murder? I did not think so. I was being forced to the conclusion," said Cataldo carefully, "that the person with the most to gain from Pellegrini's death was"—he swung a finger and pointed—"Signora Elena Pellegrini."

She was on her feet immediately, eyes flashing and breasts heaving. Gasps came from the crowd, which was lapping it up.

"This is absurd! Ridiculous! It is—"

"Am I wrong?" asked Cataldo innocently. "You do not inherit all the Pellegrini businesses?"

"That part is true," she snapped. "I do inherit all Silvio's businesses."

"Which you have been heard to say you could run better than he did."

"But I did not kill him!" she shouted. "It's preposterous to suggest that I could hit him on the head and drown him in the pool!"

"Ah, I see," said Cataldo, rubbing his chin reflectively, "you claim the frailty of your sex. You are not strong enough to have knocked him unconscious and you are not unscrupulous enough to have drowned him. H'm . . ." He appeared pensive for a moment. "That could be true, I suppose."

His next words rapped out so forcefully that Elena flinched visibly.

"In that case, you must have had an accomplice. A man presumably. Now who could that be?" His gaze pivoted to Giacomo. "We have a witness to clandestine meetings between you and chef Giacomo Ferrero."

"See!" Francesca whispered triumphantly. "Carlo did have a man at the Fica!"

Now it was Giacomo, his bearded bulk knocking his chair to the floor as he leaped to his feet. "I object to these scurrilous accusations!" he bellowed. "I met Elena at a nightclub because she wanted to talk about canceling my debt to Pellegrini!"

There were snickers at this and even a few laughs. Giacomo glared back. "It's nonsense to think that I would kill a man because he caused me to lose a star," he blustered. "I was furious when I first heard about that. I still am, but I did not kill him!"

"Please remain calm," Cataldo admonished him. "You are not being accused."

Giacomo stood there, still angry, but Cataldo's words robbed him of further argument. He retrieved his chair and sat down.

The noble figure of Captain Cataldo drew to full height. The black uniform with the bright red piping looked even more imposing. He breathed leisurely and the hiatus raised the tension in the room to a still higher level.

"When I reached this point in my assembly of the facts in the case—still concentrating on the identity of the criminal—the problem was solved." He smiled gently, proud and satisfied. The atmosphere was reaching an explosive level. No one spoke, but it was clear that Cataldo's audience did not deem the case closed at all. A puzzled look was on several faces and the man next to Francesca frowned and shook his head.

"Signor Calvocoressi?" Cataldo called out and a heavy brown-faced man lifted a hand. "Would you tell us what your doctor told you?"

"He said it was an attack of indigestion. I often have them. Sometimes they are very bad and—"

"Thank you," said Cataldo. "We can eliminate you from the case. Now, we are fortunate in having an expert on food with us. Our English friend here has had much experience in the field of culinary murder, especially poisoning"—he pointed to me—"so I am going to ask him to give us his opinions."

He sat down, gave me an expansive wave, and I came to my feet. "Much experience" was an exaggeration but it probably helped to establish my credentials.

"We had a list of four people," I began, "believed to have been the victims of a poison administered at the San Pietro. One possible means suggested was that a flower or a plant contained a hallucinatory agent. It is true that some plants and flowers do, but there is no doubt whatever that Chef Bernardo is scrupulously careful in his selection and preparation."

I could see Bernardo now, looking relieved. I went on, "With the elimination of Signor Calvocoressi from the list, we are left with only three people who might have been poisoned— or hallucinated.

"First, Signor Pellegrini. No trace could be found in his stomach of any foreign substance. This led to the possibility that the poisonous material was untraceable. He cannot, unfortunately, tell us anything about his condition so we do not know what hallucinations he may have experienced. The spilled coffee pot, the cup and saucer, the overturned chair, the zigzag trail of spilled coffee, and his fall into the pool—all these suggest it.

"That leaves us with Signora Pellegrini. She experienced hallucinations and once again, the possibility of an untraceable substance suggested itself."

A few murmurs of concern arose. Nobody liked the sinister sound of "an untraceable poison." When they had died, I continued.

"The third person reporting hallucinations was our lawyer friend, Avvocato Tomasso Rinaldo. Considering all these facts, I came to a startling thought. What if the so-called poison was untraceable because it did not exist? Only two living persons say it did. What if they were not telling the truth?"

I sat down. Cataldo rose. "Thank you, and that very clear exposition brings us to the further question: if the Signora had an accomplice, who more likely than Tomasso Rinaldo?"

Exclamations and gasps of astonishment rippled through the room at this accusation of the well-known lawyer.

Tomasso rose to his feet calmly. "Captain, you are fumbling in the dark. You are at a loss in this case and grasping at any straw. You will kindly withdraw your remarks." He sat down, cool as ice.

Cataldo was about to reply when there came a startling interruption. Another person had stood and all heads turned. It was Tomasso's wife, Clara.

"The two of them have been having an affair for some time," she stated clearly.

Elena Pellegrini swirled around and was about to rush over and start some clawing of eyes but she was restrained. She stood, eyes blazing, but any aggression on her part would be self-condemning and she realized it.

Cataldo regarded all this with a complete absence of visible emotion, but I did not doubt that he found his duty difficult.

He was a compassionate man, and accusing people known to him of murder was distasteful to him. Only the additional fact that another of these was the victim of that murder enabled him to keep to his purpose.

"She killed Silvio," Clara Rinaldo said in a loud voice.

"I didn't! I didn't!" screamed Elena and her shrill voice echoed.

"If you did not," said Cataldo, calm by comparison, "then it was Tomasso Rinaldo—and you, Signora Pellegrini, helped him."

The silvery-haired lawyer got to his feet and walked out of the room.

Cataldo watched him go, making no attempt to stop him.

CHAPTER TWENTY-SEVEN

I could hardly believe it when I saw Tomasso walking out of that room—and you just let him."

We were in one of the adjoining staff rooms in the Italvin buildings and Cataldo was sitting by a telephone, smoking a long cheroot and looking extremely pleased with himself

"Tomasso Rinaldo is a renowned lawyer," he said. "I had achieved what I wanted—I had pointed a firm finger of suspicion at him and I had got Signora Clara Rinaldo to say that her husband and Elena Pellegrini were having an affair. I knew that Clara had been frequenting the Fica nightclub and that there had been estrangement between her and her husband for some time. So when I saw the reports on her visiting the club I thought that she was the errant one. It took me a little while to realize it was her husband who was straying and she wanted to keep an eye on him."

"Elena was seen there not only with Tomasso," Francesca said. "She also arranged to meet the chefs there. They were flattered and it provided her with a cover for her affair with Tomasso."

"I have learned," Cataldo said, puffing deeply on the cheroot, "to always suspect the spouse first. It is a reliable rule to follow and more often than not, rewarding."

"But why didn't you arrest him?" I asked.

"Arrest! You Anglos are so direct. You should learn a little finesse from the Latins."

Francesca shot me a I-told-you-how-clever-he-was look which I ignored. I asked, "What about Elena Pellegrini? You haven't arrested her either."

"I will very soon. I am sure that Clara Rinaldo will provide me with ample evidence."

"I liked the way you had me accuse Tomasso," I said. "In your official position, you didn't want to do that without more evidence."

He smiled complacently. "Yes, that was good, wasn't it? I certainly did not have sufficient evidence to take it to trial. In fact, I still don't, but I will very soon. You see, much of the evidence pointing to Avvocato Rinaldo came from your experiences. For instance, Rinaldo was close enough to Pellegrini to know exactly where Pellegrini stopped on his tour to show the buffalo. He was therefore able to instruct Spezzano where to set off the firecrackers and stampede the herd."

Cataldo continued, "Spezzano was an ex-convict, and so was Perruchio, the man who tried to kill you in the Ristorante Regina. Now how many people can readily hire ex-convicts? Hardly any, but as a lawyer, Rinaldo could. He had defended many of them." He looked at me. "That was the point you picked up."

"Brilliant," said Francesca in admiration. "Both of you," she added diplomatically.

"And I suspect," said Cataldo, "that Pellegrini—at Tomasso Rinaldo's instigation—planted Spezzano at the Dorigo Farms to get inside information that would help in buying out Dorigo. After killing Pellegrini, Rinaldo realized that he had a man in the right place to dispose of you as soon as you visited the rice fields."

"I made it easy for him," I said bitterly. "I told him we were going there."

"Go on, Carlo," urged Francesca, her eyes bright. Cataldo needed little persuasion.

"Dorigo gave me a valuable clue too, although I didn't realize it at the time. He told us that Pellegrini had made what he called "legal offers" for his rice fields. There was only one way he could have made "legal offers," and that was through his lawyer, Tomasso Rinaldo."

Cataldo shook his head sadly. "I have known and admired him for a long time. It is terrible that I must now prosecute him." He puffed again and expelled a dense cloud of blue-gray smoke. "Then there was another aspect of the case—the telephone conversation with Mr. Desmond Lansdown when he told me of the dismissal of his right-hand man, Mr. Nigel Hamilton. Desmond said that Hamilton had used one of their phones. He meant one of the phones used to do Lansdown's restaurant or film business. It was easy to get a listing of all numbers called. Two were in Italy."

I was listening with interest to this part. Francesca sat as if enraptured. I felt like suggesting she go sit at the great investigator's feet.

"One was to Pellegrini and the other to Tomasso Rinaldo. Hamilton had, of course, known both of them while he was here with Signor Desmond making *Don Juan*." His face took on a slightly pained expression at the recollection of the notorious film but he persevered gamely. "That was the other factor that you pointed out to me. When Hamilton got into trouble over drugs while they were making the movie, Lansdown got him a lawyer. It was simple to find out that lawyer was—"

"Tomasso!" Francesca clapped her hands together in delight.

"Exactly. Hamilton had now lost his job, and he was calling anyone who might help him. Pellegrini was a wealthy industrialist, Tomasso Rinaldo was a prominent lawyer and widely known. Both could be helpful to him, and with an Italian mother, Hamilton spoke the language well. Perhaps neither was receptive initially, so in order to show how valuable a man he was, Hamilton told them of Lansdown's plan to hire a famous chef from this area. This may not have impressed Pellegrini but as soon as Rinaldo heard this, he knew that here was a great opportunity to do what he had been planning on doing: kill Pellegrini, and run his business empire with his widow. We know they have been having an affair for some time. Hamilton had handed him alternate suspects—"

"Me and the three chefs," I said. "As Pellegrini's lawyer, naturally Tomasso knew of the debts between them which were partial motives at least—"

"Plus the addition of some—as the English say—marital infidelity." Francesca said, darting a wicked glance at me.

"Cleverly introduced by Elena Pellegrini," I added. "So he invited Hamilton to come here and help him—he must have told Hamilton to pretend to kill me as another diversion. Hamilton, a frustrated actor, enjoyed dressing as a monk to do it."

"Exactly." Captain Cataldo was generous in his praise, glorying in his success. "Rinaldo then brought in Spezzano to do the real dirty work—including getting rid of Hamilton."

"They must have thought that Hamilton told me everything. That's why the attempts on me," I added.

"Yes. And realizing that Spezzano was a liability as you could recognize him, Rinaldo tried to get him out of the country. He brought in another ex-convict, Perruchio, to dispatch you at the restaurant."

"Me too!" Francesca cried, not wanting to be left out of a murder attempt. "Don't forget he was going to kill me too."

"And you saved my life," I reminded her.

She smiled at me warmly. "It was good shooting, wasn't it?"

"Excellent shooting," agreed Cataldo. "The first bullet went through his heart and the second was close to it."

"Do you think Spezzano killed Pellegrini?" I asked him.

"No. I have no doubt that Rinaldo did that himself. He knew about your visit to Pellegrini's cheese factory and he phoned Pellegrini at a chosen moment. He was able to get him alone in the house, and your involvement nearby in the factory offered another suspect. They may well have had an argument—possibly over business, possibly over Elena. Rinaldo had already planned Pellegrini's death, and when the buffalo stampede failed, this was a perfect opportunity. He knocked Pellegrini unconscious and pushed him into the pool."

He puffed another smoke cloud. "Food and passion. They account for ninety-eight percent of all the crimes in Emilia Romagna, did you know that?" he asked me.

"No, I didn't," I admitted. It was true. I didn't know that particular statistic—every time I heard it, the number had changed.

"Yes, that's so. Keeping that in mind made it easier to concentrate on factors that helped me solve the crime."

It was his hour of triumph and I was certainly not going to deprive him of a minute of it.

"When Lansdown hears about this, he'll want to play you in the movie."

Cataldo bristled. "I shall play myself." He looked at Francesca. "I was an actor, wasn't I? Remember that RAI film at Cinecitta?"

"Yes," she said obediently, "and you were very good too."

I was reminded of Orson Welles' comment when making a film in Rome. "Everybody in Italy is an actor. Fifty-five million of them and they all love to act. The only people in Italy who can't act are in films or on the stage." I did not think it was an appropriate time to share that observation, though, so instead I asked him, "Do you know where Tomasso Rinaldo is now?"

"Not exactly," he said, casually blowing smoke away. He must have studied the way Marcello Mastroianni did that in *City of Women*. I wondered if he already saw himself in the role of Captain Cataldo.

"Aren't you worried he'll get away?"

"I instituted a six-man watch on him before we came into this room. He can't get far. I hoped he would try, though, it emphasizes his guilt. Meanwhile, two of my investigators are interrogating Clara Rinaldo." He gave a wolfish smile. " 'No better witness than a woman scorned'—isn't that what your William Shakespeare said?" he asked, turning to me.

"I don't think those were his exact words, but something along those lines."

"What about Elena Pellegrini?" asked Francesca.

"Two other officers are taking a statement from her."

"That's your polite way of saying they're grilling her, isn't it, Carlo?"

He smiled through the smoke. "The more guilt we pile

on her, the more she'll tell us about Rinaldo." He puffed again with satisfaction. "He may be a lawyer, but he won't squirm out of this."

He rose to his feet. "Now I must ask you to excuse me. There is much to do to wrap this up." To me he said, "You may make your plans to leave anytime after tomorrow. I shall require statements from you before you go."

"Me too?" asked Francesca hopefully.

"Of course you too." He beamed and I got Francesca out of there before she could tell him again how wonderful he was.

CHAPTER TWENTY-EIGHT

I had to change flights in Rome. It is a busy airport, like all airports in capital cities. Fortunately, it was one of those days when no weather problems occurred and no mechanical faults or human errors showed themselves.

Iberia Flight 269 took off almost on time. We lifted off the runway and turned to head west over the city, and I was able to pick out the massive circular structure of the Colosseum and mentally picture it with a hundred thousand bloodthirsty fans on their feet with excitement as a handful of men and women faced the unspeakable terror of hungry wild beasts.

Within minutes, the blue Mediterranean was spread below, thin patches of cloud and haze disappearing as we climbed. By the time the flight attendant appeared with the drinks trolley, the islands of Corsica and Sardinia were visible as brown hulking shapes.

"I'll have a vodka and orange juice," Francesca stated.

After we had given our statements to Captain Cataldo at the Questura the previous day, Francesca had gone to her office to take care of requests for escorts. I went to the Ambasciatore Imperiale Hotel to phone Desmond Lansdown. I found myself hoping that she was being more successful than I was.

"Mr. Lansdown is on location," said a cool feminine English voice after I had had desultory conversations with three Spanish voices.

"I know that," I said patiently. "That's why I'm calling him on this number. It's the one he gave me so that I could call him on location."

"Mr. Lansdown is shooting right now—"

"Then please tell him to take his finger off the trigger and come to the phone."

"I'm afraid I can't do that. Can I have him call you back?"

"It took a long time to get through, so I'd rather talk to him now."

"He gave me very strict instructions—"

"Did you give him my name?"

"What is your name?"

I sighed but persevered.

"I'll see that he knows you are on the line," she said in that same neutral tone. I could hear conversations in both Spanish and English then she came back on the line. "Is this an emergency?"

"It has been a matter of life and death until now," I told her. "Now it's getting serious. Look, you wouldn't want to be responsible for a woman's life, would you?"

I had been about to say "a person's life" but at the last second, I decided to be gender-specific, making a wild guess that judging by her voice, this might get her attention. "Just a moment," she said and after a series of clicks and pregnant pauses, there was a spatter of Spanish in another female voice then that East London drawl came through, loud and clear.

"Lansdown here. A woman's life is at risk, you say? Not anybody I know, is it?"

"I just said that to get through to you. You're not a prisoner in Leopold's castle yet, are you?"

He laughed. "No, I'm still crusading against the infidels. They're nice chaps really, Spanish army in real life. What's so important?"

I told him. The whole story since our last conversation.

"Well done," he said admiringly. "Jolly well done. My congratulations to Cataldo—and you too. A great job . . . Rinaldo, eh, the lawyer fellow . . . yes, congratulations indeed. Now, what about the chefs?"

"I have a full report for you. Shall I send it to your London office? Or do you want me to send it there?"

He was silent for a moment. "Tell you what," he said finally, "bring it here."

"Bring it? There? You mean Spain?"

"Yes. A decision this important needs careful consideration. We need to discuss it. There'll be a lot of questions I want to ask you. When can you come?"

"But you're still on location, aren't you?"

"Shooting on location is mostly hanging around for several hours so as to get five minutes in the can. I can arrange for us to have plenty of time to discuss this."

So it was that I started to make plans to fly to Madrid. I reached for the phone to talk to the travel desk at the hotel then hesitated. Instead, I phoned Francesca.

I told her what Lansdown had said, adding, "Why don't you come too?"

"Me?"

"Why not? You deserve a vacation."

"I do?"

"Certainly. After all this stress, being nearly killed . . ."
It took her a full half second to agree. "You're right."

Full instructions were awaiting us at the car rental desk at the
Madrid airport and Francesca said, "I'll drive," which suited me
fine. It was a sunny day, warm and with a slight breeze. We
headed west in the direction of Salamanca. Spanish drivers are
not quite as macho as the Italian speed-merchants, but on the
autopistas, Spain's equivalent of the autobahn, they are no
slouches. To Francesca, they were probably just dawdling.

After an hour and a half of driving, we turned north and
climbed into the Trabancos Mountains. The temperature
dropped noticeably, but the air was clear and sparkling and
within fifteen minutes, we could see the location site ahead of
us on the edge of a great escarpment. It looked like Tent City.

There appeared to be enough tents to accommodate an
army, then I recalled Lansdown's comment that they were using
the Spanish army as extras for the battle scenes. They were a
colorful array, and as we drew nearer, we could see the Spanish
flag, red and yellow, fluttering over many of them. Other tents,
many larger and multishaped, stood a distance away, and close
to them were several marquees capable of holding a couple of
hundred people each. Various types of mechanical and electrical
equipment was scattered everywhere, thick cables coiled like
black snakes. Parking lots contained cars and trucks of all kinds.
Trailers in every size and in haphazard patterns constituted a city
of their own.

On a hilltop across from the escarpment was perched a
castle, an icon from another world. Flags in dazzling colors flew
from the battlements and it was possible to espy sentries with

long pikes but they were stationary, and I supposed they were dummies. Other figures moved, though, and the sun glinted off metal now and then. Massive towers looked impregnable, although I learned later that one of them was fiberglass.

Francesca's eyes were bright as she surveyed the scene. "Just like the old days for you?" I asked. "On location?"

She nodded. "I haven't seen many as large as this, though."

The recently leveled road was hard-packed sand, and we swirled dust as we drove to a guard gate to receive directions. Colored marker posts identified the various areas and we followed the yellow ones to a large square tent. We could hear voices inside.

"How do you knock on the flap of a tent?" I wondered but Francesca just grinned, pulled the flap aside, and called out, "Desmond, are you decent?"

He came out, clearly puzzled by the voice, then he smiled broadly and gave her a big hug. He released her to shake my hand. "Didn't I tell you she was a great guide, assistant, and helper?" he asked me.

"Crack shot and saver of lives too," I assured him.

He was wearing what looked like a leather harness, bulky and padded with big shoulder guards. His pants were of leather, too or a plastic that looked just like it. They were tucked into massive boots, and it was then that I realized he was towering over me.

He chuckled. "It's the boots. Give me about five inches extra height. Now I'm almost as tall as Richard. This way, you don't have to shoot me standing on an orange crate, do you, Bob?"

The latter was addressed to the thin, partly gray-haired man who had emerged from the tent. He had a strong face and a firm hand grip as Lansdown introduced him, and I recognized his name at once. Robert Stewart was considered one of the most experienced directors in the film business, renowned for his historical epics.

"If you were wearing authentic armor, you'd need a reinforced steel platform," said Stewart with a slight smile.

"Hope we're not interrupting," said Francesca breezily.

Stewart shrugged. "It's okay. We were just going over the shooting schedule for the next few days. Some rain is forecast and we have to finish this sequence before it gets here. In any case, I have to go and talk to the military unit. Armies today fight differently than they did a thousand years ago." He gave us a half wave and left.

"So," said Lansdown, "come on in and sit down." He pulled the tent flap aside. "I suspect that remark about Francesca's crack shooting has more to it. Tell me all about it."

Inside the tent, a large trestle table was covered with drawings and pages of script with colored overlays presumably showing changes. Canvas-backed chairs were scattered around. A radio receiver and transmitter was on a stand—it looked large enough for worldwide communication.

Telephones were on a rack on the wall with wooden partitions between them, and some opened wooden shipping crates were piled high with Styrofoam bubbles. An air conditioner was an accouterment I had not seen in a tent before.

We told him everything, filling in all the details between our phone conversations. Francesca interrupted me to add points, and when she described shooting the ex-convict, Perruchio, in the Ristorante Regina, I completed her account. "She shot him right through the bottom of her handbag! First shot in the heart, the second close to it."

"Incredible! Bloody amazing!" He looked from one to the

other of us. "I want you to know I had no idea that this would turn out to be such a dangerous job. All I wanted to do was pick a chef—and here you get involved with murderous monks, assassins who are ex-cons, buffalo stampedes, dangerous gas sprayed on you from a crop-spraying plane. It's all too much." He paused. "That last episode—it sounds familiar somehow."

"It did to me too," I admitted. "I still can't think why."

"Well, anyway, I'm jolly glad you're safe and sound. And that Nigel—who'd have thought it? Poor old Pellegrini. I liked him. The captain's a great character, though, isn't he?"

We agreed.

He asked more questions. He asked about buffalo, about the belltower on top of the duomo in Modena, about the rice fields, and finally shook his head in admiration. "Extraordinary! I've got to hand it to you two. I'm interested in all kinds of details—always have been. Nearly everything fascinates me."

A cell phone buzzed and I looked at Francesca. "It's not me," she said indignantly, and Lansdown said, "It's mine. I leave it on the table here. Don't want it to go off while I'm riding a horse into Jerusalem in the twelfth century." He talked briefly and said to us, "I have to get the rest of my makeup on. Then we're shooting a scene with the castle in the background. Why don't you come with me, we'll have a spot of lunch, I'll be clear for a few hours, and we can get down to business."

Two very competent women dabbed and patted Lansdown's face with powders, creams, and lotions while another combed and recombed his hair. "Need another color touch-up tomorrow," said the latter, squinting critically. "Sun's bleaching you out."

"Very tactful of you, Emma," Lansdown said. "It's really the gray showing through."

She squinted again, tilting her head. "We can take care of that too."

I had expected the donning of the suit of armor to be a long and painstaking task but modern technology had the answers. Thin aluminum was surface-treated to look like shining steel, and the separate units for the body and the limbs had tiny hinges. It all clipped into place quickly. A wizened old Spaniard carried the massive helmet outside. "Not," said Lansdown, "because it's heavy. It's not, it's plastic and aluminum, but it's bloody hot in there, even with the visor open."

The set was a beehive and the main camera was the queen. Everything buzzed around it. The assistant director was the boss on the set, telling the dolly operators where to move, yelling questions to a camera technician staring at his light meters. A voice called out "Move that brute!" but before I could ask Francesca whom he was referring to, two men wheeled one of the massive light stands a few feet. Robert Stewart, the director, was aloof from all this, talking to the script "girl" who was at least his age.

"That's what I used to do," said Francesca, looking on a little wistfully.

"Wish you were back in the business?"

"No. Assisting food detectives is much more exciting."

"It's like the film business in some ways, I suspect," I told her. "Long periods of boredom punctuated by minutes of activity."

"Yes," she said softly, "but what activity!"

A Spaniard, active and voluble, seemed to be the assistant director. "Gotta getta going!" he was shouting, clapping his hands. "Don't wanna fall behind!"

The director nodded. He had walked over to join another

man standing by one of the cameras. "I've seen him before," Francesca said. "He's the director of cinematography, one of the best."

"Sound okay?" the director shouted and a response came. "Lights?"

Another okay and one of the makeup women came out with Desmond Lansdown. The director gave him a critical examination, nodded, and turned him into position. Bob Stewart went over to the camera, spoke briefly with the director of cinematography, then came back and moved Lansdown again, the aim being to get him and the castle in the same shot.

"Too much glare off the breastplate!" a voice called, and the armored figure was moved yet again. I was awaiting the traditional "Roll 'em!" but that had evidently been lost with the celluloid decades for all I heard were "All right, Des?" and a few more words. Then Lansdown was standing imperiously, head raised, looking at the castle.

Off camera, something moved, a signal of some kind and with the camera still running, Lansdown reached up and slowly took off the helmet. He did it so that it appeared to weigh fifty pounds. The camera dollied in, a slight whir presumably being the slide of a zoom lens. A gust of wind caught the flags and for a few seconds, they unfurled fully. Lansdown took several steps. Then Stewart called out "Cut and print!" and it was all over.

"That wind came just at the right second," I said to Francesca, but she smiled and pointed to Bob Stewart who had a cell phone to his ear. Francesca said. "He was giving directions to the crew on the battlements when to start the wind machine. You don't think they'd leave that to chance, do you?"

CHAPTER TWENTY-NINE

"Not as good as Benson's Brasserie," commented Lansdown, "but pretty good food nonetheless."

The large marquee served as a restaurant for the "upper crust," as Lansdown humorously referred to it. The director, the assistant director, the director of cinematography, the communications manager, an accountant, the electrical supervisor, and a handful of others were in there at lunchtime, and Lansdown had a word or a wave for all of them.

Lobster salad, giant shrimp in a garlicky sauce, fresh bread, and a bowl with a bewildering variety of fresh fruit made a delightful meal, and we had a couple of bottles of Castilian wine, the wine of the region. "Miles and miles of open plains around here," Lansdown commented. "You wouldn't believe they could grow grapes that yield wines this good. None of them travels well, so nobody gets to know about them. *Vinos verdes*, they call them." This one was a blend of grapes from Treixadura and Torrontes, and it was sharp and biting yet fruity at the same time.

During the meal, Lansdown told us of his fascination with the character he was playing. "Poor old Richard Plantagenet has been getting a raw deal from historians for a lot of years. A hundred years ago, they had him pegged as 'the worst king ever to sit on the English throne.' Said he was 'a bad son, a bad husband, a selfish ruler, and a vicious man'. Then, on top of that, they said he was a homosexual, though it seems that may be more a reflection on our times than on Richard's."

"The view is different today?" I asked.

"They seem to be getting nearer to the truth now. Both Richard's parents were French, did you know that?"

"No. We think of him as so essentially English."

"He was brought up in France and spent more than three-quarters of his life there. More than any other king of England, though, he belongs to the world of romance and legend rather than the world of history. It's understandable—the bravest warrior of the age, leading a great crusade to the Holy Land, captured while returning to England, imprisoned in a castle, finally returning home to wrest back the throne from his rascally brother, John."

"Which viewpoint did your screenwriters use?" I asked.

"They've had to bring in as much of the romantic element as needed for a movie. Generally, though, they show him the way historians today see him—as a military genius, a very capable ruler, and a brilliant political strategist."

Interested in everything, Lansdown was clearly ready to go on about Richard, but across the restaurant marquee, Francesca had seen a stunt man she knew from a couple of Roman epics. He had made the transition from chariots to one of Saladin's commanders, so she went with him to talk about old times while Lansdown and I went to his trailer, a massive Winnebago that he jokingly called his 747.

It was luxuriously furnished, and we sank into plush armchairs while Oriental carpets spread on the floor and oil paintings on the walls made it hard to remember where we were. A silent air conditioner kept the temperature and humidity at comfort level, and Lansdown stretched out his legs and said, "Right.

Now's the crunch. What about these three chefs?"

I didn't take out my notes. I wanted to give them to him verbally before I did that.

"I'll give you a thumbnail sketch of each before we get into details. Let's begin with Giacomo Ferrero, chef and owner of the Capodimonte. He's a huge, bearded character, looks like Pavarotti, extroverted, boisterous, noisy, opinionated. Been in kitchens all his life, stays fully involved in all aspects. He's a fine organizer and a stickler for precision. His aim is to offer nothing less than perfect food and flawless service. He believes in thorough professionalism and is a hard worker."

"First out of the gate." Lansdown grinned. "Off and running, may be hard to beat."

"The food is excellent, service too. From an extracurricular point of view, he owns part of a vegetable distributor and has stock in a trucking outfit that handles mostly foodstuffs. One final point."

Lansdown leaned forward attentively.

"He is about to lose one of his three stars, according to gossip."

"Gossip!" he said contemptuously.

"Well, you're in the entertainment business, which is lubricated by gossip. I know you're in the restaurant business too, so you know that it's taken more seriously there."

He looked unconvinced. He shrugged, though, and asked, "Any basis to the gossip?"

"Not as far as I know."

"Married?"

"Yes." I decided not to enlarge on the sultry charms of Anita so I just added, "She is not active in his business."

"All right. Next?"

"Ottavio Battista, chef-owner of the Palazzo Astoria—"

"Heard he's a bit of a prima donna." commented Lansdown.

"You can say that again. But he's imaginative and more than that, he can see the possibilities of food combinations that nine out of ten chefs would miss. He's unusual for that brilliant a chef, too, in that he always seems to have an eye on costs. He's not a penny-pincher but he has more awareness of economy than most chefs. He can get away with clever touches—he leaves the pink coral on grancevola, spider crabs. He can make simple dishes into special dishes. Do you know strangolopreti?"

"Don't think so. What is it?" He was all attention at the chance of learning something new.

"It's gnocchi filled with spinach. Seasoning the spinach with chives or marjoram is as far as most chefs go—even the better ones. Ottavio adds garlic and caraway, a real daring idea. A lot of chefs try challenging things like that and many fail. With Ottavio, he seems to have an instinctive flair for knowing, just knowing that they will work."

"And on the negative side?" Lansdown asked.

"The man's a mess, personally. Looks like a reject from a rehab clinic. He's a tyrant in the kitchen too. All he needs is a whip—though his tongue is just as effective. He treats his crew as if they were galley slaves."

"And how do they react?"

"I won't say they love it, but many of them have become chefs elsewhere and several have gained stars."

"He's a woman-chaser as I recall from the earlier survey when we still had a lot of candidates."

"They swoon over him as if he were, well, a movie star," I said straight-faced.

Lansdown grinned. "Surely women don't do that?"

"There are rumors."

"Okay." Lansdown nodded. "And the third, that'll have to be Bernardo Mantegna. Bit of an odd duck from all accounts."

"He is a genius with flowers and plants. From a culinary point of view, probably one of the best-informed people in Europe. Yet he doesn't let them dominate. He likes to make use of them as much as he can, but he is superbly talented with conventional dishes."

"Sort of a Zen character, isn't he?"

"Different, yes, but not eccentric. He admits to being totally immersed in his approach to cooking as being also an approach to nature. There's one difficulty that has to be faced— his wife hates London."

"Impossible," said Lansdown promptly.

I smiled, expecting him to say that. As a barrow-boy on the North End Road in Fulham who had progressed to one of Britain's most visible exports, he was a fervent Londoner at heart and not likely to understand how anyone could dislike the city.

"She even faked an affair with another of the chefs because she wanted to help him get the job, thereby making sure that Bernardo didn't."

"Is she involved in his business?"

"Deeply. She does the books, handles the money."

"H'm." Lansdown sighed and rose, going over to an elaborate bar. "Get you anything while we judge the finalists?"

I had a glass of *palo cortado*, a style of sherry slightly less rich than the *oloroso* and from the famed Valdespino bodega, the oldest family in the sherry trade. Lansdown opened a bottle of Spanish beer, San Miguel. "Can't beat Young's or Fuller's," he said, keeping up his loyalty to English beer, "but this is not bad."

He returned to his seat and put the beer in front of him. "Now let's see your notes and get down to some nitty-gritty."

We spent the rest of the afternoon discussing, reviewing, arguing. The time was punctuated by another sherry and another beer and then another. We covered every aspect in the decision-making process and we were nearing the selection of a name when a knock came at the door.

"Mr. Stewart asks if you could come and look at these dailies, Mr. Lansdown," called a voice.

"I still call them rushes," Lansdown said. "Shows how long I've been in the business, I suppose." He called out an agreement. "I'm co-producer on this picture," he said to me, "so Bob likes to keep me involved."

"You and I are close to making a choice."

"Yes. Might be a good idea to sleep on it, though. When are you planning on flying back?"

"I have a flight to London at one o'clock tomorrow afternoon, and Francesca leaves for Rome and Bologna an hour later."

"Why don't you do this then?" Lansdown said. "We keep a few rooms booked at the Parador de Salamanca. Stay there tonight and we'll finalize this in the morning. Bob and I have a meeting tonight with the fellows responsible for the Spanish army." He chuckled, "I don't mean the generals—these are from their War Department. We're going to use two thousand soldiers in the scenes coming up and we don't want to have to keep them a day longer than necessary. Neither do the Spanish—they might have a war sneak up on them."

So it was agreed, and I went in search of Francesca, wondering if the movie bug had bitten her again and if she was right at this moment signing up for the next epic.

CHAPTER THIRTY

The paradors of Spain are hotels par excellence. Most are castles, abbeys, and monasteries converted with superb taste and flair so as to provide all the modern comforts while losing none of the medieval magnificence. The Parador de Salamanca is, unfortunately, not one of these. It is a modern building, multistoried and constructed in the early eighties when the tourist boom was at its height. Still, it is well up to the standard of a good hotel. The one area in which all the paradors are lacking is food. It is true, there is the initial disadvantage that Spanish food is not one of the foremost in Europe, but the guest at a parador has to be satisfied with mediocre meals which do not make the best use of the country's produce, especially the seafood.

When Francesca and I returned to the location site the next morning, rows of cavalry soldiers were drilling on a wide plain where they could be photographed against the backdrop of the castle. A soft breeze ruffled multicolored banners and pennants. Puffs of sand rose from the horses' hooves, and it was a sight to stir the most sluggish imagination. The director of cinematography was with his camera operators, studying angles and distances, and the site was a buzzing hive of preparation.

Francesca found a script girl to chat with and I went to Lansdown's trailer. He was studying my notes as I went in and he waved a sheet. "You did a good job. Now it's time to wrap this up. Who's our man?"

"Your preliminary review was well done," I said. "You came up with three chefs who all like to cook. That sounds like a simple requirement, but chefs today have so many facets and are expected to be in so many fields that it's easy to overlook the basic point. These three have been cooking all their lives. They have a lot of experience but they are not rigid—all continue to strive to get better. All three have another characteristic too—they are aware of the standard stylized cooking techniques but they are not afraid to experiment. Any one of them could do a fine job for you."

"I think so too. Anything else?"

"All the three have outside interests," I went on, "but none of them wants to be a Wolfgang Puck or an Alain Chapel or a Paul Prudhomme. I don't think you want a chef who is thinking more about his upcoming TV series or his twenty-four-volume set of cookbooks or jetting off to Tokyo to open a cooking school. I think you want a man who is dedicated to cooking good food."

He grinned that insouciant grin he had employed to such good effect in the remake of Kipling's "Soldiers Three" in which he had co-starred with Sean Connery and Roger Moore. "You're right," he said. "That's what we want. We have three like that so the question is, which one?" He paced around the large living room of the trailer, talking as he did.

"Have we both decided?" he asked.

"I have," I told him.

"I have too. We'll compare choices and if we differ, we'll hammer it out."

"Okay. You first, it's your restaurant."

"No, you first—you're the investigator."

We grinned at each other like a couple of schoolboys.

"Right," I said. "Ottavio Battista."

He stopped pacing, sat in a big leather chair. "You surprise me. I thought you were going to go for Giacomo."

"He would be an excellent second choice," I said. "It's a near thing. Here's the way I reasoned. I ruled out Bernardo. He's brilliant, original—in fact, almost unique in his imaginative use of plants and flowers in his cooking. He may be a little too original, though, for your purpose. Bernardo is great in his own kitchen but in someone else's—"

"I don't interfere in the kitchen," Lansdown said, aggrieved.

"But the day would come when you— or your partner— might. And in any case, you want a chef who is a superlative Italian chef above all else. You don't want a chef who is passionate about a different aspect of cooking. You couldn't tighten the reins on Bernardo's enthusiasm for his plants and flowers. The main point that ruled him out in my estimate, though, was his wife. They are a devoted couple, and as she detests London so much, it just wouldn't work."

"Strange woman," Lansdown said, shaking his head. "Okay, so Bernardo is out."

"It was hard deciding between Giacomo and Ottavio. A minor item was one of the things that settled it. Ottavio had one of his sous-chefs reducing milk by a technique that must be centuries old. He was preparing *lait d'amandes,* the almond milk that preceded coconut milk and makes such an enormous difference to many dishes."

"Still," Lansdown objected, "it is, as you say, a minor item."

"It says more than just that—it's an indication that Ottavio is willing to incorporate the best elements of foreign cuisines.

Oh, I know you want an Italian chef who cooks Italian, but in today's world even the most passionate specialist has to know how to make use of the best available from other cooking styles."

"How does Giacomo compare in that regard?" Lansdown asked.

"Giacomo believes in professionalism and precision, but that kind of dedication is just not him."

"Plus he's losing a star."

"I paid no attention to that," I said. "It wouldn't be fair. I don't know who said it or why."

Lansdown got out of the leather chair and paced again.

"Interesting," he said. He took a few more paces. "I reached the same conclusion that Ottavio was our man, though obviously not for the same reason as you. But I thought his manner and his attitude might have put you against him."

"There is the one proviso. You would have to keep him in the kitchen. I don't see it as a problem for you, though. You know about public relations and the value of customer confidence, so you would want to have a smoothie up front anyway."

He studied me for a moment then he chuckled. He broke out into a laugh and held out his hand. "Jolly well done."

"Just routine," I said with a grin.

I didn't add that it was just routine once you forgot a terrifying monk with a knife, a high parapet on top of a cathedral, a robot plane spraying gas, a killer at the controls of a six-wheeled monster, and an assassin with an automatic.

The espresso machine in the coffee shop at the Bologna airport rumbled and vibrated in a determined if futile effort to compete with the noise of the Boeing 727 rolling past the window where we were sitting.

"I hate long good-byes," Francesca said, idly watching the silver shape slide by, "remember Marcello Mastroianni saying that to Sophia Loren in *Sabato, Domenica e Lunedì?*"

"*Saturday, Sunday and Monday*, yes, but I always thought that was a strange statement for him to make in the circumstances," I said. "They were dragging him off to prison."

"No," she said with a firm shake of her head. "You're thinking of *Ieri, Oggi e Domani.*"

"*Yesterday, Today and Tomorrow?* I thought that was the one where he was dying of multiple bullet wounds."

"That was *Dall'Alba al Tramonto, From Dawn Till Dusk.*"

"He wasn't in that film," I objected.

"He was. He didn't want any billing, that was all."

The espresso was so strong that one more bean would have refused to dissolve. When I had recovered from another sip, I asked her, "Why didn't he want any billing?"

"Something to do with tax."

"Are you sure?" I asked.

She fixed me with her of-course-I-am look, her chin upraised. "I worked on the film. I should know."

"So how did you enjoy being on the set again? Did it give you the urge to dig out your union card?"

She stared out of the window. "Only temporarily. I prefer the escort business—oh, and the investigating business too."

"Not thinking of taking out a private eye license, are you?"

"Not really. It's too hard on the clothes and the accessories," she said disdainfully.

"That escort service—you keep mentioning it, but you never tell me about it. Just what services do you provide?"

"It varies according to the client's requirements." She stirred the thick black liquid and took a delicate sip.

"You're not going to tell me, are you?"

"It's confidential," she said with her lovely smile. "Just like your business."

"As far as my business in Italy was concerned, you knew as much about it as I did," I complained.

"I told you many times, in Italy everybody—"

"Knows everybody's business. Well, maybe you're right, maybe you should stay with the escort business—whatever it is, it must be safer than investigating three chefs turned out to be. You don't have to shoot people, which reminds me," I added, "I want to thank you again for saving my life. Sorry about your handbag, but at least it died in a good cause."

She shook her head sadly. "I'll never find another handbag like that one. Did I tell you it was a limited edition?"

"No, you didn't, but I'm putting it on my expense account. Desmond will understand."

She brightened. "Oh, you don't have to do that. It's guaranteed."

"Against gunshots?"

"One of my sisters-in-law manages the shop where I bought it." Her dismissive tone turned into one of her delicious giggles, and it was then that the PA system announced that passengers on Flight 067 to London were invited to board now.

She walked with me to the gate.

"When will you come back to Italy?" she asked without looking at me.

"As soon as I can. When will you come to London?"

We stopped at the Passengers Only Past This Point sign. We kissed.

"Remember that other Mastroianni film?" she asked as she turned to walk away.

"Which one?"

"*Uno di Questi Giorni.*"

I hadn't known that Mastroianni was in that one—perhaps he was experiencing another of his tax dilemmas. If pressed, I would have guessed that film featured Gina Lollobrigida and Vittorio di Sica. Not that it mattered. I turned it into English in my mind.

Some Day Soon.